RANDOM HUSBAND

Janie Gordon

AdVintage LLC

To my husband, Eric, and my daughter, Shauna, my first and second readers who even liked the shitty first draft.

PREFACE

I started reading romance novels before puberty hit —probably because puberty took its sweet time arriving. Stuck in a poor public school in a poor small southern town, I scored the triple-whammy by also being painfully shy. Thank God for books. I'd hide under a tree at recess and read my book, escaping into a fantasy world of playful banter, love, and always, always a happy ending.

Here's my first story. Well, the first story out in the world for someone besides my family to read. And let me be honest: It's a story. It's not a work of literary art. You won't find page-long sentences full of references to the imagery of Canterbury Tales or even Shakespeare. It's a story about a woman who takes chances, adores her sister, and wants to build a life for herself without waiting for a man to make all the first moves. Like me, she doesn't take herself too seriously, and she makes mistakes but tries to learn from them, intent on rising above her challenges. And like me, she believes there's always a "Yes." You just have to find it. Or make it happen.

I hope you say "Yes" to my story. I hope it gives you a chance to stretch out on the couch and relax. And I hope you laugh along the way.

Sincerely yours,
Janie Gordon

CHAPTER 1—ABBY

Twenty million dollars.

Million dollars.

What did the amount even mean?

When I bought the single lottery ticket, I let the machine randomly pick my numbers and never looked back. I'd forgotten I had a ticket until newscasters kept making a fuss about the winning ticket purchased from the Gas Hutch near downtown Savannah. That place sells the best iced tea, and you can get a fresh cup any time of the day or night. Maybe they put a little mint in there for extra flavor.

But I digress.

I rolled across my bed toward the bedside table, where I'd laid the lottery ticket. Staring at the pastel paper, my stomach churned, and I was pretty sure vomit would follow—not the bad kind of vomit after too many spicey margaritas at Repeal 33, but a good kind of sick that says I just won twenty million dollars.

Thank goodness I found my ticket at two-fifteen on a Tuesday because I don't know if I'd have survived an entire weekend waiting for the lottery office to open. As it was, I called and asked for information. "Um, what if I won the lottery?

What happens next?"

The woman on the other end of the line sounded tired. "Honey, if you won four dollars, cash in your ticket at any lottery dealer, like a convenience store in your town."

I poised the phone on the pillow beside me and used speaker. My hands shook too much to hold both the phone and the ticket. "No, um, I mean the twenty-million one." A giggle bubbled up along with the tiniest bit of my lunch: a grilled-cheese sandwich with a side of sweet-potato tots.

"You best not be messing with me right now."

"No ma'am, I'm not messing with you. I'm holding the ticket." *Please, lady, please give me some closure here.*

I pinched myself.

Was it actually possible I'd move out of this roach-infested apartment? As a journalism major fresh out of college, I'd signed a lease in a feeble attempt at independence. One annual lease had turned into six. My plan included another year of saving and a move to a lavish two-bedroom apartment in the same building.

Big dreams.

Now my vision expanded to include a grand old Victorian house like the ones I could never have afforded, even if the magazine granted me a promotion and a raise.

I reminded myself to breathe.

My bedroom filled with beeping noises, and I

assumed the woman plunked phone keys. "Hold on, hold on! Oh, my sweet Jesus, hold on!" More beeping. Five long minutes later, she returned to the phone. "Listen now, you got to do a few things before you bring in that ticket. Child, you don't want people knowing you won the money. Get yourself a lawyer first thing. A lawyer will hide you from the world so nobody knows where the money went. I reckon a lot of other things need to happen, but get a lawyer first."

"Yes ma'am." My head buzzed with too much energy or too little oxygen. I took a deep breath. "Thank you for the advice."

"Sugar, I'm tickled blue you won the money." She chuckled, and it was the warmest sound I'd ever heard. "God bless you, and God bless the people you love. 'Y'all are headed down easy street."

Fifteen seconds later, I headed to my sister's house to wave the ticket in her general direction. She would freak out! There wasn't a doubt in my mind I'd share the wealth, although I found out later twenty million really meant a little over seven million.

Still, seven *million*!

⚭

Three months later, when the money finally rolled into my bank account, I was still trying to give it away.

"Take it!" I threw up my hands. "You have to take it."

3

Ricky, my brother-in-law, reached around me to open the fridge and pull out two Miller Lights. "Tell you what, Abbigail. I ever hit a snag and can't pay my bills, you'll be the first person I call." He handed me a cold beer and went back to the living room, the *cha-chunk* of his recliner saying, "case closed."

Back when I'd bumbled through life as a scrawny fourteen-year-old tomboy, Ricky had married my sister, Karen, only a month after our mom died of breast cancer. On day one, *poof*, Ricky had a family, but he never complained, taking on his new responsibility as casually as he did everything. He played the role of both brother and father, or at least my image of a father based on zero experience with one. My favorite piece of fatherly advice was, "Life unfolds. You live it, enjoy it, and don't be an asshole."

He's sarcastic as hell, but a current of love runs through every snarky comment.

I followed him and blocked the TV. "But Ricky," I might have whined. "You never have to work again."

"What?" His shocked face wasn't convincing. "Dump my superpower?" He leaned forward as much as his reclined position allowed. In what I call his "serious" voice, he said, "But Abby, you offering is what matters most." Sitting back again, he picked up the TV remote. Next, he'd turn up the volume like he always did to let me know the conversation was over. Before he clicked the plus sign, he added, "Everybody should work. It's good for the soul. Keeps you grounded."

"Not if you're rich!"

My sister had warned me he wouldn't bend.

Karen ambled downstairs. "I told you so." She walked by Ricky on her way to the kitchen and rubbed his shoulder. "The kids are building a blanket fort. Let's watch a movie tonight."

Eli or Prissy squealed from upstairs. It was hard to tell which one because Eli's ten-year-old voice was years from deepening. If history repeated itself, Eli would soon boss his sister, claiming his three extra years of breathing put him in charge, and they'd clamor for Karen's divided attention.

I followed her to the kitchen, sulking. "Millions. Sitting in the bank, gathering dust."

"I don't think it works that way." She pulled a bag of popcorn from the cabinet. "And how much dust could it gather in two days?"

"*Right*? I can't believe it took so long to get everything worked out." I leaned against the doorway, too antsy to sit still. "But it's real now. I —we—can spend it."

"*You* can spend it." White-cheddar popcorn tumbled into a bowl.

I giggled. "Today I moved my clothes to *The Drayton*."

"Swanky hotel!" She clutched the bowl to her

chest, a light over the sink creating a halo of fuzzy brown hair, probably full of static from building a blanket fort. "Want to stay for a movie?"

"No thanks. Luxury calls my name." I waltzed toward the front door. "I have a big day tomorrow."

She called after me. "What's happening tomorrow?"

But I couldn't say...mainly because she might not approve.

⨑

I slept badly in my down-covered, fluffy-pillowed sanctuary, probably because wealth churned in my stomach like acid. By the time the sun came up, I'd been wide awake for hours.

Being rich would take some getting used to.

After a long, hot shower with enough water pressure to rinse the shampoo from my hair, I pulled on a yellow sundress and headed to the *Women First* offices for the magazine. Today I would confront Edith, my editor, and free myself from the tyranny of employment.

By the time I stood outside her office, I'd checked my bank balance five times.

Yep, I was still rich.

My mouth tasted like metal. After years of bowing to Edith, today I'd bow out.

I pushed open her door.

She barely offered me a glance before returning to pages on her desk. "Knock much?"

Deep breath. I stopped myself from checking my balance again. I'd practiced my speech. Today I'd tell her she was demanding, caustic, and rude. And she smoked too much. She smelled like stale cigarettes, and I hated when she breathed in my face, standing too close while she yelled. I'd never again darken her desk, rush to meet a deadline, or listen to reasons why I couldn't have a raise. I was out, out, out!

Clenching my fists and my jaw, I stomped to her desk, daring her to ignore me.

She ignored me.

"Um." I cleared my throat.

Nothing.

"Um, I quit." It came out in a high-pitched squeak.

She glared at me over impossibly small glasses. "Why?"

Crap, I hadn't thought of that. I'd promised Karen and Ricky to keep the lottery private so no one would take advantage of me. But I hadn't come up with a cover story.

"I just quit."

"Yeah, we've established that. Why?" She stuck her pen behind her ear.

"Um, no reason." I felt twelve years old.

"So. A talented writer and social-media star dumps a job dedicated to helping women for 'no reason.'"

A talented star? *Now* she compliments me? For years, I would have killed for a pat on the back from this woman, and now she offers words of affirmation. To top it off, she made me feel like I was abandoning all women, not her, specifically.

"Maybe I could stay, if you really need me." If "women" really needed me.

"Nope, *Women First* will survive." She pulled the pen from behind her ear and started writing again, probably shredding someone's hard work. "Good luck with your 'no reason' life."

I backed toward the door, feeling behind me for the handle. If quitting meant sweet freedom, why did I feel so empty? Sure, the small, regional magazine wasn't exactly changing the world, but I'd always seen it as noble...

No. This is exactly what Edith wanted. The magazine would be fine without me to push around.

In the parking lot, I paused beside my jalopy and checked my balance again.

Still there.

I'd left the windows open to keep the car cool; the AC had died before my time. The driver's door creaked open enough for me to scoot in and start the engine, suffocating me in a cloud of smoke. I coughed like Edith on a cigarette break. My eyes watered. This piece of junk wouldn't last another week.

Then it hit me. I could buy any car I wanted.

Holy shit. I could buy *any car.*

I pushed Edith and *Women First* from my

mind and tugged a smile to the surface. *Let's have some fun.* My phone's GPS app led me to a dealership an hour away in Hilton Head, South Carolina, where I parked and made my way to the showroom.

Six hours and four-hundred gawks later, I drove away in a red Porsche 911 with more features than I'd ever understand and more horsepower than I'd ever use.

My trade-in covered the free pen they gave me to sign for the new car.

I spent the day at the beach, sitting without the benefit of a towel and getting sand in key places, basking in my first day of unemployment. By the time I ground part of the beach into the Porsche's floorboard, the sun raced toward the horizon like a horse thirty yards from the barn.

Time to go home...to my hotel room.

My sticky, salty skin burned from the relatively tame rays of late spring, the first day-long kiss of vitamin D in months. Today had been incredibly bizarre; too much excitement, too much stimulation, too much change.

As I drove back to Savannah, my jittery stomach felt like a caffeine overdose although I'd only bought water at a shop along the boardwalk. Every survival instinct told me to *go home* to Karen and Ricky, sit on the couch, and binge watch whatever show they liked, as long as it wasn't reality TV. I cringed when shows made people—contestants?—seem foolish.

But I couldn't go home.

Not tonight.

Not in this car.

I stroked the fine leather of the steering wheel, imagining Ricky's face when he saw the car. His expression would leech the fun from my impulsive purchase, because, damn it, I cared what he thought. And I wasn't ready to admit I'd quit my job. No matter how often I told myself I'm an adult and can make my own decisions, part of me recognized I wasn't acting like the person they'd helped raise. So yeah, wrapped up in my musings and hesitation was shame.

Denial to the rescue.

I'd distract myself with a decaf cappuccino on the way to the hotel. I avoided my usual coffee shop on Liberty Street, where they might ask about the fancy car, but Savannah boasted coffee on every block.

I screeched to a stop next to Historic Coffee Roasters on West Park Avenue and eased a few inches forward into a spot marked for street parking. Determined to act carefree and fun —enjoy the wealth, baby!—I hopped out and admired the car in the pink light of early evening. On the wide sidewalk in front of the coffee shop, only a woman and her toddler strolled away. Blame the uncharacteristic quiet for my behavior: I kicked off my shoes (no need to scratch the paint job), crawled on the hood of the car, held my phone high in front of me, and snapped selfies.

I puckered my lips toward the windshield. *Click click.*

I reached down and cupped the side-view mirror. *Click click.*

I draped across the hood, leaning on one elbow and trying my best to look sexy. *Click—*

"Want me to take your picture?"

I jumped and nearly dropped my phone.

Right in front of me, a respectable four feet from my sports car, stood the sexiest man I've ever seen. No, wait, I don't mean handsome, tall, muscular, even though he was all those things. I mean heart-in-the-stomach, eyes-popped-open, toe-curling sexy. He flaunted short black hair, a dazzling smile, and dark-blue eyes I hoped belonged to his entire family; they were too gorgeous for one person.

To be fair, he might not have "flaunted" them, but I would have.

"I can get a picture of you and your car." He held out a hand that could have modeled for Michelangelo's *David*.

I couldn't *not* comply. My fingers brushed his palm when I handed over the phone.

His hand exuded warmth.

My heart worked overtime while my tongue lazed against my teeth, refusing to budge. *Words, Abby. Now.* My effort resulted in a blurted, "It's not my car!"

CHAPTER 2—MAX

"I, uh, borrowed it." She didn't sound convinced.

Her big brown eyes drew me closer. "Okay, it's not your car." I pretended to frame a picture of the Porsche, but I zoomed in on her. Dark-brown hair fell across her shoulders, in sharp contrast to the bright yellow dress. "Ready?"

"What?"

"Ready for the picture?"

"Oh. Yeah. Thanks."

Barefoot, she leaned against the door, her arms folded across her chest. Then she smiled.

My stomach raced down a roller-coaster mountain.

People say the eyes reveal depth, a person's soul, but a smile shares their humanity. Her smile radiated warmth, kindness, and a playful spirit. She embodied the girl next door, the woman parents want to meet, a lover and best friend.

While I stood there, staring at her face through the phone, she tipped her head to one side. "How does it look?"

She meant the picture I hadn't taken.

I clicked the photo. "Good, great." Handing

the phone to her, I avoided touching her skin again because already my thoughts were too involved with a stranger. Tonight, of all nights, I needed to focus.

My hand went to my jacket pocket and patted the small box there.

Rather than look at the picture on her phone, she stared at me, and the fading light wrapped us together as only dusk can do. Four feet apart became three feet, then two. I'm not sure which of us moved, or if we both did, but closer felt right. I'd like to think I wouldn't have touched her, wouldn't have kissed her, wouldn't have begged her to drive us away in her gaudy car. She seemed so vibrant, and I wanted her sunshine to brighten my world for a—

"Hey there, handsome!" Zoe yelled from her car window.

I backed away from sunshine woman, and we both turned toward my date.

Right. My date.

"Thank you for the picture." The woman climbed into her borrowed car while I stood on the curb, wishing I'd touched her hand after all. As I watched her drive away, I told myself the spell, the attraction, was a preview of cold feet, a natural and harmless reaction to my big plans.

Zoe yelled again. "Take your time, Max." Her tone said, "Move your ass."

After I slid into the passenger seat, Zoe leaned over to receive a kiss. Her cheek felt soft and perfumed and familiar. My life snapped back into focus, and I banished sunshine woman from my thoughts.

Strange how the mind can play tricks that mean nothing.

I patted my pocket.

Zoe, "the One," had met my family over Christmas and earned a double thumbs up from my dad, a single "okay" from my mom and older brother, and silence from my younger brother, but he avoids interactions when he can.

With my thirty-third birthday in the rear-view mirror, I'd started thinking about settling down, and Zoe checked every box. She was pretty —I mean jaw dropping—and nice to waiters. Her job as a restaurant supplier threw us together, though I figured her weekly check-ins meant more than work. Hell, she'd asked me out the first time, insisting I'd enjoy roasted kangaroo at Alligator Soul, a little basement restaurant for people who wanted to pay for atmosphere. I can't say I liked the kangaroo, but I liked ending up at her loft after dinner.

Tonight, a year after our first date, I walked her toward Alligator Soul, rehearsed words running through my head. I followed Zoe down the steps below street level, entering the small restaurant through a heavy prohibition-thick door. A bar glowed along the left wall, and on the right, two archways led to dining tables meant for two but stretched to four when needed.

I appreciated the low lighting and gentle jazz drifting on the smell of grilled meat that I hoped would be beef rather than kangaroo.

The maître d' seated us right away, and we ordered pre-dinner cocktails before the waiter described the specials. Zoe avoided eye contact, which should have made me suspicious, but my mind scrambled with the proposal. Was I doing this? How could a person ever be sure about such a big decision?

Sunshine woman popped into my mind, but I dismissed her again.

Cold feet were a bitch.

After the drinks arrived, we toasted—like we always did—before taking a sip. I reached in my pocket and pulled out the light-blue box, holding it in my lap.

"Max." Zoe lifted her chin and finally looked me in the eyes. "We've dated a year."

Okay, go time.

"Yes, a good year." I smiled and fumbled with the box under the table. My heart thumped in my ears. "Zoe, I'd like—"

She held up a hand, palm toward me. "Wait. I need to get this out before I lose my nerve."

I stopped fidgeting. My heart thudded harder.

After folding her hands on the table, interweaving her fingers to create a fist, she said, "I'm breaking up with you."

What the hell? My mouth dropped open, but I didn't speak.

"You are not emotionally available. I gave you six months to open yourself up to me, and you stubbornly remained closed off."

Six months? We'd dated a year.

"For the past six months, I've seen other people." She held up her hand again, but I hadn't uttered a word. "It's your own fault. I needed to be sure about my decision. Several of my lovers want an exclusive relationship, so I have some difficult choices to make. If you had behaved better, I wouldn't be in this position."

Several "*lovers*?" My vision clouded, but I saw her clearly, maybe for the first time. I should have yelled or banged my fist or stormed out, but none of this felt real. Couldn't be real.

"I'll admit, you're handsome. When I first saw you, I fell hard, but you won't commit." She paused. "Max, I'm trying to process the breakup. Are you listening?"

I nodded, somehow stuck to the seat as though I'd lost free will.

"You need to learn about women; I recommend you start reading *Women First*."

Women First must be a trendy new book about the G-spot, but she'd never complained about sex.

The more she talked, the more I tuned out, so it's fair to say I wasn't a good listener. I flagged the waiter for a double bourbon and let my mind drift.

Whenever I feel like crap, I think about the

good parts of my life. Zoe? Okay, scratch through that one. My apartment is pretty awesome, sitting above the coffee shop in what Zoe had called a "charming" area of town. All I knew was I got to walk right downstairs to work, ready to roast coffee beans any time the mood struck me. The smell always made its way upstairs, wafting around my apartment like a friendly ghost. Buying the building and opening Historic Coffee Roasters had been the best decision of my life, and after five years, I'd never regretted it once. Right now, I itched to go home and wander around the closed shop, breathing deep and checking on my little slice of the world.

Zoe's mouth kept moving. And did I see tears in her eyes? What the fuck?

Maybe I'd head to Jamaica for another round of coffee tasting. Or set up a session with another roast-master to learn new techniques. I could travel and up my roasting game, ready to dive in with a new offering. Owning a business meant keeping things fresh, slipping in surprises for customers and adopting the better changes. Lately I was feeling comfortable leaving my kingdom in the hands of Anuli, my manager, in spite of her need to curb her sweet tooth or start paying for the sugar high she got at work. I wondered if we knew each other well enough for an honest discussion about healthy eating, but before the thought trailed away, I admitted I'd never overstep the boss-employee boundary.

"Are you listening to me?" Zoe delicately patted a napkin to her eyes. Those polyester napkins weren't absorbent and would never soak up tears. Give me a good old fashioned paper napkin every time. Louder, Zoe said, "I'm giving you some constructive feedback."

What happened to the "it's not you, it's me" line? I wanted that little gem right about now. Why had I ever thought she was pretty? Or hot?

With an exaggerated huff, she stood and dropped her napkin on the table. "I'm going to the ladies' room. We'll talk more when I get back." She tottered away on high heels, her hips swinging side to side in a tight red dress.

Oh yeah. She was hot. I was going to miss that. And by that, I meant Zoe's body. When she was out of sight, my brain went back to rational thought. Damn. Maybe she was right. I mostly enjoyed the physical part of our relationship— and the discount I got on paper products. Petty thoughts, but they released me from the chair.

I once read we should fake it till we make it, so I embraced the mantra. I downed the rest of my bourbon, got up, smiled at onlookers, and walked out. I didn't pay the bill either, which brought a smile to my face I didn't have to fake. An hour was plenty of time to let someone blather about my faults, and the coffee beans were calling my name.

In the weeks to come, I'd think about Zoe's comments, at least the ones I heard, and I'd probably try to change. People are supposed to grow, I guess. I don't listen well, I don't share my feelings often, and I don't know much about women, all true. But in my own defense, because I felt I needed *someone* in my corner right now, I grew up the middle child of three boys; we never understood the mystery of women. Sure, we had girlfriends and a few girls who were friends, but nothing takes the place of a sister telling it to you straight. Family is forever, which gives siblings a lot of freedom with each other.

A sister would have gentled us.

The breakup stung, but my heart didn't shatter, a fact that should have told me Zoe wasn't "the One" after all. When I thought about how close I'd come to proposing, my gut ached like the time my brother had suckered me into a hotdog-eating contest. My almost fiancé had slept with other people. For *six months*. Tomorrow I'd schedule an STI test and let anger wrap any sadness in an airtight bag; no way would I grieve for the stranger I'd nearly married.

Sunshine woman shimmered on the edge of my thoughts.

This time, I welcomed the distraction.

CHAPTER 3—ABBY

I laid in bed and stared at the ceiling. A stupid green light flashed in a stupid smoke detector. Once I saw it, I couldn't look away, damning the device for disturbing my sleep.

Truthfully, fractured images of a dark-haired man holding my phone destroyed sleep, but I intended to purge those thoughts by tomorrow. The man clearly belonged to the woman who'd interrupted whatever might have happened between us—if anything. A chance encounter wouldn't distract me from making better decisions.

Starting tomorrow morning.

First, the mid-life-crisis Porsche had to go. I'd return it to the dealership and accept any financial loss. I intended to trade in a car that screamed, "Notice me!" for one that mumbled, "I do okay."

After I settled the car issue, I'd contact a realtor to find a home. Living in a hotel room sucked. For as long as I could remember, I'd coveted Victorian houses, so buying one made sense.

From now on, I vowed to spend my money wisely and get my new life in order.

◫

By noon, I'd dumped the Porsche, suffered through a team of good-old-boys pointing, laughing, and shaking their heads, and acquired a sensible blue Volt. Next stop, the old Victorian I'd coveted since the age of sixteen. A web search at three a.m. had revealed my dream house on the market, which I took as a positive sign from the universe. The three-story beauty nestles on a modest plot of land surrounded by an elaborate wrought-iron fence, with a backyard full of indigenous trees, shrubs, clusters of flowers, and a brick patio only a few blocks from the historic district.

I parked outside the fence fifteen minutes before my appointment; I wanted to drink in the Savannah charm of this house without a realtor. A few minutes of quiet, me and the house.

The gate creaked as I opened it, but the house drew my attention. The exterior glowed in the sunshine, a warm brown with cream accents, and the roof and sweeping concrete steps contrasted in a rust red. For years, I'd walked by this house, peering into the backyard and fantasizing, but not until today did I allow myself to fall in love.

I'd pay any amount to make it mine.

My home.

Standing on the walkway, craning my neck upward to see the highest wavery windows, I thought about the builders at the end of the nineteenth century—how they'd survived a yellow-fever epidemic and built through a catastrophic hurricane, how they'd felt the pressures and the losses of the Spanish-American War, how they'd created a work of art and refuge lasting so much longer than their lifespan. Inside my body, gratitude welled, far too big for the space. I didn't faint or swoon, but I did cry. Not a boo-hoo sloppy mess, but a release of tears to make space for so much wonder.

"Hi there!" A voice chirped behind me. "I'm Camila."

I wiped my tears before turning around, intent on looking like any normal twenty-something buyer with a load of cash and no job. It occurred to me she'd ask what I did for a living —code for "where did you get the money?"— and I still hadn't planned a cover story. Maybe today I'd be a trust-fund baby...or a hedge-fund manager, if I had any idea what the heck a hedge-fund manager did.

"Hi, I'm Abby. Thanks for meeting me so quickly."

"Happy to do it. You're going to love this gem. I understand the sellers already have three offers. You'll want to move quickly." She led the way to the front door. "The door's tricky." She jiggled the key in the lock and tried the knob several times. "Dang thing."

Finally, she swung open the door and stepped inside, blocking my view. "Welcome to your new home. As you can see, it's been completely renovated." Camila gestured with flailing arms, but I still couldn't get a clear look.

I wanted to tell her I didn't need the hard sell. I didn't even need a nudge. After slipping past her, I gawked first at the hardwood floors, then at the curved mahogany staircase, then at the peach-colored walls reflecting sun streaming through stained-glass inserts at the top of several tall windows.

The online pictures hadn't captured the quiet, the peace that existed between Camila's eager words.

I bit my lip to stop "I'll take it!" from bursting out.

The living room flowed into the kitchen, with stainless-steel appliances, a white farm sink, and a butcher's-block island. I tuned out my agent as she followed me upstairs, where I lost count of the bedrooms and bathrooms because each new room captured my full attention. The devil on my shoulder whispered that furnishing the house would cost a fortune, but the angel on the other side reminded me I was rich.

I smiled.

Camila led the way to a final room on the second floor. "The spiral staircase leads to the third level, which would be perfect for a study, office, or retreat from your family." She knocked on the railing, and the sharp *ping* told me it was made of iron. "Everything about this house is solid as a rock." I glanced up at the opening in the ceiling while she inhaled. "Are you married? Kids?"

"No to both, so far."

"Oh." She looked puzzled. I braced myself. "You know this house is expensive..."

As if a woman couldn't possibly afford such a house without a man. Well, I couldn't have afforded it on my salary, so she was right. This time.

"Yes, I know the list price. But since they have other offers, I'll offer more."

Camila's eyes widened. "If you don't mind my asking, what do you do for a living?"

I do mind. "I'm a hedge-fund manager."

"Oh! What a coincidence. My husband works with Citadel. Which fund are you with?"

Crap, crap, crap. "You wouldn't know it. It's a small fund, um, called..." I saw my car from the window. "Voltage. The Voltage Group."

She frowned.

I turned toward the landing. "Well, I'd better get going. Loads of hedge-fund meetings this afternoon." Jogging down the stairs, I chattered to keep her from asking more questions. "Busy investing, monitoring, researching and stuff to do. You know how it is."

I didn't stop until I reached the gate. Camila followed at a reserved pace, locked the door, and approached me, still frowning. My next words would soften her attitude.

"I'll take it. Please offer twenty-five percent over asking. If you think the offer's too low, go higher." *I want this house. I need this house.*

She smiled a tight-lipped grimace. We still had a problem. "I'll have to confirm your finances first."

"Of course!" I walked backward to my car, giving her a two-thumbs-up atta girl to let her know my finances wouldn't cause a problem. "The Voltage Group has been good to me." As I drove away, I glanced in the rearview mirror to see her staring, probably noticing the Volt badge gleaming on the back of my car.

Six days later, the owners accepted my offer, and I asked Camila to open the house. Karen would arrive any minute, and I'd reveal my first and last home. I'd been avoiding my sister, spending my days at the beach and my evenings in a sterile hotel room, because I wasn't ready to tell her or Ricky I'd quit my job. I kept reminding myself it was my decision to make, but no rationalization could bring me to their door.

Karen joined me on the front steps, where I stared in the open door and crossed my fingers Camila would make herself scarce. I looked forward to a big reveal, and Camila's constant chatter wasn't part of the plan.

"Ta-*da*!" I opened my arms wide, proud of the sun-dappled walkway and wide front steps, proud of the extravagant investment in the home, the history, and my own life.

"Oh. My. God." Karen's jaw dropped as she scanned the entry, staircase, living room, and tall windows. "Abby, it's absolutely gorgeous. I can't believe you bought the house you've talked about for years."

"Yep! And wait till you see the rest." I crunched my shoulders around my ears and clenched my fists, dancing like a kid offered a trip to Disney World. "It's *perfect*." I grabbed her arm and pulled her inside.

We toured the house twice while Camila caught up on phone calls. Through Karen's eyes, I saw the sloped floors and the cracks in the ceiling, but nothing diminished my devotion.

I've never needed perfection—only character and potential.

Back on the front steps, Karen hugged me. "I love it."

"Will you help me buy furniture and decorate? I have so many ideas!" I also needed something to do with my days. My skin couldn't take much more sun worshipping, and as much as I loved reading, I couldn't sustain my new habit of eight hours a day.

"You know I will. Keep me posted." She walked down the steps.

"We could start right now." *Please don't leave me. It's too early in the morning for me to fill another whole day.*

"Can't. I need to pick up the kids from a sleepover." Already at the gate, she opened it and waved back at me.

No! "How about after?" *Please don't leave me here alone.*

"I wish I could, but Ricky's coming home early so we can do yardwork." She opened her car door.

Don't leave!

"Maybe tomorrow. Go ahead and get started. You have great taste!"

She left me. I watched her drive away, feeling as deflated as any air mattress used more than once. I couldn't muster the energy to pump myself up again. Nor could I get excited about another day reading on the beach.

Maybe I'd drive up and down West Park Avenue and scope out the crowd for tall, dark, and handsome. Sure, he might have a girlfriend, but no one could blame me for looking.

I yelled a goodbye to Camila and ran to my car before she could leave the house. Without pausing to consider my goals, I drove to West Park and toured down the street until I came to Forsyth Park, where sanity returned and forced me to park the car.

For the rest of the day, I ambled through the thirty-acre park, admiring the live oaks and intermittently sitting on benches and reading until the pages blurred. By six o'clock, I gave up pretending the day relaxed me; I practically quivered with unspent energy.

Although I urged myself toward the hotel—

the empty, bleak, too-much-white hotel—I ended up at Karen's house. Right about now, she'd be serving a hot dinner. Ricky and the kids would be talking about their day and planning their tomorrow. Their busy, chaotic tomorrow.

I didn't bother to knock. "Hello! It's Abby!" I slammed the door behind me to punctuate my arrival. "Anybody home?" But I knew they were. I could smell the charred meat from here. Ricky must have grilled his famous burgers for dinner.

My mouth watered.

"In here!" Prissy called from the kitchen.

Then, as smooth as room-temperature butter, Karen ordered, "Pull up a chair. Burgers and fries tonight." By the time I sat, she'd already set an extra plate on the table.

Ricky piled food on my plate.

I bit into the juiciest burger on the planet and closed my eyes, savoring the flavors. Conversation swirled around me, and I savored that too. Mixed with the peace of home was a longing to create and nurture my own family. Today I'd acquired the house; tomorrow I'd swipe right on Tinder. I opened my eyes, chewed, and grinned. My life felt back on track.

People say luck is random, but it's not. Life can encourage luck.

I wouldn't have won the lottery if I hadn't played.

I won't find a partner if I don't try.

"How's your burger?" Prissy poked a finger in

the bun I held.

"Better without your finger in it." I teased.

Prissy giggled.

Ricky explained in excruciating detail his latest job in a run-down apartment building with a sewage leak.

I screwed up my face, mostly to make Prissy and Eli laugh.

Out of nowhere, Ricky's laser focus turned to me. "How's work?"

"You know, work is work is work. Nose to the grind. Plugging away. Going the extra mile." I glanced at Karen, who blinked at me then studied a tomato slice. *She knew.* I never told her, but she knew. Then again, she'd never missed one of my stories or posts, and days had passed in a vacuum.

Ricky, Prissy, and Eli stared at me. The kitchen quieted. I whispered, "Bending over backward...blood, sweat, and tears."

In the silence, I took a huge bite of my burger and couldn't force the bolus down my throat. After sticking a wad of it in one cheek, I swallowed a bit and worked on the cud.

Ricky glanced at Karen, then returned his attention to me. He laid the burger on his plate and wiped his hands on a napkin. "What's going on, Abbigail? Did you get fired?"

Karen cleared her throat, but I couldn't face her. They'd raised me to contribute good to the world, and in their minds, contribution meant a rock-solid work ethic. I didn't disagree.

But I was rich. And money bought leisure time.

Right?

I swallowed the last of my bite. "I didn't get fired." Everyone stared. A car drove by. "I quit."

CHAPTER 4—MAX

Closing time. Anuli appeared in the roasting-room doorway. "I haven't seen Zoe in a while." It wasn't a question. But it was.

"She's probably been busy." I checked the roaster's temperature gauge, trying to appear preoccupied.

"I might need more cups soon. Is she still our rep?"

Clever. Anuli rarely dropped a subject she set her mind to.

I gave her my full attention. "Yes, she's still our rep, but somebody else might be helping out for a while." *Hopefully*.

She squinted at me. "What's going on?"

I didn't want to tell her, but she wouldn't leave it alone, and I couldn't hurt her feelings. "We're on a break."

"*Dang it*, Max!" Her fierce reaction surprised me. "You've been moping around for days. I figured something was wrong." She entered the small room and patted my back. "Are you okay?"

"Definitely okay, thanks." I hefted a bag of beans from the corner, a move requiring Anuli to back up. The last thing I needed was my employee's pity. Besides, I didn't want to

31

encourage a gossip habit and run the risk of losing my privacy.

She took the hint and returned to the counter. A few minutes later, she leaned in the doorway and handed me a scrap of paper. "Here's Keisha's number. She's fun, popular, and bubbly. Call her. Ask her out."

Bubbly? How did a woman bubble? And I hadn't cared about popularity in high school; I definitely didn't care now. "Anuli, I don't—"

"Sure, sure. Big, strong Max doesn't need any help." She turned away and waved over her shoulder. "Stop being so grumpy. Ask her out."

I tucked the paper in my apron pocket, where it would stay until I remembered to throw it out. "Bubbly." I shook my head. No way would I cold-call a woman. How desperate did Anuli think I was?

Twenty minutes later, I locked up the shop, turned off the lights, and headed upstairs to scavenge for dinner. My fridge coughed up an old pack of hotdogs and a block of green cheese. Laughter drifted through my windows from the sidewalk below. Porsche woman popped into my head, and I brought my half-eaten, cold hotdog to the nearest window, investigating the source of joy. Two blonde-haired girls—probably teenagers—leaned in close to each other and pointed at a tattooed boy on a skateboard.

I hated to admit it, but I missed Zoe. I missed my family. I missed Porsche woman. The pink early evening would turn dark too soon. I missed the attention of an interesting person.

Ten minutes later, I called bubbly, popular, fun Keisha.

◐

"Over here!" A pretty woman I assumed to be Keisha waved from the bar with both hands over her head. She'd chosen to meet at Jazz'd tapas downtown, where live jazz music bounced off the walls in a steady stream of wailing saxophone.

When I arrived beside her, she smiled and jumped up and down, displaying an impressive jiggle in her chest area I tried not to notice. Subdued lighting glowed against her luminous dark skin. The top of her curly hair came to my nose, probably because she wore spikey high heels, as bright pink as her tight dress.

"Hi, I'm—"

"Max! I know! Anuli told me everything."

Everything?

She raised a hand to the bartender. "Two shots of tequila, kind sir." The woman vibrated with energy. Literally vibrated. The bartender thumped two full shot glasses on the bar, and Keisha thrust one at me, sloshing some over the side.

Well, I had asked for company, so I might as well join in. I held up my glass. "Cheers."

"No!" She shoved her hand between my mouth and the drink, spilling more of the

33

liquid. "We have to document our first date." A cell phone appeared, and Keisha smooshed her body beside mine, clicking through several poses while I faked a smile. "For my followers."

When she pulled away, I raised my glass again, watching her over the rim to make sure I followed her rules. A flash left spots circling the room. I blinked. She snapped pictures of me as I drank, returned the glass to the bar, turned to face her, pretty much every unexciting move I made. Her followers would wonder where she'd found such a dolt.

She held up two fingers to the bartender. Before I could say anything else, she squealed, "Isn't he dreamy?"

I assumed she meant me, and I felt like I'd transported to an Archie comic. Who was she talking to? Had she brought friends? The packed bar offered no clues; people surrounded us, but no one seemed particularly interested.

After we downed a second shot, she grabbed my hand and pulled me to the dance floor, where I stepped side to side like Frankenstein's monster as she undulated around me, clicking pictures every few seconds. She clutched the front of my shirt and pulled me forward to talk over the loud music. "I need pics so I can blog about this later!"

I'd never felt so old and dull.

She yanked me toward the bar, yelling, "Let's get out of here!"

What a relief.

The bartender leaned over the bar, eyebrows raised in question for our next order, but Keisha nodded toward me. "He'll pay the tab."

Which I did.

Outside, my ears rang in the aftermath of the bar, but I heard Keisha well enough.

"Sorry about all those pictures." She squeezed my arm as we walked down Barnard Street. "I'm a model, actress, and social influencer."

"Sounds...interesting." What else was I supposed to say? "What have you acted in? Maybe I've seen it." *Doubtful.*

"Only background work, so far, but I have tons of followers, so it'll happen."

Curiosity got the best of me. "Where do you work?" That dress wasn't free, and she had to eat.

"I told you."

"Yeah, but I mean for money?" Tacky question, sure, but *come on.*

"I live with my parents while I attend SCAD."

Good lord, a college student. What had Anuli done? "How old are you?"

She howled like I'd asked a hilarious question. "I turned twenty-one last week." With impressive balance on high heels, she ran ahead of me to strike a sexy pose. "I'm holding up well in my old age, don't you think?"

"Twenty-one is young." *Really young.*

Keisha waved away my comment. "Not in show business. Tons of people get discovered in their teens." She held up her phone. "I can make you famous, even if you are creeping toward old fart." Pictures flashed, certain to paint me as a startled zombie.

"I don't want to be famous." We walked side-by-side again.

"Everybody wants to be famous, or they're lying to themselves." While she studied her phone, she tripped on a sidewalk crack. "Hold on, I have to rate Jazz'd." She typed with impressive speed, reading her words aloud. "Dinner was a supreme disappointment. The chef must have the night off or spent too much time getting high in the back alley. But my date and the dancing were hot!" A *whoosh* signaled her live post.

"Did you eat before I got there?"

"No, dummy. I didn't eat tonight. But I had to post something, and people love to complain. I give the people something to hate, something to talk about."

Why had I not planned an escape? In the movies, a call gives the guy an out. I didn't want to be rude, no matter how unfair and vicious she was, but I couldn't get through an entire evening with her.

I pulled out my phone. "Oh, shoot. My mom texted. She depends on me..." Shit, I had to be careful; Anuli knew my parents didn't live in town. And my mom would flick me in the back of the head for pretending she relied on me. If anything, I rely on her.

"Up to you, but I have to review this date, and

so far, it's not going well." She stopped walking and folded her arms across her chest.

"Do you want me to call you a car?"

A streetlight illuminated her impressive scowl. "What do I look like, a tourist?"

"Okay, if you're sure." I turned in the other direction.

"Don't you dare *think* about leaving now if you want my followers to like you."

I heard the shutter sound of her phone taking pictures of me as I walked away.

Before I made my getaway, Keisha screeched, "Wait!"

My teeth pressed together, but I was raised by a Southern woman, so I made my manners and turned around. Keisha frowned at her phone and held one wait-a-minute finger in the air. "Go figure. My followers love you."

Still clutching her phone in one hand, she jammed both fists on her curvy hips.

A pink shoe tapped.

"Want to make a sex video?"

CHAPTER 5—ABBY

I stared at the plaster ceiling, my head resting on silky pillows chosen by a decorator who had promised to work fast as long as I paid a premium.

After another two weeks of unemployment, I wallowed under boredom thick enough to drown me. What the hell do retired people do with their days—one after the other, in a string of *blah* hours that tie them to the couch streaming shows or standing at their front door scrounging for conversation crumbs.

Ricky was right: Everybody needs a purpose. And damn it, I missed writing, the deadlines, my followers. I missed sending pro-women messages into the world...or at least a small part of it.

I missed work.

I needed work.

I needed Edith.

I rolled out of bed, my stomach tightening more with every minute closer to seeing my old boss. Unless I wanted to race to the bathroom every five minutes, I'd better grovel right away. Even with certain destruction looming, I paused to appreciate the interior decorator's work. She'd painted the master suite Wedgewood blue and furnished it with a four-poster queen-size bed and antique dressers. The adjoining bathroom held a clawfoot tub perfect for long soaks. Although my stomach squeezed in protest of the day, beauty and good vibes floated around the edges of my consciousness, giving me strength.

Forty-five minutes later, I stood in front of Edith with my hands clasped together, practically praying she'd say "yes."

"I made a mistake. By quitting. I made a mistake."

Edith stared over the rim of her glasses, silently demanding I keep groveling.

My legs shook. I wanted to sit in one of the uncomfortable chairs flanking her desk. "I shouldn't have quit. And I'm here to ask for my job back." I needed a sip of water. A gulp. A gallon.

She didn't move. "So do it."

"Do what?"

"Ask."

"Can I have my job back?"

"No." She dismissed me by squinting down at the paperwork in front of her.

"No? *Why*?" My whine sounded like the time I'd asked my high-school boyfriend why he broke up with me.

"Because you quit without a reason and without notice."

Fair.

"I'm sorry. I, um, was going through

something." It wasn't untrue.

Edith paused and peered at me again. "What something?"

"It was a family thing," I lied. "I can't really discuss it."

She leaned back and tented her fingers like any good nemesis would. "Okay, you can have a job."

Yes! This was more like it. I'd been damn good at my job. Of *course* she'd let me come back. I'd been silly to worry. "I can pick up where I left off."

With a shake of her head, she barked, "*No.* You can have *a* job, not your old job, which you slammed in a dumpster. You'll freelance."

No way. She meant paid by the story. I had to remind myself I didn't need the money; I needed the work.

"Okay, I accept your terms."

"You haven't heard my terms." Edith smiled, revealing smoke-stained teeth. Like a nemesis.

What now? I considered walking out, but I'd come too far in this groveling adventure, and my curiosity begged for closure. "What terms?"

She dropped the bomb. "You have twenty-four hours to come up with a project for articles, posts, followers, and ads. I don't mean a story. I mean an entire campaign, with multiple stories."

"Do you have a project in mind?" *Please have a project in mind.*

"Nada. Pull one out of your ass." She went back to her papers. "And it'd better be good.

Otherwise, no job for you."

As I drove away, my guts churned like the TV static in Poltergeist, supercharged by the three cups of coffee I'd gulped this morning. I could return to my big, beautiful, lonely house or visit my sister either to vent or for emotional support, whichever could be managed on short notice.

Easy decision.

I let myself in and marched into Karen's kitchen. This time of the morning, the kids were in school, and Ricky was off fixing a septic system, clogged toilet, or something else to do with bodily functions guaranteed to keep me miles away from plumbing. With three people gone, the house should be quiet, but pop music played from a Bluetooth speaker and added to the chaos of unfolded laundry, unwashed dishes, and the kids' latest art projects.

Karen busied herself at the stove, laying bacon on paper towels to suck up grease. Without turning around, she said, "Morning, sunshine. I'm making breakfast, round two."

I plopped into a kitchen chair and waited for her usual, "What's up?" so I could unload my dilemma. I thought about declining breakfast until my stomach settled, but Karen would give me an earful because, as she puts it, I'm "ridiculously skinny."

Not true.

Everyone has an ideal weight, and mine happens to be a smaller number than hers. She's also at least three inches taller than my five feet, six inches. I often remind her she's beautiful at any weight, a truth echoed by Ricky through fifteen years of marriage.

Karen's voice broke through my thoughts. "I have some exciting news." She turned from the stove with a wide smile. She had that look in her eye again, the one saying she's pregnant. I glanced around the sunny yellow kitchen as though a bouncy seat or other clue would present itself. Finding none, I went with my gut.

"Congratulations." I grinned.

"For what? I haven't told you the news yet." She slid a plate piled high with eggs, bacon, and toast in front of me. "Eat."

I examined my plate. "The eggs are wet." With both hands, I rescued the bacon and toast.

"What are you, five?" But she picked up my plate and scraped runny eggs back into the hot pan.

Seriously, who eats wet eggs? Cook those suckers brown and cover them with ketchup. "No, I just don't eat raw baby chickens."

"Gross." With a scrape of the pan, she scooted the eggs around, making them edible. "Back to me. My news."

"Another bundle of barf and poop and sunbeams? Soon you'll have a whole croquet team." I shoved an entire piece of bacon into my mouth, pausing to savor the world's perfect food.

"Croquet doesn't have teams."

"Exactly," I mumbled around the mouthful of bacon.

"Maybe this new baby will call you Aunt Abby."

I swigged my coffee to ease the food down. "I'll never be *aunt* anything. I'm only twenty-nine, which means I'm young and hip. Hip Abby. Maybe your kids can use my new name. Starting today."

Karen laughed and piled egg pebbles on my plate, exactly the way I like them. She poured her own cup of coffee and sat at the table. "When am I going to be an aunt? I need some kids to spoil."

"You've got kiddos covered with your own rugrats." I grinned to let her know I was kidding. "The minute I start dating someone, you'll know. You know everything about my life."

"Now that you mention it, I'm still mad at you for not telling me the day you quit your job."

"About that..."

"Uh-huh?" She folded her arms.

"Long story short, I quit like a spoiled trust-fund kid, bored myself to tears and sunburn, and asked Edith for my job back this morning."

"Holy crap." She dropped her arms and leaned forward. "What did she say?"

"To prove myself, I can freelance."

"*Freelance*? After years with the magazine?" Bless her, she always took my side, often against karma. "Edith is a—"

"It's fair, and I accepted her terms." I glanced

out the window over the sink. Now the hard part. "But for the job, I have to come up with an entire project on my own. Something big. Something ensuring subscribers, followers, and ad revenue."

"Ouch. Got any ideas?"

"Not one."

"Come on, let's rally. What would hook people on your Instagrams and tics?"

My sister's stubborn ignorance is endearing. I've told her a hundred times to say "Insta" and "TikTok," but she keeps missing the boat. I can't decide if she does it on purpose, but it still makes me laugh every time. "I need something fresh, trendy, *hip*. Something sure to grab people's attention and give me plenty to write about for a while."

"You could cover fashion trends."

"Ugh." I noted my sweatpants and flannel shirt, neither of which screamed "fashionista."

"How about make-up tips?"

"Shoot me."

Karen pushed back her chair and walked her cup to the sink, leaving me to shove another piece of bacon in my mouth. Heaven. Over her shoulder, she pointed out, "You could date people for the project." The *clank* of dishes nearly drowned her out.

"It's been done thousands of times."

"With every single time different in some way. That's what makes two people together so interesting!" She clucked her tongue like she'd offered the perfect story. "Maybe you'll find your soulmate out there."

Always a romantic, my sister couldn't get enough of romance novels, rom-coms, and happily ever after. "Karen, I love you. You know I do. But there's no such thing as a soulmate."

"Everyone has a soulmate. You have to open yourself up to finding him."

I appreciated her blind faith in cosmic energies and serendipity, but they weren't realistic when it came to relationships. Did she see Ricky as the only possible person for her? Sure, he's a great guy, but they'd had ups and downs, like everyone else. How could I ask the question gently? Always opting for the straightforward approach, I blurted, "Is Ricky your soulmate?"

She stopped washing dishes and faced me, focused on something above and beyond my head. "Oh yes." The woman practically swooned. "That big, strong, beautiful man is my one true love." Karen closed her eyes and hugged herself, smiling like she'd won the lottery.

"Okay, that's fair." I knew a losing argument when I saw one. "But what about arranged marriages? What chance do those women have to find their soulmate?" I wasn't trying to destroy my sister's theory completely, but entire cultures survived with marriages planned like a merging of companies. Men and women who didn't exactly follow their hearts still lived happily, shared dreams and children, and built long futures.

After sitting down again, my sister seemed to consider the question. "You make a good point. Maybe it's luck. Maybe it's fate."

"Or maybe life throws us together with people at the right time in the right place, and as long as we're open to a match, we do okay."

With a frown broadcasting her skepticism, Karen asked, "Are you saying *any* two people can be happy together?"

"Basically, yeah. I think so."

"Where's the magic?" She sounded concerned, but I stuck to my argument.

"No magic. Two people trying to get along. Seems pretty easy as long as no one is rude, abusive, or cheats."

Karen raised one eyebrow. "Well, there's your story."

My story? I couldn't have heard her right. "Are you saying I should look for a husband?"

"No, I'm saying you should marry the next guy who comes along. If it fails, I'm right, but at least you're dating again. If it works, you're right, and I get a brother-in-law and maybe some nieces and nephews." She shrugged her shoulders. "It's a win-win."

Typical Karen. Nuts. Ever since we were kids, she'd suggest outrageous opinions, and we'd bounce the ideas around for a while, coming up with more and more outrageous angles, always acting like the idea could really happen. "We're too old and sophisticated to compete."

"Chicken." My sister grinned. "What have you got to lose?"

"My life! I could marry a serial killer!"

"Oh, come on, what are the chances the UPS guy or the nearest accountant will kill you? And besides, you could do a background check."

Just for fun, I ran with her proposal (lame pun intended). And to be honest, other ideas weren't bursting forth. "He'd have to be about my age."

Karen played along, tapping her fingers on the table. "And sexy. Real eye-candy."

I bit into jam-covered toast—a stall tactic. Not one to be dissuaded, my sister continued her signature intense stare. I swallowed. "But I don't have to have sex. I mean, it's not off the table, but it couldn't be required, either."

With a sober nod, my sister agreed. "Sex should always be a choice."

"True…" I drew out the word as another stall tactic. "How long would this fictional marriage have to last before I'm declared the winner?"

"Forever. Isn't that your claim? Any match can work?"

"Yeah, for sure, but for the sake of argument, when would you concede?"

"Ooh, fair question." She wiped table crumbs into her hand and dusted them onto an abandoned plate. "A year?"

"Six months?" I countered. A year seemed like a very long time. Heck, six months did too, but we were in fantasyland anyway.

Karen shook her head. "Tell you what. I'll admit you're right about random pairings at the three-month mark."

"Holy shit. This little chat could turn into a kick-ass project." My heart picked up a notch.

"Yeah, yeah." She grinned.

I ignored her verbal pat on the head and offered another rule. "And he has to live in my house, so we'd be stuck with each other. In separate bedrooms." I leaned back and grabbed a piece of unopened junk mail and a pen from the counter. "Wait, let me write this down."

Dishes were pushed across the table, and Karen leaned on her elbows. "Good! You'll really get to know each other in three months. After the honeymoon period, what? You tell the guy he can leave?"

I scribbled copious notes. "Or he can decide to stay married."

Karen frowned again. "What about you? You're half the relationship. What if you want out?"

I stopped writing and looked up. "I see what you mean. Okay, at three months we each get to decide. If we both want to continue, we do. But if one of us wants out, we divorce. Will that work?"

"Write it down!" Karen pointed to the envelope I'd nearly filled with my scrawl.

"Now, how do you get a normal guy to go along with this?"

"Easy." I leaned back, confident in my answer. "Me! A happy marriage to me."

My lovely sister made a *pth-th* noise with her tongue. "How can you sweeten the deal?"

I thought for a few seconds, examining the "Live, Laugh, Love," "Choose Joy," and "Money Can't Buy Love" driftwood planks above the sink. *That's it!* "A prenup promising twenty thousand dollars when the marriage ends."

Eyes wide, Karen leaned back. "The guy has to choose between staying married to you or taking the payout?"

"Exactly!" I wrote it down. Although I didn't believe in magic when it came to relationships, I wholeheartedly believed in the magic of the written word. As I read over my notes, the plan began to take shape. What did I have to lose? Soon enough I'd be in my thirties, and I hadn't had a lover for more than a year, after which we'd remained friends or at least acquaintances. Besides, I'd never hidden my drive to build a career, which meant most of my energy over the past several years went toward writing.

No harm, no foul.

I couldn't exactly wait for my career to build again; today I started from square one.

Karen gave me her serious face. "Do you *want* to get married?"

The past weeks of relative solitude had

brought home the fact that I wanted a partner. I was ready for a long-term commitment, as long as the guy didn't have skeletons in his closet or a trunk full of emotional baggage. People could say I didn't need a man to complete me, but what should matter most is how *I* feel. I wanted a relationship. I wanted marriage. I wanted love. If there was no shame in flying solo, there should be no shame in admitting loneliness. I didn't want a husband because society told me I should; I wanted a husband because my heart ached for him.

I could have written my thoughts, where I could read, reflect, and revise, but I couldn't organize the words for my mouth. For now, I'd focus on the magazine campaign, a step removed from my own ruminations on love.

In the silence, Karen covered my hand with hers. "Stick with articles about fashion and make-up. This one's too personal."

"Which is exactly what makes it perfect." I grinned to ease her worry.

She must have read the change in tone because she removed her hand and raised an eyebrow again. "You're not seriously thinking of doing this, are you?" She shook her head like she'd already decided for me. "Think of all the reality shows out there tossing people together. It's been done a thousand—"

"With every single time different in some way. That's what makes it so interesting!" I had her. "Think about it. I won't ask people to be dishonest, I won't exploit them or humiliate them, and I won't televise their worst qualities, some of which could be scripted. I'll seek a marriage partner for myself and tell the truth at every step." *Yes! This would work.*

She bit the inside of her cheek. "Fair enough. I can see the differences, and no one can own romance anyway. But you're my sister! I'd worry about you." But I saw the grin pulling at the edges of her mouth. She was intrigued, exactly the response I could expect from my readers. And from Edith.

The envelope taunted me. I practically itched to write this series of articles, already considering the interesting possibilities. I'd take my readers along for the entire ride, from sharing the plan to executing it and reporting each day's progress. I could call it "Random Husband."

I grinned across the table. My world was about to turn upside down.

I dropped the pen and picked up the envelope, tapping it against my free hand. "Why would you worry?"

My sister laughed out loud. "Because your husband will be a stranger!"

"Every new relationship starts as strangers, but most people date, have nights of wild sex, or take on roommates. Right now, thousands of people are opening themselves up to a stranger, and ninety-nine point nine percent of the time, everything is fine."

"But—"

"What we're talking about is no different from what people already do."

"The marriage part is different."

"Why? What makes commitment a problem?"

I read Karen's discomfort, but I waited. She shrugged and looked toward heaven. "Marriage is forever."

There you go. She saw what I saw. I considered not responding, but she had laid it out so beautifully, teed up and ready to go. I swung. "Nearly fifty percent of marriages end in divorce. I expect your marriage to last forever, but no way are all of them keepers."

"Well, damn."

"Tell you what. I'll keep you in the loop every step of the way." Truth was, I planned to keep everyone in the loop. That was the point. I'd show two random people could be content together. Logically, I knew there would be hiccups, but I also knew for sure every relationship had problems to overcome. And three months would fly by, hopefully as a preview to a long, fulfilling marriage.

"You'll run a background check?" Karen asked, more an order than a question.

She's in. I saw it on her face.

I jumped up and kissed the top of her head.

"I promise." Well, I promised for the magazine. But I recognized a winning idea when I saw one, and this idea would blow Edith's sagging panty hose off. All I had to do was make sure the concept would work in the non-Hollywood world of Savannah, Georgia. I couldn't present a half-assed idea to Edith. I needed a test case.

Karen stood and hugged me. "Be careful!"

I extricated myself and my precious crumpled envelope and headed for the front door. "Always!" But my mind was already on the next step: Find a husband.

CHAPTER 6—MAX

Avoid a wife. Avoid a fiancé. Avoid women.

If Zoe incinerated my faith in women, Keisha stomped on the ashes.

Every afternoon around three o'clock, Keisha showed up at the store, pretending to talk with Anuli but ostensibly scoping me out. Who knew rejection wielded so much power, especially after one hour-long date?

As the clock inched toward three, I considered hiding in my apartment, but damn it, this was my store, and I couldn't abandon work over a minor—no, major—inconvenience. From behind the counter in the back of the room, I glanced toward the door every three minutes, dread co-opting my attention. I'd given Anuli the day off, hoping her absence would mean Keisha wouldn't show.

I glanced up again.

Keisha blocked the front door, wiggling hello with her fingers.

Shit.

She'd already seen me. No time to escape.

"Hello, future lover!" Her voice echoed around the crowded room, bounced off the wide expanse of concrete floor, and accosted my ears.

By the time she reached the counter, I steeled myself to firmly tell her I wasn't interested. Manners be damned. Two weeks of dodging advances was enough.

"Hi, Kiesha. Anuli's off today."

"I know, dreamboat. I counted on it." She reached across the counter and patted my chest. It took all my control not to step back.

She batted her obviously fake eyelashes while purring in what she must have thought was a sexy voice, "I wanted your full attention, mister."

"Keisha, look—"

"Hear my offer." She reached across the counter to touch me again; this time I did step back. Is this what women put up with from men, stalking, pawing, and ignoring polite hints to go away?

I gave her the line I'd wanted from Zoe. "It's not you, it's me." There. Case closed.

"What the hell does that mean?" She frowned but then shook her head as though dispersing my negative cloud. "Never mind." Her next words boomed, as though she needed an audience to approve. "The point is, I don't think you understand what I'm offering: a no-strings-attached sexual relationship. Is my generous offer clear enough for you?"

Customers leaked out. Tables opened. I raged.

She held up her phone and clicked pictures of either herself or me, depending on which way the camera faced. I opened my mouth to offer my own nugget of clarity, but she kept talking. "I only ask you to help me document the affair. I've polled my followers, and they want to see more of you. Don't you want to be famous?"

This woman, this *girl*, was ridiculous.

"No." This had to stop. "I don't. Sex is private, I'm private." I stopped short of telling her I wouldn't have sex with her in private, either. She should have gleaned that from my first rejection.

"Good god, how *old* are you? Join this century, already. Nothing is private, and you should do whatever feels good."

Fine.

Whatever feels good.

I walked from behind the counter and looked down at her. She smirked and held up her phone to document my agreement. "There you go, Max, show me what you're made of. Show everybody." The phone blocked her face.

For a second, I hesitated. Everything I said and did would be captured. Then I realized I didn't care. Hell, maybe people needed to hear it.

The phone loomed closer. "Keisha, I don't want any kind of relationship with you. Period. And I'm asking you to stop coming to the coffee shop. I work here. Your friend works here. The operative word is 'work.'" I placed a hand on her shoulder blade and guided her toward the door. "Please post this and tell your followers I'm not interested in them or fame or you."

We reached the door. I held it open for her. She stumbled out, glancing back and still holding up her phone. As the door closed, she videoed me, which I assume continued as I walked away, fuming too much to smile at gawking customers.

Within an hour, Anuli stormed in and plopped her enormous purse on the display case. "What have you done?"

I didn't bother to play dumb.

"She's nuts." I said it with no enthusiasm. A strong reaction would have meant I cared.

Anuli closed her eyes and shook her head. "Her posts are trashing you *and* the coffee shop." She opened her eyes and bit her lip. "Let's assume she doesn't have enough followers to impact business."

"She'll calm down, right?"

"Watch your back."

I took her advice. Every time the door opened, I clenched up, tense and waiting for disaster to strike again in the form of a woman scorned, but as the minutes passed, I relaxed enough to focus on customers and remember why I loved the shop. The smell, the smiles, the steady stream of work, filled me with a sense of well-being and purpose.

Kismet rewarded me; Porsche woman strolled in the door.

Of all the coffee shops in all the towns in all the world, she walked into mine.

I saw her through the glass of the roasting

room tucked behind the counter, my eyes drawn to her the minute she appeared, almost as though I'd been waiting for her, searching for her. Only I wasn't. Because women were trouble. But this one, this woman, might be different. I told myself she was different.

She ordered a coffee from Anuli, then wandered around outside the roasting room before leaning against the wall, adjusting her stance, her hands, and her gaze, fidgeting with her whole body. I thought about the one middle-school dance my mom had made me attend. The boys huddled in clusters of false bravado, pushing each other and laughing, and the girls propped themselves against the opposite wall, trying to project "pretty and available." Every once in a while, a couple of girls would amble over to our side of the gym, where we bragged about them wanting to be closer to us. Now, as an adult, I tried not to make much of this woman choosing a spot nearby. After all, there were no open tables.

Either way, I wanted to make some kind of contact with her, so I stared. I won't make excuses for it. I wanted her to see me. Every move I made was meant to get her attention, especially smelling those toasty beans, making eye contact, and smiling before turning away from her.

She saw me. I know she did. My heart kicked up a notch, but I reminded myself I needed a break from women.

Did she remember me?

I glanced her way again.

My ego wavered. Apparently she didn't remember me or didn't care; her attention focused on the room. A table near her opened, and she made herself less uncomfortable, less conspicuous. I was thrown off when she lounged back and opened her knees, like she was trying to communicate "Come and get it," but she quickly sat up and crossed her legs, changing the message to "I'm a spinster librarian with cats."

Intrigued, I stopped pretending to work. She stood, and I felt a moment of disappointment, but she bought another coffee and changed tables. What was she searching for? *Who* was she searching for? Of course, a woman like her would be attached. Maybe she was married. I needed to get a grip on my libido and live in the real world where a beautiful woman didn't waltz into my life and announce, "I'm available."

Besides, I wasn't interested.

Wasn't.

Interested.

Still, I watched.

She abandoned her chair and approached a man sitting a few tables away, walking like she'd forgotten how. *Come on, man*, I silently shamed him. *Look at her*. I'd have been much smoother than the dolt with the computer. For no good reason, I felt a pang of jealousy in my guts. I wanted to hear their conversation, but the spinning arm of the cooling tray behind me filled the air.

I needed to get back to work. But instead, I stubbornly held my spot, trying to unravel the mystery before me. They'd probably leave together, wrecking my sad little fantasy.

I couldn't have guessed—or understood—what would happen next.

CHAPTER 7—ABBY

Wow. My heart thumped in my chest. I couldn't decide if the handsome barista or my mission was to blame.

The mission.

I forced tunnel vision to keep me on track. So what if the barista was mystery man from my Porsche past. A man with a girlfriend wasn't part of my plan.

Crossing the floor had required one cautious step after another, each step punctuated with a silent reminder that my job and my future were mine to control. Master of my destiny. Captain of my ship. Owning my truth.

I examined the target. He appeared to be in his late twenties or early thirties, had dark blond hair, and I suppose brown eyes, but it was hard to tell because he kept frowning at his computer screen. He wore nondescript pants and a "Yee-Haw" T-shirt, which I assumed to be ironic.

Fortune favors the bold, right? Tell it to my racing heart. As I grabbed the back of a chair, I thought I might throw up, pass out, or keep walking until I was safely back home. I paused there, wondering what the hell to do next. He didn't immediately glance up, so I raised my cup in his direction and asked, "Can I buy you a cup of coffee?"

His head snapped up. "Huh?"

Okay, he might not be eloquent, but nobody's perfect. I tried again, throwing in a nervous laugh. "Coffee. Would you like some coffee?"

The poor man frowned in confusion. "I already have coffee, thanks."

I closed my eyes for a second to regain a shred of dignity. It didn't work. My head told me to *run away*, but my reckless hand pulled out a chair, dragging the metal legs against the concrete in an teeth-rattling *screech*. "Would you like some company?"

I sat.

If a person's face could slam its shutters and display a "closed" sign, this man's face did just that. What could he be thinking? Oh crap, he probably figured I was a hooker, drinking coffee and randomly turning tricks in a coffee shop during the slow afternoon hours. A working girl trying to make a buck.

He stared, mouth open. "I don't have any cash with me, sorry."

Oh! He thought I was panhandling. I tried to ease my intrusion with a smile. "No, I don't need money." I'd better come up with a cover story to get past this horrible crash-and-burn approach. "Sorry, my sister told me I couldn't meet a nice man at a coffee shop, and I was hoping to prove her wrong." I scooted my chair back a little, expecting him to come around. "I only wanted to say 'Hi,' so hi. I'll leave you alone now." Offering my most charming and innocent smile, I raised my coffee in salute.

"Wait!" He closed his laptop. "Don't rush off. We're just getting to know each other." With an exaggerated wink, he extended his hand. "I'm Jeremy." We shook, grinning at each other, and he added, "Nice to meet you..."

"Abby." I had his full attention, and I patted myself on the back. He was handsome, appeared to be single, and had no obvious red flags. Well, I didn't love the wink thing, and his fingers felt delicate and soft, but other than those anomalies, Jeremy seemed fine.

He leaned forward, a sure sign he was interested. Bingo. This was easier than I thought. Now I needed him to agree to marry me. I leaned forward, mirroring his posture to encourage his subconscious. Jeremy's pupils dilated, which meant he had spent the morning at the eye doctor, the afternoon sun was bright, or he liked me. I was pretty sure it was the latter.

I was crushing it.

With another exaggerated wink for no apparent purpose, Jeremy asked, "What do you do?" Another wink. "Besides meet nice men in coffee shops?"

I tried to ignore his facial tic. This was my opening for what I *really* wanted from him. With a smile, I laid it on the table. "I'm glad you asked. Actually, I'm a writer for *Women First*, a magazine devoted to women's issues." When he bent back a little, I knew he thought I was driving down a political road, and he did not want to be my passenger. I clambered out of the hole I was digging. "I write about things like exercise, nutrition, and relationships."

He relaxed and smiled again. "Sounds cute."

Cute? Who says "cute?" As in, "That girl is so cute with her thoughts and words." Still, I had a job to do. "Yeah, it's great. Right now, I'm working on a relationship piece. Here's the idea: Two randomly-paired people can get married and create a happy life together."

He nodded, clearly trying to act interested in my cute idea. "Fun." The last of Jeremy's coffee found its way into his gullet.

I was running out of time.

"I plan to try it out."

Still nodding, he grinned across the table at me. "Super fun. Like in some cultures with arranged marriages." I could have explained arranged marriages demanded a lot of preparation and weren't entirely random, but Jeremy was now examining my chest region, so I was pretty sure he wouldn't process such valuable information.

I forged ahead. "I plan to marry someone I don't know and show we can get along."

My companion froze like a rat who suddenly came upon a screeching human. "Huh?"

I talked faster and stretched toward him. "I'm hunting for a husband, but it's only for three months, then we'd both decide if the arrangement is a success."

Jeremy cut his eyes right, then left, as though someone might offer him a way out of this conversation. I covered his hand with mine, irrationally thinking the gesture would hold him to the table. It did not. With a weird little grunt reminiscent of a belch, he closed his computer, tucked it under his arm, and got to his feet, all the while avoiding eye contact with me.

The money!

I forgot to tell him about the money.

I jumped up as winky, delicate-fingered Jeremy power walked toward the front door. "Wait, I can pay you!"

CHAPTER 8—MAX

"Wait, I can pay you!" bounced around the room.

If I'd been drinking coffee, I'd have done a spit take. Pay him for what? A woman who looked like her didn't need to buy sex. Hold on, why had my mind gone straight to sex? The guy could be a contractor, and she needed him to build a fence or back porch.

Or sex.

She might be asking for sex.

The idea was definitely more entertaining and made me smile. I felt laughter in the back of my throat but nearly labeled it indigestion before recognizing I was having a good time.

Heads craned in her direction, coupled with whispers unrelated to the wonders of coffee.

I stared, emerging from my sanctuary for a better view. The woman might be nutty, but she was entertaining, and her quirkiness wasn't directed at me, thank god.

Shit.

She stormed toward me. I couldn't tell if she was angry or embarrassed, but her cheeks flamed red. I kept smiling, not even sure why I wanted to. She stopped on the other side of the counter and handed me an empty cup. For a minute, I felt sorry for her. Whatever she'd come here for clearly hadn't gone as planned, and now she had to do the walk of shame across the room to the front door.

Through clenched teeth, she said, "Thank you for the delicious latte."

I wanted to come around the counter and hug her to let her know she could pay me for sex any time. Instead, I said, "Glad you liked it."

I'll be damned if her cheeks didn't turn a darker red. Her embarrassment was palpable. Then she nodded at me once like we'd made a deal and walked away. I wanted to peek behind the curtain and know about the woman who blushed so easily. I had absolutely no idea what her life was like and not a clue about her personality, but I was intrigued by her story, whatever it might be. I think my slight infatuation was based on the firm belief I'd never solve the riddle; today's snafu probably meant she'd never set foot in my store again. She'd remain a mystery, and eventually I'd stop wondering about her.

Halfway across the room, she turned back and locked her eyes on mine. I forgot to be embarrassed for watching her exit.

She leaned her head to one side. "Have we met?" I couldn't tell from her expression if she knew the answer.

"Have we?" I kicked myself for playing it cool.

Her smile disappeared, and she shook her head. "My mistake."

I watched her leave, the door closing silently behind her, willpower rooting me to the spot. *Wait! We've met. I remember every detail, every nuance, every smile.*

I might have, too, if Keisha hadn't rushed in, shoving dread in front of her like a train scooping an unlucky cow from the tracks.

CHAPTER 9—ABBY

He didn't remember me. I'd made no lasting impression. Then why did I remember every second of our interaction, right down to the pink color of the evening air? Silver lining: The sexy barista wouldn't alter my budding plan for Random Husband. I refused to live in fantasy land, demurely waiting for the universe to provide Mr. Right.

Back in my sister's kitchen, I prepared to bounce ideas at her like a client with her therapist. I didn't need her to talk—merely listen.

I plopped down at the table and patted the top. "Come sit. I need help."

From behind me, she said in a monotone, "These clothes aren't going to fold themselves, and the kids will be home soon." I heard the unspoken message: *Get your ass over here and fold.*

I trudged to the counter and picked up some of Ricky's boxers. Holding them up with two fingers, I graced Karen with an "ew" before opting for a tiny pink T-shirt. Now that I had her attention, I relayed the entire coffee-shop debacle. When my beloved sister stopped laughing, I prompted, "Are you finished? May I continue?"

She wiped her eyes with a sock. "There's more? Oh, please. Please continue."

"I explained my offer. I was direct and clear, but he ran away. How can I describe it better? What did I do wrong?"

Karen made a valiant attempt to stop smiling and give my problem the serious consideration it deserved. "You talked."

"Yes, that much is obvious. It's how people communicate other than charades. Are you suggesting I act out my plan?"

She shook her head while folding a huge T-shirt. "No, you talked. But not everyone is like us, direct, straight to the point. Some people need time to think and process."

I threw up my hands in a most unappreciative gesture. "I could talk veeeerrrrrry slowwwwwly."

Rolling her eyes toward the ceiling, she sighed. "Or?"

She'd better be talking about buying a rowboat because this "or" business wasn't helping. If I couldn't talk or play charades, how would I communicate the— *Oh!* Wait a minute. I covered my open mouth with a hand and stared wide-eyed at Karen. "I could *write*!"

"There it is, folks. A writer can write."

"Yes! I knew I'd find a solution. I barely needed to toss some ideas at you." To let her know I was joking, I channeled my new friend

Jeremy and gave her an exaggerated wink.

She paused her folding marathon. "Is something in your eye?"

"No, I was winking."

"Well stop it. It's creepy."

She wasn't wrong.

Before we could outline the new plan, the kiddos barged in for an after-school snack, then dredged up an absurd amount of homework. Minutes ticked by as first Eli then Prissy insisted on another piece of cinnamon toast, a second glass of milk, and some hugs from mom as Eli attempted "new" math, and Prissy read a book for a sticker and a school party at the end of the week. I finally had to promise I would check their progress in thirty minutes, a declaration that sent them racing upstairs with the wild glee only children can feel.

Once again alone with our thoughts, we both leaned against a kitchen counter and tweaked the project. Obviously, I'd write the details in an article and promote the hell out of it on social media.

Karen asked, "How will you review the candidates? Or will you randomly pick from resumés?" Apparently, her job was to poke holes in my plan.

"Hmm, might be a little too random, even for me. I think I need interviews."

"Okay, makes sense."

"But I'd rather have a buffer between me and

the candidates. Someone could maybe interview them and give me input." I smiled with more teeth than necessary. "Two heads are better than one."

"Here we go." Her ChapStick-covered lips pressed closed.

"Come on. It'll be fun, and we might not get any candidates. Look what happened this morning."

My stubborn sister folded her arms across her chest. And caved. "Okay, let's say I'll help. I don't want to meet people here." She gestured around her modest kitchen like it was a mansion full of priceless heirlooms. But I got her point; I had learned the importance of privacy.

"What's public and safe? The library?" I asked.

"Too quiet for interviews."

I clapped my hands together. "Historic Coffee Roasters!"

She pursed her lips in thought, but I already knew it was the perfect setting. With a nod, she said, "Okay." Shooing me away like an errant dog, she added, "Now get upstairs and play with your niece and nephew."

Φ

The next morning, an hour before my deadline expired, I sat in Karen's driveway and reviewed my notes on Random Husband.

Like a coward, I called Edith rather than appear in her office. I prefer rejection from a comfortable distance.

I would say she gushed, but Edith doesn't gush. Basically, she said, "Okay, this better be good." She actually agreed to the payout if the marriage failed, as long as ads covered the expense. In her words, "Otherwise, you and I are going to have a talk about debt."

"Don't you want to know why I'm willing to make this project so personal?" I was ready to explain that people had died for love, kings had given up thrones for love, and I wanted a happy ending.

"None of my business. If it sells, it sells."

"But I have a whole speech."

"Save it for the project." I could almost hear her slicing edits into a colleague's article. *Scritch scritch*. Like a rat shredding paper for a nest. "Some rules: All materials and interactions will be public. Applicants must agree to an open-book marriage, at least for the trial three months. Not negotiable."

"I figured." I'd present any truth in a loving way. Edith couldn't write my words for me.

Just when I thought I was in the clear, her voice scratched across the phone waves. "Nobody wants to see you marry a freeloader. Applicants have to earn at least eighty-thousand a year."

What? "Where did you get such an oddly specific number?"

"Last time I checked, it's what *you* made when you had a job."

Ouch. "But a paycheck shouldn't—"

"We don't want a bunch of money-grubbers competing only for a payout. This is supposed to be a real match."

She cared about my happiness? "I appreciate your concern, but I doubt anyone would—"

"I've made my decision." Edith coughed into the phone. She wouldn't bend.

"Any way I could have an assistant?" I pushed my luck.

"Minimum wage, and you find one." Her very un-Edith assent told me she loved the project. "I don't have time to—"

"Got it!" Karen wouldn't take money from me, but she'd have to accept payment directly from the magazine for her work.

I emerged from my self-imposed phone booth and swaggered across the lawn, giddy with my reclaimed title of "writer." After rapping a playful knock on the door, I used my key to enter.

"Heeeeeeere's Abby!" I giggled at my reference to *The Shining.*

Karen grudgingly agreed to payment, and we ironed out the project details to make sure we hadn't missed anything. Because Karen's voice is gentler than mine, we agreed she would speak voiceovers to posted pictures. And because I'm a control freak, I reminded her she had promised to accept applications on my behalf. In fact, I reminded her she was *excited* to meet and interview a few potential brothers-in-law. Essentially, I was doing her a *huge* favor, adding spice and excitement to her life, a fact echoed by Ricky when he came home for lunch and caught me goading his wife.

He pulled Karen into a bear hug, growling playfully into her hair. "Honey pie, think about it, you'll get to hang out with lonely men all day. Sounds like an exciting time to me." He grabbed a sandwich off the counter and walked past where I typed at the kitchen table, patting me once on the top of the head and saying, "boop," like he'd done since I was a teenager. "Abbigail, keep her out of trouble." He disappeared to plunge someone's toilet, leaving us to our important work.

In the article, I explained to readers the psychology behind relationships, including the finding that opposites do not attract, or if they do, it's a temporary match doomed from the start. In truth, similar people attract, especially those with overlapping core values, such as religious beliefs, desire for a family, and agreement on lifestyle choices like level of physical activity. As long as two people are minimally attracted to each other and share similarities, they should have a good chance together. I also covered the randomness of attraction, which is mainly based on who we're thrown together with and how often. This bit of research explains why people end up sleeping with their co-workers. It's not necessarily a mid-life crisis; an administrative assistant simply spends plenty of time with the boss.

Next, I laid out the plan.

I would randomly pick my husband. As long as we felt some attraction and shared similarities, we should be able to make a marriage work. Despite supreme discomfort, I admitted a successful candidate must earn at least eighty thousand a year (proven by the past twelve pay stubs) in a reputable job. In other words, no drug dealers, although I assumed they wouldn't have pay stubs to share. I also explained the magazine would run a background check to make sure a candidate didn't have a history of bad decisions, such as bankruptcy or imprisonment.

On a whim, I added the stipulation he couldn't have an ex-wife because prior marriages brought more baggage than I needed.

On a second whim, I added no children. I wasn't prepared to deal with extra houseguests.

And no pets. A cat or dog or pot-bellied pig might be fun, but I wasn't open to a tarantula or boa constrictor, so why unbolt that door?

The new husband would live in my home, with separate bedrooms, for a minimum of three months, at which time we'd each decide if the marriage would continue. At the very least, we'd evaluate the success of the relationship. Finally, I added the money promise. Dissolving the marriage would mean twenty thousand dollars popped into my ex-husband's bank account, no muss, no fuss.

In the final paragraph, I announced the interviews at Historic Coffee Roasters from ten in the morning until two in the afternoon next Friday. A link sent interested candidates to a form asking for a picture, annual income, personal history, and general interests, which I modeled after popular dating sites. If Karen was able to pick a few candidates, Edith would have the magazine's legal team run a background check and verify relevant details, such as employment.

After I finished a rough draft, I wrote preliminary hype for Karen to read as a voiceover to pictures of the magazine cover, the coffee shop, and locations across downtown Savannah. We focused on TikTok, Insta, and YouTube for now, agreeing we might later expand to other platforms. More hype would preview the first article, teasing readers into buying and reading *Women First* to get the whole story. Posts would also give me time to fine-tune the article and brainstorm about what came next.

I had a ton of exciting work to do!

After kissing my sister on the cheek and accepting the sandwich she packed "in case I got hungry," I drove home to relax in a long, hot bath. A bubble bath continued to be my favorite luxury and where I did my best thinking.

Long ago I'd learned to write a first draft and spend time mulling over ways to improve the piece, a smooth few days because changing is always easier than the first pass. This particular series had so much potential, starting with those social-media teasers I needed to turn over and craft in my head.

As I settled into neck-high bubbles, apprehension shimmered in the periphery. A husband? Was I willing to marry a stranger? But really, the man would simply be a glorified roommate, several of which I'd had during college, and sharing a home had been easy. As for the marriage part, I still firmly believed finding a life partner was random. Relationships—good, healthy relationships—moved from getting to know each other to adjusting for the other person and ultimately settling in for a long-term commitment, where sexual interest waned and small habits became annoying. After all, we're not married to ourselves, leaving us exposed year after year to someone else's foibles, with their gentle but ever-increasing weight. Lurking in the shadows of a wedding, divorce wrings its hands and smiles, waiting...always waiting. Certainly, in today's world, that specter often tiptoes into the light and becomes the elephant in the room, larger and larger until two people go their separate ways.

I had to remember my thoughts so I could write them down later. A sizzle of excitement ran up my spine as interesting new avenues opened. In every direction my mind turned, a fun possibility sent me racing down the road. I don't remember ever being this excited about a story, and this story held a motherload of installments.

Yes, the idea was pure gold.

I saw no downside. Even if only a few qualified men applied, I had a good chance of making the series work.

⚙

By Friday, my introductory article had been out for three glorious days. Social media had been abuzz for a few days longer, and other than the usual haters, people jumped on the idea like gnats on a sweaty face. Several followers demanded I accept applications from women, but since I'd promised honesty, I wasn't willing to feign sexual interest to make people happy. I encouraged women to seek wives in the same way I was seeking a husband. Truthfully, I admire people who speak (or write) their mind, as long as it's done in a peaceful way, and for the most part, my dissenters were kind. I also appreciated the chance to write about sexuality and remaining authentic regardless of societal demands.

As I'd expected, response soared higher than any previous piece, and every day brought an exponential increase in followers. The magazine pulled in plenty of sponsors and ads, which meant a satisfied editor and job security.

But mainly, this storm of activity was just plain fun.

I love my job.

At ten o'clock, I planned to sneak into the coffee shop and watch the action from a distance. I looked forward to sipping a fantastic cup of coffee while listening to Karen interview whoever might show up. I'm not exactly famous, but my avatar did appear on my work, so I dressed in an old pair of ripped jeans, a T-shirt claiming "Savannah is for Lovers," flip flops, and a Savannah Bananas baseball cap with my hair pulled back in a ponytail. To be safe, I added big purple sunglasses light enough to wear indoors.

Not knowing what to expect, I parked a few blocks away and meandered through Forsyth Park, pretending to enjoy the live oaks and mossy lace but really trying to calm my galloping heart. Today was a big day. Maybe not as big as my impending wedding day, but today held the potential for pleasant surprises. Fingers crossed that at least one candidate was similar to me and attractive, along with the other stipulations the lawyers would confirm.

Karen and I had thought of everything.

I breathed deep, feeling a joyful giggle threaten to break free, and turned the corner to the coffee shop.

And stopped.

Men of every shape and size crowded the front door, apparently trying to be the next person inside. Some sat at outdoor tables, their eyes glued to the front door. A few sipped coffees. From my vantage point on the corner, I'd have guessed more than fifty men stood outside, and I frantically tried to see if the flood had leaked into the building where my innocent sister held court. Unfortunately, the window tint and angle of the sun prevented me from seeing inside.

Head bowed, I repeated "excuse me" as I nudged my way through the front door. I suppose they let me pass because I clearly wasn't their competition. Once inside, I made a beeline straight to my little corner by the roasting booth. Three women worked the counter, but no way was I getting a coffee because the line was at least thirty men long. Instead, I wedged myself against the back wall and perused the room.

I shouldn't have been surprised when the big, dark-haired barista barged behind the counter. He did not look happy. His strong jaw clenched, and he squinted across the display of masculinity before turning his blazing blue gaze on me. His expression didn't change. I felt like a kid being reprimanded for making a mess in the house.

At least now he'd remember me.

The thought gave me little comfort.

I turned away, feigning interest in the superb paint job on the crown molding. To my surprise, he appeared at my side, gruffly shoving a paper cup of coffee in my hand and placing sugar and cream on a table. I noted the "to-go" nature of the gift. We stood side by side for a few seconds before he spoke.

"Is this you?" He gestured toward the room.

I could have pretended not to understand the question, but I had a feeling that game wouldn't work with him. Instead, I added Splenda and cream and sipped my coffee before responding, "Maybe not." I didn't make eye contact, preferring to watch Karen attempt crowd control.

She was going to kill me.

"Hm. Probably it is." Then he walked away. Rude. But the coffee was much appreciated, so I decided not to make a snarky comment.

A few rumination minutes later, I returned to the problem at hand. Karen gestured at a couple of men leaning toward her. If their frowns, bared teeth, and wild hand motions were any indication, no one was happy. I suppose I should have been flattered by the turnout, but I still hadn't completely digested the glut of interest. These men wanted—were willing—to marry me? If only a third of them qualified when the lawyers did their work, the task of choosing would be overwhelming. I assumed the problem held a solution, but right now I had to get Karen out of there.

Mistakes were made.

Likely this wouldn't be the first misstep, but I often told myself mistakes help lead us in the right direction, like a sheepdog nipping at heels to say, "Not that way, *this* way."

What I couldn't do was reveal my identity and add to the mayhem. But somehow, I had to urge Karen to excuse herself and then disappear. Tell them anything. She could say she has to pee, say someone else is coming in to take over, or say she has raging, debilitating diarrhea. Get out of there. We'd regroup in her kitchen and devise a new approach.

After seeing the turnout, it made more sense to start with the paperwork, fact checking, and background checks. Then I could go over the "dating" profiles of qualified candidates, after which Karen could conduct interviews. It might take a lot of convincing to get her to agree after today.

I scanned the room for the hunky barista and saw him working behind the counter—still frowning. I held my coffee in front of me like a shield and approached his left flank.

CHAPTER 10—MAX

Porsche woman had returned.

Probably not by accident, her appearance aligned with a sea of loud guys, with one woman huddled in the middle of the room, clutching a clipboard like a ship's mast on turbulent water. Men surrounded her table, yelling, frowning, and handing her papers. Too many voices bounced around the room for me to make out what anyone said, but the general feeling was pandemonium. At least most of them made their way to the counter, which was great for sales, but the three servers scrambled around, running into each other, almost as frazzled as the woman at the center of the commotion.

The chaos in the room was nothing compared to what was in my head.

I was torn between elated to see mystery woman and annoyed she was involved in this mess. Either way, I'd intended to sweep her off her feet the next time I saw her. A few days had passed since Keisha apologized—in front of Anuli and a camera—for her social-media terrorism, a contrite, although public, spectacle restoring some of my faith in women.

Unfortunately, mystery woman had avoided

eye contact and feigned interest in the ceiling. No encouragement there.

Since a friendly chat wouldn't work, I'd adjusted my strategy to a slightly grumpy business owner who wanted answers, hoping the approach would give me the upper hand —and some confidence. But after our brief interchange of my accusation and her vague denial, I'd had to walk away before I lost my super-cool image and needily asked her what was going on. *Please, pretty, hot, awkward lady, what are you up to, and can I play?*

Abandon and regroup.

I had only served three coffees when I felt her scrutiny. I glanced up to see her headed straight for me and mentally patted myself on the back for walking away, leaving her to make the next move. I gave her my best "sexy-intense" look and waited for her approach. Time for her to come clean on what was happening here.

She held my stare with a sexy-intense gaze of her own, and I gave her props for being able to pull it off behind bizarre purple glasses. "Excuse me. Can I ask for a favor?"

What the hell? A favor? No explanation? No flirting? I folded my arms. "Ask away." This should be good.

"Would you please take a note to my sister?" With a gesture toward clipboard woman, she grabbed a napkin and a pen from my counter and wrote, "*Abort mission! Meet at your house!*" She held out the drooping napkin. "I appreciate this."

I examined her face, still trying to figure her out, and damn if she didn't look up at me with big brown puppy-dog eyes, vulnerable and trusting at the same time. Way to bring out the protective urges in a man. What the hell. I had no choice but to help. Careful not to touch her hand because I really wanted to, I accepted the napkin and turned toward clipboard lady.

"Wait!" She grabbed my bicep and squeezed. Reflexively, I tightened, and when I faced her again, I saw something in her eyes that stirred lower parts too. I've been around long enough to know lust when I see it. She squeezed my arm again. Her pink tongue touched her top lip, and I almost forgot I was annoyed with her.

With a little shake of her head, she jerked her arm away. "Can you please wait until I leave?" Those brown eyes pleaded with me again, and I was toast.

I almost blurted, "Only if you come back," but I didn't want to show my hand, so I pressed my lips together and watched her walk away.

Again.

After the door closed behind her curvy ass, which about ninety percent of the men turned to watch, I carried the note to her sister. They did resemble each other, but the woman was clearly the older sibling. When I tapped her on the shoulder, she jumped. The nearest gaggle of men quieted, and the sister turned to me with a frown.

I handed her the napkin. "Your sister sent this." I should have walked away, but I stayed, hoping she'd offer an explanation.

Instead, she held the note to her chest and looked at me with soulful eyes in need, and I assumed she'd taught her younger sister how to look pitiful. She mouthed one word. "How?"

How is right. How did I get in the middle of this? But she seemed overwhelmed, and I couldn't leave her there. I leaned down and spoke into her ear so she could hear me. "Go around the left side of the counter, to the kitchen."

"But—" She gestured to the teeming room.

"I'll take care of it." *Somehow.*

She weaved through the mob toward the back, ignoring their shouted questions.

I turned my attention to the crowd and announced, "Sorry everybody! The lady wasn't feeling well and had to go home."

The crowd erupted with groans and angry shouts, none of which made much sense to me because I couldn't single out one person's voice. A couple of guys tapped me on the shoulder, and one of them loomed a few inches from my face to ask, "What the hell are we supposed to do now?"

"Dude, I don't know what you were doing *before*, so *now* is a big mystery to me."

For a second, he looked confused, but he rallied. "We're trying to bag a rich wife. And now she's gone."

I was speechless.

All of this was to marry off clipboard lady? She seemed attractive enough to find a husband the old-fashioned way, but times were changing. Don't get me wrong, I wish clipboard lady and her sister had asked me before bringing their strange transaction to my business, but I planned to make the best of it.

I raised a hand to the crowd and whistled using my other hand. The piercing sound silenced the room, buying me a few seconds. "Drip coffee is free with the purchase of food. We have sandwiches with fresh-baked bread and great desserts. Please form three lines at the counter."

From the back of the crowd, someone shouted, "What about the interviews?"

"I'm sure someone will get in touch with you soon."

I turned and walked toward the kitchen, determined to get some answers from clipboard lady.

She was gone.

CHAPTER 11—ABBY

When I arrived at my sister's house, Ricky's truck was parked outside the garage, where he rummaged through tools. He wouldn't side against his wife, but it couldn't hurt to bring him in the loop. I parked on the street and approached as he tossed a tool in his truck.

He glanced up. "Hi, Abbigail. What's cookin'?"

I lounged against the side of his truck and tried to appear nonchalant. "Oh, not much. Well, it's good news, in fact." He cut his eyes at me, already suspicious. "What I mean is, plenty of guys seemed interested in getting married. The place was packed."

Ricky frowned. "How many? And where is Karen?"

At least I had his full attention. "Here's the thing. A lot. I slipped her a note to run away and meet me here."

His mouth dropped open. "She's still there? Abby, tell me you didn't leave her there."

"I had to! I couldn't exactly waltz up to her without blowing my cover." I studied my shoes because meeting his eyes wasn't working for me.

"You're not an undercover detective busting

a drug ring." He shook his head. "If she's not here in three minutes, we're going back to get her."

I would have defended myself again, but Karen drove up and parked behind the truck. She shut her door very carefully, which told me she was holding her temper. Slowly, she strode toward us, and I braced myself.

When the three of us stood together, Ricky broke the silence. "Hey babe, how was your morning?"

She stared at her husband.

I examined their faces, back and forth, holding my breath while I waited for what might happen next. Karen grinned, shrugged her shoulders, and kissed Ricky on the cheek. "Another typical day in Abby's world."

The tightness in my chest released. God how I loved these people.

Ricky nodded. "Yep, our Abbigail does keep things interesting." He put an arm around his wife and walked toward the house, leaving me behind as though I hadn't witnessed the entire exchange.

I followed like an imprinted duck and entered the door they left open for me. By unspoken agreement, we met in the kitchen. I sat in my usual spot and talked fast. "Listen, I think I've figured it out. We can have people apply to the magazine, let legal do the fact checking and background checks, then they can funnel qualified candidates to me. I'll review pictures and their interests. When I've narrowed it down to people I'm attracted to, we'll come back to the interviews." Out of breath, I waited, wide-eyed in my innocent need for help.

Karen laughed out loud. "Don't give me that look. I *own* that look." After a conspiratorial glance at her husband, she turned back to me. "Sounds like a plan."

I jumped up and hugged her. "Thank you, thank you, thank you!" Then, for good measure, I hugged Ricky, who patted me on the back in his usual "yeah, yeah" way.

⌽

For the next week, I churned out apologies, adjustments, and new plans to our readers and social-media followers. I was pleasantly surprised to see they loved the mix-up, probably because it was real time and real life. Their reaction sent messages of "we're all in this together" and "nobody's perfect." As our follower list grew, countless people sent supportive comments, telling me to keep trying and keep them posted. A wedding planner contacted Edith and insisted on donating services and buying ad space. Soon after, a well-known local dress designer promised to create my dress...and buy ad space. And so it went, people jumping into the plan and spending money. The magazine corporate types went wild, and my celebrity status moved up a few notches, a goal that, I have to be honest, made me feel loved and successful.

Occasionally, it occurred to me I made a living by working rather than living on lottery money, and I felt proud of my little personal secret. Ricky was right, accomplishing something is better than sitting on your ass doing nothing. Well, I mostly sat on my ass, other than occasionally practicing yoga, but I was working, and I did try to move my ass to various places. Unfortunately, my new favorite coffee shop wasn't an option so soon after the interview disaster. I figured I'd lay low and let any hard feelings cool off so I could eventually return. I loved working at home, but everybody needs a change of scenery once in a while.

It took a few weeks, but legal got through more than five-hundred applications. When they removed anyone with a sketchy history and those who didn't earn at least eighty thousand over the past year, the pile shrunk to about a hundred applicants. Next, my job was to view pictures and check for some overlap in our interests, omitting people who, for example, spent every spare moment base jumping or collecting insects. Basically, I reviewed a hundred dating profiles.

I whittled the list down to thirty-eight qualified applicants and blasted out social media posts about interviews beginning soon. After all, there's only so much I could know about a person from a piece of paper. It was time for my sister's help. I practically skipped up her front walk before bursting into the kitchen with my laptop and a smile.

I sang, "Good morning, sunshine!"

As usual, the Bluetooth speaker played music, and this time it was Jason Isbell, one of my favorites. While I hummed along, I searched the bottom floor for any sign of life. Karen tottered down the stairs in her pajamas, fluffy green pants topped with a gray sweatshirt I'm pretty sure belonged to Ricky. She didn't look so good.

With a *thump* down the final step, she wiggled her fingers in a sorry excuse for a wave. Her trudge said she carried the weight of the world on her droopy eyelids. "Morning, Abby."

"You look awful." The comment earned me a frown. "Are you sick?"

"Nah, first trimester stuff. It'll pass." She trudged toward the kitchen.

"No way." I held her shoulders and steered her toward the couch. "Rest. I'll make you some tea with honey." In our family, tea with honey cured everything.

"Thanks." She didn't try to stop me but stretched out on the couch and closed her eyes.

I'd probably seen my sister sick five times in my life, and two of those were from drinking too many sangrias at Thanksgiving. Her mothering had taught me what to do in case of such an emergency. After tea, she'd need to rest, not in bed, hidden from the family, but in the living room, where she could stay part of the action. When she was up for it, she could watch TV and have some broth and crackers until she was ready for ginger ale and orange-vanilla ice cream. The final step was a warm bubble bath while sipping flavored soda water. Karen preferred lime.

I headed to the kitchen to get started, calling back, "Some tea, or do you want me to cook?"

She must've been feeling better, because she said, "Please don't cook. I want to get well."

It's no big secret I can't cook, but in my defense, Karen has always performed the job well. She never needed my help. Then when I moved out, it seemed cheaper—and easier—to buy prepared food, go out to eat, or come home for a meal.

When I brought the tea, Karen sat up against the pillows I stacked behind her. "Thanks. I'm already feeling better. We need to schedule those interviews."

The only thing I wanted more than the interviews was for her to get well. "Oh, I'm not quite done with my part," I lied. "I have a few more to review."

She cut her eyes at me and tasted her tea. "How many more?"

"Um, ten or twelve." I snuggled at the other end of the couch. "What movie do you want to watch?"

I have to give my sister credit; the woman bounces back fast. By midafternoon, she insisted on skipping the bubble-bath portion of the healing process and dressed in sweat pants and a T-shirt before heading to the kitchen. The kids would be home soon, and today's snack was home-made pizza rolls with a spinach smoothie. *Blech* on the spinach, but I looked forward to the pizza rolls.

After closing the oven door, she sat across the table from me. "Let's have it. I know you're finished with your part. Show me the winners."

I didn't bother to stick with my lie. Instead, I pulled up the candidates on my computer and scooted it toward her, coming around to sit close by. "It's alphabetical by first name, not by ranking." I clicked open a file and read over her shoulder. "Albert is an architect who enjoys long walks, quiet afternoons in the park, and gourmet cooking."

"Does he like to *do* the cooking or only eat the gourmet meal?"

"Good question." I clicked to the next file. "This is Anthony. He runs a hedge fund, likes fine dining, and volunteers at a soup kitchen on Sundays."

Karen clicked on the picture to enlarge it. "You like a ginger?"

"I'm not against a ginger." I peered at the photo. "He's got a nice smile."

"The descriptions don't tell you much about

what you might have in common. Anyone can say they like long walks or good food."

"True, but I've ruled out people with interests I couldn't get my head around, like ice fishing and swinging."

"*Swinging*?" She lifted an eyebrow in judgement. "Someone admitted to sharing sex partners?"

I had to roll my eyes at her naïveté. "You'd be surprised what people will admit or even brag about. One guy shaved his teeth to points and said he's a vampire." I shrugged, and to make her chuckle, I pointed out, "Hey, he passed the background check, *and* he's an accountant."

I got my reward when Karen threw her head back and laughed. "This is so much fun."

After studying my list, we cut it down to thirty-two candidates, a doable number. I had prepared a one-page list of interview questions, including, "Why do you want to do this?" With a bit of luck, no one would say they needed the money for a loan shark or a heroin fix. Most candidates would likely say they were too busy to seek out women, date, and take the time to develop a long-term relationship. And since I had opened the pool to anyone between the ages of twenty-five and thirty-five, candidates might be ready to settle down and commit to one woman.

When I went over interview questions with Karen, she pointed out what should have been obvious to me but wasn't. At the bottom of the sheet, she scribbled, "Are you open to fame?"

She was right; every aspect of our marriage would be open to the public, beginning with the wedding, which would be flooded with the press and fans. The ceremony would take place in Forsyth Park, with everyone invited, and the reception would be a by-invitation event at Savannah Station. The magazine had tentatively set the big day for the first Saturday in September, anticipating cooler weather in the Coastal Empire.

I added one more line about fidelity. Although I wouldn't promise sex, I wasn't okay with my husband running around on me. He should be able to keep it in his pants for three months if we didn't do the deed, but I harbored some expectation that part of our marriage would be physical. I balked at a *requirement*. Nothing kills the libido faster and more completely than an obligation to perform.

Karen nodded her agreement then sat back. "Let's get started meeting in person."

Panic welled in my stomach. "Now? Are we ready? Right now?" Suddenly, the preparation and waiting didn't seem nearly long enough for an event this huge, and I regretted letting followers know the interviews were back on track. I tried to swallow past the growing lump in my throat.

Smiling, Karen squeezed my shoulder. "How about this? Pick from the men we omitted today.

I'll interview one person tomorrow for practice, then we can make whatever adjustments are needed."

Her concession sounded good. One man, then full stop. Regroup, revise, rethink. I exhaled the stale air I'd been holding. "How about no-shirt man?" I pulled up his file. "He looks pretty good, and it's not like I said people *had* to wear clothes."

"Shows poor judgement, though. And maybe some narcissism." Karen picked up her phone and checked the number for candidate Larry. While she pressed the buttons, she added, "But he's for practice." She put the call on speaker.

Larry answered after the first ring. "You've reached Larry, and I'm right here live and in the flesh. What can I do to make your life better?"

I motioned for Karen to hang up. *Hang up!*

She ignored me. "Hi Larry, I'm calling about your application to Random Husband. Would you be able to interview tomorrow morning at nine?"

"Hell yeah! Say where, mama. I'll be there."

I slapped a palm to my forehead. Practice. This one was for practice. Jeez.

Karen remained professional even though I wanted her to *hang up*, already. "Thank you, Larry. The interview will be at Historic Coffee Roasters on West Park Avenue. I'll see you at nine."

"You betcha!"

And that was that. Our first interview.

CHAPTER 12—MAX

Weeks had passed without a visit from mystery lady, at least while I was working, which was most of the time. Maybe I'd missed her. I casually asked my manager, "Have you seen a customer, a woman, with big purple glasses?"

Anuli regarded me like I was nuts, but she let me down easy. "I reckon I'd remember if I'd seen her. Naw."

Unfortunately, I had no better description. "What about the woman who was in here a few weeks ago when a bunch of men came in? The one they crowded around?"

"So weird! But I haven't seen her either. Not since then." She reached in the display case for tiramisu, and I noted the empty shop. At seven in the morning, we'd only been open a few minutes, but our first rush would start soon. "Is something wrong?" she asked.

"No, I was just curious. I guess they've moved to another coffee shop." I felt the slightest bit betrayed. What was wrong with *my* store?

With a shake of her head, Anuli sat the treat on the counter. "Nope, the woman with the crowd stepped back to fix a few things. I thought you knew. Heck, I thought you were part of the whole business since the lady met people here."

"What?" I handed her a fork. "I'm lost. Tell me what you know." Then, remembering Zoe's complaints, I added, "please."

She scooped tiramisu into her mouth and swallowed before answering. "It's a long story, and it went viral on TikTok and Insta." She pulled a phone from her back pocket and read something before continuing. "The project is called Random Husband. It's a pretty cool idea."

"Yeah, I heard she's looking for a husband. What else?"

"The marriage only has to last three months, and at the end, the man gets twenty thousand dollars!" I must have balked because she nodded, "Uh-huh, a big payout if the marriage doesn't work."

"Why would anybody marry a stranger?"

"Did I mention the twenty thousand dollars? And he'll be famous because the whole shebang will be tracked on social media and written up in *Women First*."

The plan started to make more sense as a publicity stunt. I shook my head. I don't care how much money was on the line, I'd never agree to those terms. My brief stint in Keisha's world had shoved more than enough publicity my way. I had to ask, "Did those men know what they were getting into?"

"Oh, for sure." Anuli tucked the empty plate and fork into a bin for dirty dishes. "Hundreds of men applied to be her husband—way more than we saw the one day." She typed on her phone for a minute and handed it to me. "This is the post about interviews starting tomorrow. They'll be here in the shop, which I guess is her home base. That's why I thought you knew about it." A customer walked up and ordered a skinny cappuccino with two shots of vanilla and whipped cream, requiring Anuli's attention.

I skimmed the post and squinted to see the writer's avatar and the name "Abby Lynn." It did look like clipboard lady, but the avatar had slightly longer hair and, because it was a cartoon, looked younger. At least the men who applied would see her during interviews, so no surprises on the wedding day. Purple-glasses woman must have been trying a low-key approach to marrying off her sister on the first day I saw her, but it was a better tactic to let the men meet their future bride in person.

I didn't envy any man who would become part of the circus. Thank goodness my infatuation with the sister kept me out of the spotlight.

I had some reading to do.

To stay in the loop.

For my shop.

Honestly, any conscientious business owner would do the same.

I retrieved my phone and downloaded Instagram, a simple process dragging on longer than it should have since I forgot my app-store password. After entering personal information, I maneuvered through requests to find contacts and add a profile picture, all of which reminded me why I avoided downloading apps. Finally, I clicked into the *Women First* account for Random Husband and learned that interviews would begin at nine o'clock.

Based on the previous round of interviews, we should prepare for a crowd. I'd ask a few people to come to work at five tomorrow morning; we'd fill the display cases and cooler with desserts from Coastal Bakery and bake fresh bread for the sandwiches we'd make. To be safe, I'd roast our most popular coffee flavors, with enough options to keep me busy through the night. Rope line dividers for the outside space would funnel people through the front door.

I tried not to think about the sister, mystery lady with the purple glasses, but my mind kept wandering. Since she'd been around during the botched computer-guy attempt and the group interviews, she might show up tomorrow too. Would she be as pretty as I remembered? After a month, I couldn't be sure.

Tomorrow would offer another chance to make some progress, and I wouldn't squander the opportunity. I hadn't found success in life by being timid, opting instead to go after what I wanted. My older brother always gave me shit about my single-minded determination to find the "yes" in every situation, but I liked my life and gave credit to my pig-headed attitude. Granted, my relationship with Zoe wasn't a good example of either success or determination; I'd let her walk away—okay, technically I'd walked away—without running after her. But relationships are completely different. If someone doesn't want you, why tank your self-esteem by begging?

My prior interactions with mystery lady were so brief they almost didn't count. I'd make tomorrow count. When she came in, I'd abandon work to bring her a latte with Splenda, and she'd thank me. Then I'd ask her opinion of the coffee, explaining my role as roast-master. She'd be duly impressed. Hopefully during the interaction we'd touch; I wanted her soft hand on me again. Man, did I want her hands on me. I pictured silky dark hair fanned out on my pillow, big brown eyes pleading with me like they had over the napkin note. I didn't have to imagine the look because I'd seen it.

"Hey!" Anuli's voice made me jump like a randy teenager caught in the act of self-discovery. "Do you want me to restock the paper products while we're slow?"

I cleared my throat and turned away, mumbling, "Sure, sounds great."

Where was I? Mystery woman would be impressed. Right. Then I'd invite her into the small roasting room, where we'd stand next to each other, and I'd explain the process. She'd probably ask questions, smile, step closer... Next, we could go one of two ways. I could kiss her. I definitely wanted to kiss her. I can learn a lot from a kiss, not the least of which is taste. And boldness. I prefer a bold kisser, a woman who's not afraid to suck my tongue or slip her own tongue past my lips. I can taste—

"Max!" Anuli tapped me on the shoulder, and I jumped again. "Here's the inventory list. Can you place an order?"

"Sure, sure." I accepted the list from her. Great. An order meant I had to contact Zoe, but she might still have another rep covering Savannah. Or maybe she'd changed her territory and wouldn't come back. I was being childish, but I didn't want to talk to her again. Time hadn't softened my attitude toward her, and I sure as hell didn't want to hear more about what a loser I was.

Maybe that's why I focused on mystery woman. She meant a clean slate, a do-over, with a woman who hadn't seen my flaws, or at least didn't have a strong aversion to them yet. I glanced at the roasting area, letting my thoughts wander back to the seduction. If we didn't kiss right away, I would ask her out. We'd have dinner anywhere other than Alligator Soul. After dinner, she'd come home with me, and we'd start with the kiss.

CHAPTER 13—ABBY

For this morning's interview, I changed my tactic and planned to arrive before Karen. After pulling on a pair of tattered jean shorts, a black tank top, and comfy black ankle boots, I pulled my hair under a hat and donned my cute purple glasses. A parking spot opened three blocks from the shop, providing a great excuse to meander through the park. From several yards away, I tucked behind a live oak and scoped out the shop's front walkway, spying on my own life. The coast was clear. Oddly, a series of line dividers spanned the outside seating area and led to the front door, but I saw only four people sitting outside and no one in line.

Reconnaissance complete, I approached.

I opened the door and firmly stopped myself from searching for the hunky barista. Maybe it was my imagination, but the room smelled rich with coffee and baked bread, more so than usual. Sure enough, the counters overflowed with mounds of thick bread loaves and trays of baguettes. Inside the cases, colorful desserts made my mouth water. The owner clearly expected a crowd; we'd better stay out of the way during this morning's interview.

Still not letting myself peek toward the roasting room, I approached the counter and ordered my usual and a baguette with butter and strawberry preserves. Four servers scrambled to pull together my order in record time, seemingly grateful for the distraction.

While I searched for an out-of-the-way table, a few more customers trickled in, bought coffee, and scattered around the room. No one opened a computer or stared at a phone. Instead, they scanned the room as though searching for someone. It occurred to me they might follow my story and waited to see the candidate, a likelihood Edith insisted we encourage. When I'd tried to change her mind, she kept saying some version of, "This is business, and there's no business without customers." For Larry's sake, I prayed they'd keep quiet. Although Larry had agreed to open himself up to scrutiny, I wanted the process to stay gentle. Maybe I was fooling myself. I'd already seen some snarky comments related to my posts, but the people here seemed relatively happy, like they expected good news.

I found a seat behind a retail rack of bagged coffee and opened my laptop, planning to take notes on what I saw and heard. Karen would arrive soon, and shortly after her, narcissistic Larry. Today I was more excited than nervous because I couldn't take shirtless guy seriously. He wasn't a contender.

While I waited, I pulled up the folder

containing applicant files, determined to stay busy and not think about the barista who may or may not be working behind me. I thought about his blue eyes and short black hair, a little messy and sexy as hell. And that bicep. Whew. The last time I'd seen him, a little beard stubble roughened his face, which, coupled with a growling voice, added to his air of danger, or at least no-nonsense.

Thank goodness he wasn't a candidate in my plan because I brought with me a sizable dose of nonsense.

As a case in point, part of me acknowledged I should have tracked down the shop owner and asked permission before bringing interviews here, but I had no idea our first attempt would be such a fiasco. And from now on we'd carefully schedule interviews so no more than one or two men showed up at a time. I did mention Historic Coffee Roasters in my articles and posts, but the owner should be grateful for the free advertising. Besides, in my experience, most business owners didn't stay too involved, preferring to leave the day-to-day operations to hired help. It seemed a shame to me, and not the way I'd run a business, but I guess today's world didn't run on mom-and-pop operations.

I thought again about the brawny barista and kept my back to the counter. Proud of my phenomenal self-control, I smiled and sipped my coffee, staring at the front door. My sister would arrive soon, and we'd move forward with the plan, giving me something to focus on other than the blue-eyed man.

I didn't have to wait long because Karen was always early. She arrived at ten till nine, scanned the room, and gave me a little wave before setting up shop smack dab in the middle of the room as if to say, "I'm here. Deal with it."

Ballsy move, sister.

She had her trusty clipboard and a pen, which she clicked open and closed while scanning notes. A minute later she walked past my table and tapped on it without stopping on her way to order coffee, quickly returning to her seat as the minutes ticked by and my heartrate kicked up a notch.

Right on time, Larry strutted through the door. Maybe it's not fair to say he strutted, exactly, but I perceived it since I'd already made up my mind about him. People tend to see what they expect. While I chastised myself for stereotyping the guy, he approached Karen and spoke loud enough for the entire room. "Helloooo, mama! You look different from your picture, but I like *all* the ladies."

Karen smiled her not-amused smile and waved her hand toward a chair across the table. With a prolonged *screech*, he pulled out the chair and sat, lounging back as though he was the only person she'd need to interview before declaring him the winner. Glancing down at her clipboard, she dove right in. "Larry, can you tell me why you're interested in being the Random Husband?"

"Affirmative! My friends will tell you I'm an adventure guy. Give me a thrill, and I'm there. This set-up looks like a pretty intense adventure, am I right?" He stretched forward and ran his index finger down Karen's arm, and I almost burst out laughing when she jerked her arm away. He continued as though he hadn't noticed. "And the money sure doesn't hurt."

A few notes scratched onto the page. "Mm-hmm. Mm-hmm."

While Karen silently reviewed her next question, good old Larry piped up, "But I bring good mojo to the table, sweetheart. My friends will tell you I'm great in the sack. The bedroom, the kitchen, anywhere you want, I'm on top of it." He reached out for Karen again, but she turned sideways to avoid his touch.

All business, my patient sister explained the sex issue. "Larry, I should tell you sex is not a guaranteed part of the deal. It likely won't happen." Well, she was right about that. If I married this man, I could not see a world where I'd want to be intimate.

For some reason, this revelation seemed to strip away Larry's false bravado, maybe because he knew he wasn't interviewing well. He started to sweat. I don't mean a glisten or a glow; I mean a full-on flop sweat running down his face, trickling past his nose, and dripping from his chin. After wiping a beefy hand down his face, he said, "Sorry, I came from a killer workout. I bench three-hundred pounds, easy."

It didn't make sense he'd start sweating from a workout after five minutes of being dry, but I felt sorry for him anyway. The sweat continued. Soon there'd be a puddle in his chair, where I could only guess his butt was sweating as profusely.

Gross.

I know my sister well enough to see she was trying to look anywhere other than at his sweaty face, but she had no choice. She asked, "Do you understand being chosen means the first three months of your marriage would be shared with *Women First* readers and social-media followers?"

"I'm counting on it!" He wiped his face again, but at this point he simply smeared his secretions around.

From behind me, the hot barista approached Larry and dropped a stack of napkins in front of him, turning around without saying a word. On the way to the back, his route would bring him past me again. Should I make eye contact? Smile? Feign interest in my computer? *Crap*. He stopped at my table and pulled out a chair without making so much as a single screech across the floor, and I raised my eyes enough to watch his bicep flex in the process. Man, I definitely needed to stay busy. Without my permission, he sat across from me, leaning one forearm on the table and dangling his hand off the edge casually, a body position that made me feel uptight and awkward by comparison.

I looked up. Those same intense blue eyes stared, but today he seemed friendlier. One side of his mouth turned up a little in what I guess was a half-smile. In a voice as warm and comforting as towels pulled fresh from the dryer, he said, "Latte with one Splenda, right?" He pushed a cup across to me, almost like a peace offering, but I doubt he saw I was at war with myself in such close proximity to him.

I behaved like a reasonable patron. "Thank you. You're so thoughtful." Steam drifted from the cup's sip opening. To show I was a nice, grateful person, I drew a long mouthful and immediately spit it across the table, including the arm he had resting there. "Oh god! I'm sorry. It was hot. Really hot. I should have blown on it. Blowing would've been good."

The whole time I stammered, I tried to wipe off his arm with the single, tiny napkin I held. It was no use. I must have spewed a full mouthful because light brown dots were everywhere. My cheeks flushed, a terrible reflex leaving me more embarrassed than I already felt.

I dabbed his hand with the wet napkin. No wedding ring.

Out of nowhere, he said, "I'm the roast-master."

I stopped cleaning him. "What? Oh, I kinda figured."

"Do you like this blend?" He acted like nothing had happened, completely ignoring the wet table. "I've been working on it for a while."

I couldn't decide if he was acting strange or trying to change the subject from my blunder, but I went along, hoping the hot blush on my face would dissipate. "It's delicious. I usually ask for this darker roast because it tastes..." Nuances escaped me. I could no more name subtle coffee flavors than identify "notes" of wine.

"Like chocolate?" He finished for me.

He was right. But then again, I could always taste plum, apricot, and pine when a sommelier insisted. Once, I tasted leather in a cabernet because I was told to, but why someone would want to drink leather escapes me. "Exactly. Chocolate. And maybe a hint of leather."

With a deep laugh showing what appeared to be perfect teeth, bicep guy left me breathless. Damn, he was handsome. I could stare at him all day. "Yeah, leather was the toughest part. I had to choose between old horse saddle or worn-out cowboy boots."

He stood, showing off his size—or standing like people tend to do before they leave.

I wasn't ready to watch him go. And yes, I planned to watch him walk away and enjoy the view. But not yet. "What do you do as a roast-master?"

"I'm glad you asked." He held out his hand. "Want to see?"

I grasped his hand and stood. Yep, he was at least five inches taller than me. And yep, I wanted to see whatever he wanted to show me. He dropped my hand and led me to the roasting room, where he opened both doors like he was revealing a piece of art. When he turned back and guided me inside with a hand on my lower back, I had the urge to walk backward and increase the pressure of those warm fingers. Too soon, he dropped his hand.

Silence has never been my friend, and now was no exception. "How long have you been a roast-master? Are you going to cook some beans now? How long does it take?" Maybe if I asked enough questions, I'd stop itching to touch him. I don't mean grab his crotch or anything; I'd settle for an arm, his back, his sexy beard stubble.

He laughed, which did nothing to quell my need to touch him. "I apprenticed for a few years before going out on my own to learn new techniques, new machines, but I didn't consider myself a roast-master until about seven years ago." He glanced down at me. "I'll show you how it works."

Although he left the doors open, we stood inside near the silver machine. In such a small room, I could almost feel his breath on my neck. Okay, he was nowhere near my neck, but a girl can dream. My throat tightened when he bent to pick up a fifty-pound burlap bag of beans, offering a fantastic view of back muscles in play under a shirt stretched taut. They might have rippled. With a knife from the windowsill, he cut a slit in the bag and hefted it over his shoulder to dump into the funnel above his head.

Definitely rippled.

In my mind, I pressed both hands to his shoulders and felt the bunching and rolling of the individual muscle groups, massaging down to his lower back. Why stop there? Those loose jeans didn't exactly display a tight, muscular ass, but I knew in my heart it was there.

I licked my suddenly dry lips. "Did you go to college for this?" More questions. Jeez, I was like a chatty fifteen-year-old girl surfing her first rush of hormones. I might as well start swirling a piece of my hair and biting my bottom lip.

Hunky barista dropped the empty bag in a corner. "No, in college I majored in chemistry." He shrugged one shoulder and grinned, making me need to twirl my hair. "But I ended up using some chemistry as a roaster." Reaching over my head, he pulled a handful of beans from the funnel while I tried not to notice how good he smelled. Like soap. Plain old soap, not cologne, thank god. I breathed deeply until my head buzzed like I was going to hyperventilate.

In his hand, he held little green beans. With the other hand, he picked one out and offered it to me. "Feel it."

I nearly laughed out loud. *Feel it*? Did he know he was flirting? I bit my bottom lip and held out my hand to receive his gift. It seemed dense, an observation I shared. "It's harder than I thought it would be." I rubbed it between two fingers.

For a second, he paused, and I suspected he felt the heavy attraction I struggled with. He leaned closer, touching my shoulder with is chest, and I swear I heard him inhale near my ear, not at all like a man with a girlfriend.

Maybe there was no girlfriend.

Just a sister.

An aunt.

A friend.

When I glanced back, he was looking over my shoulder at the bean I held. How he managed it, I don't know, but he didn't seem to be swimming through the molasses of sexual innuendo that threatened to pull me under. He smiled down at me like our bodies weren't throbbing with the need to—

"The heat will make it better." He mumbled. When I glanced up, his eyes were closed. He felt what I felt.

He might as well have offered me an engraved invitation to his mouth. Without turning my body around, I stretched up and pressed my lips to his. No, I didn't attack him like in the movies, shoving him against the window

116

and frantically unzipping his fly, despite the thought blasting through my mind. But neither did I kiss him like you might kiss your mother when you're three. I tested the density and softness of his lips under a little pressure. What I didn't expect was how much I liked it. I could blame the piercing shot of heat through my body on the riskiness of the kiss, but I'd be lying. It was the man. The heat settled between my legs, where my body—without my permission—prepared to procreate. If I had to guess, I'd say the kiss lasted ten minutes, but the logical synapses still firing told me it was less than a minute.

Enough, I told myself. Let him go, already. I pulled my lips away and set my heels on the floor, but I kept my eyes on his face to see his response. I didn't wait long. He dropped the handful of beans into a nearby trash can before laying his hands on my shoulders and turning me to face him. *Oh, baby, please kiss me.* With a Mona Lisa smile, he gently removed my glasses and laid them on the windowsill, clearly preparing for something epic. *Yes, yes, yes!* When he turned back toward me, his smile was replaced with an intense look. An I'm-single look.

I held my breath.

Very deliberately, he leaned down, still holding my shoulders, until his lips met mine. He wanted me. My hands reached up and felt his razor stubble then his hair before settling on a neck I wanted to kiss. No one had ever felt so good. He ran his hands down my back and pulled me closer, urging my mouth open with his lips. Instinctively (thank you, Mother Nature) I received his tongue over and over again, acutely aware of the primitive desire to have more than his tongue inside me.

When he dared to pull away, I stood on tiptoes and held his head with both hands. I wanted to taste more of him. With a moan I think came from me, I slipped the tip of my tongue in his mouth, gratified when he tightened his hold. It took every fiber of my being to stop myself from rubbing against the impressive erection between us. The only reason I stopped was a vague awareness of other people in the coffee shop. Hell, my own sister could see us—

My sister! The interview! I pulled away and backed up as much as possible, shouting, "Wait!" The hottest man on earth looked as confused as I felt. I turned around in time to see Karen walking out the front door. "I'm sorry, I have to go!" Before he could respond, I jogged after my sister, hoping nothing unusual had happened during the interview.

I saw her rounding the corner. On her upper back, a wet handprint glistened in the sun, and I hated missing the entertainment of Larry patting her on the back. "Karen!" When she turned around, I tried to read her face, but she wasn't giving anything away. I trotted over to her. "Meet at your house?"

She nodded once. "Yes." Then she turned on her heel and walked away, leaving me to wonder what she was thinking and whether she'd seen me making out in the back room.

I wandered to my car while my unruly mind wandered back to the kiss. The hot kiss. The taste of his mouth, the clean smell of him, and those strong arms pressing me against his body. A little thrill started in my stomach and expanded downward. So hot. The heat begged me to return to the coffee shop, but I had to be firm, shaking my head to remind myself I had a job to do. Steamy sessions with a barista didn't fit the plan.

I also knew better than to make out with an employee at their job, where anyone might see. What had I been thinking? The servers were standing around, bored, surrounded by overflowing display cases and counters, while I put on a show. I couldn't undo it, and my future daydreams wouldn't want me to, but I could probably drum up some business for them.

I sat in the car and opened my laptop. Now feeling virtuous, I worked on several posts about Historic Coffee Roasters, reminding my followers about the great coffee and food. In a stroke of inspiration, I posted a contest for the day, inviting people to share a picture of their visit. I urged them to respond with a close-up of their favorite item at the shop, maybe a beautiful dessert or a fancy cappuccino, with the best picture earning a free year's subscription to *Women First*.

⏀

"I kissed him." Confession is good for the soul, right? But I also told my sister about it because I felt giddy and wanted to blather over a dreamy boy.

Pathetic.

"You kissed who?" Karen sat across from me at the kitchen table and frowned.

I barely stifled a grin. "The gorgeous barista at the coffee shop." When she still seemed confused, I added, "The one who brought you the note when we first tried the interviews." How could she have missed such a perfect specimen of a man?

"If you say so." She played it cool. "But tell me about the kissing part."

Gladly! It's all I wanted to talk about. "Actually, I kissed him first. We were in the roasting room, and he was really close and smelled amazing, so I kissed him. Right on the lips with no warning. I guess I realized I was going to do it, but he didn't, so—"

"Whoa! Slow down!" She held up both hands like a crossing guard. "I meant the why, not the what. Why did you kiss him?"

I gawked at her. What didn't she understand? "He's gorgeous."

She laughed, either at my wide-eyed expression or my terse reason. "I gathered that much, but what about the interviews, the marriage…the plan?"

"Yeah, I know." She was right, of course, but I wasn't quite ready to let it go. "I'm not married yet?" It was more of a question than a statement since what I did was wrong in the face of impending wife-hood.

Karen looked to the right with unfocused eyes, struggling for a solution. With a snap of her fingers, she said, "How about inviting him to apply? It's a little past the deadline, but we can fudge the dates."

Damn it. My misery didn't change the answer. "First, I wouldn't feel right about breaking the rules. And second, he's a barista, which means he can't make anywhere near eighty-thousand a year." *Damn Edith*. "Edith's trying to rule out men who would marry me only for the money, remember?" As I said it out loud, I felt certain my sexy barista wouldn't be so shallow.

"You could make an exception."

I shook my head to let her know it wasn't an option. "Rules are rules." But rules weren't the biggest problem. I doubted this man had heard about the contest, and I'd bet money he wouldn't subject himself to public scrutiny during a three-month trial marriage. I'd learned my lesson during my botched approach to computer guy. Plopping Random Husband on barista's head would be a disaster. My cheeks grew hotter just thinking of his likely response. Sometimes it's hard to see personal behavior objectively, but from a distance, my project seemed strange.

Karen examined my face and watched me blush. To her credit, she didn't mention it. Instead, she moved on with her problem solving. "Do you want to change locations for interviews?"

"Yes, but I've already put a ton of hype into this place, and I don't want my readers to see me as flaky."

She chuckled, and I politely ignored it. "Then we need to schedule more guys for tomorrow. The questions worked fine, and as long as I bring a towel, tomorrow should go smoothly." Rolling her eyes at the towel comment, she reached for her phone.

"Oh my god, right? Larry, aka no-shirt guy, was pouring!" I giggled. "Who could have seen that coming? Thank goodness you're meeting guys in person." I'm a little ashamed to admit we spent a while cracking jokes at Larry's expense, but the belly laughs felt good. Finally, I wiped away my tears. After opening my laptop, I pulled up candidate files and turned the screen toward my sister.

She clicked through until she located a phone number. Before she sent the call, she asked, "Will you come to interviews tomorrow?"

Great question. Every fiber of my being wanted to, and good kisser wasn't the only reason. My job included writing about these experiences; I'd lose the details if Karen provided second-hand reports. Still... "I'd better not." My heart sank to my stomach, but it was the right decision. "Can you video them?"

Always a good sport, she shrugged. "In for a penny, yadda yadda. We'll need the tripod from the attic, but video is an easy fix." While we waited for the first call to connect, she said, "Ten to two works for me, and I can be back here before the kids come home from school. I should be able to get through eight interviews."

"Perfect." I reminded myself to be happy the plan was moving forward. The eligible candidates were attractive and had interests similar to mine. I should be grateful. After we narrowed the pool to five or six, I'd meet with each of them in a final interview. I could require a kiss to gauge their expertise, but I'd only compare it to this morning. This whole infatuation was such bad timing.

With Karen busy scheduling meetings, I headed home, excited to write about colorful, narcissistic, sweating Larry. I'd tell the truth in a kind way. Everybody walked around with both good and bad in them, and Larry was no exception.

CHAPTER 14—MAX

I didn't know her name. I did know she tasted good, but I could blame that on my coffee if I wanted to. And I'd stood there watching her run away.

The roaster would never feel quite the same; now it inspired erotic images. If mystery woman had filled my mind before, it was nothing compared to what my future would hold. I gave in to infatuation. When would I see her again? Would I get her damn name? To be fair, I didn't know if I'd ever told her mine either. Exchanging names seemed like a great first step, but we were already way beyond small talk, at least in my mind. I envisioned us dating, enjoying walks and happy hour, and having sex on every surface of my apartment.

My body hardened again at the thought.

What now? I needed to roast the beans I'd already dumped in the machine, but suddenly I needed to move more than the room would allow. The gym seemed like too much work. Cleaning the store was always a possibility, but we'd been cleaning since early this morning for the crowd we never saw. Whenever mystery woman was around, I felt five minutes behind, like I'd missed some crucial piece of information, and scrambled to catch up.

I walked past Anuli, who, as always, kept herself busy and insisted the same of her co-workers. When she glanced up and smiled, I wondered if she'd seen me macking on a customer. With a nod warning, "Don't ask," I announced, "I'm going out for a while."

I stepped into the sunshine and walked toward the park, aiming for the fountain. Water was one of those constants, soothing and life-affirming. The flow cleared my head. Maybe it was time to recalibrate with a visit to Macon, home to my parents and two brothers. It would also give me a chance to see how Anuli ran the place without abandoning her too long. At this point, the three-hour drive sounded appealing, getting me out of my usual space and changing the scenery as much as miles of bland interstate could do.

I'd been avoiding my parents, mainly my mom, since my last visit when I'd brought Zoe home to meet the family, a huge deal for everybody. Mom would want to talk about the breakup, offer advice, and try to make me feel better, none of which seemed particularly enjoyable. What is it about moms that makes you love them from the bottom of your heart but get annoyed when they speak? Picturing my mom in the kitchen making peach cobbler, I had to smile. Another failing of children is we can't get past the larger-than-life "mom" qualities we grew up with, even though my mom is an accomplished psychology professor. I never picture her as Dr. Barbara Murphy, teaching a class of eager sophomores or in her lab running experiments; in my mind, she's always cooking.

When I visit, my older brother, Frankie, and my younger brother, Justin, sleep at the house so we can drink too much beer and stay up late talking and playing poker. Frankie was named after my dad, Frank, a transplant from Detroit who embraced the warmth of Georgia when he found a manufacturing job near Macon. Dad would slap me on the back with a man-hug as soon as I got home, then he'd explain in detail the improvements he'd made to his beat-up old Caddy, a project in progress for eight years.

Justin would keep to himself other than a few beers and fewer hands of poker, but he enjoyed being with family. As far as I saw, my baby brother never had a girlfriend, preferring to float through life without a partner. Maybe one day he'd leave his self-imposed shell and talk to me, share his secrets, but I wouldn't push. All I could do was wait.

The only chaos during my visit would be when Frankie's wife and kid arrived. Frankie had married Cynthia straight out of high school as a result of a faulty condom, and after she'd lost the child, they stayed together. A surprise baby three years ago brought Natty into the family, and the fat kid melted my heart the first time he puked on my shirt. Kids change so fast. I figured he'd be more of a little terror now than a few months ago.

I stopped walking and sat on a bench near the fountain, deep in my own head. Natty was one of the reasons I'd considered marrying Zoe. Part of me was ready for a family. The other part of me was terrified.

An image of mystery woman pregnant and baking in the kitchen popped into my head, and I had to laugh at the sexist thought. Once again, I realized Zoe might have been right about me. Although I would never have described the image out loud, it *was* my default. Was I an asshole, or was I just fantasizing about my version of a happy moment, like a woman might fantasize about a man who doted on her with puppy-dog devotion? Nobody really expected a partner to be such an over-the-top fantasy, but a few minutes of selfishness would be nice.

Good lord, when did I get so philosophical?

I guess I couldn't completely escape mom's training in psychology. I could almost hear her response to my confession about Zoe. "Don't worry, the universe will bring your ray of sunshine when the time is right." She'd pull a peach cobbler from the oven before offering advice. She always offered advice. "You have to be patient, but you also have to participate. Encourage luck. What's the next step?"

I knew what was coming because she'd constantly urged me to get out of the house. When I was a kid, I hid in my room and read books, but mom would beat on the door and insist I "enjoy the world" and "make it happen." I assumed "it" was whatever new experience she imagined for me, but I never asked. Today "it" would be making better progress with mystery woman.

The plan to kiss her had gone well, other than when I blurted out I was a roast-master with absolutely no segway from her spitting coffee on me. I cringed at the memory. *Focus on the positive*; I could hear my mom's voice. Okay, so the kiss had gone well—very well. In retrospect, I should instead have planned to get her name first, what she does for a living, her favorite color, the things people tend to learn before they taste each other's tongues.

I felt myself hardening and struggled to clear my head of sexy images, some real and some imagined. What's the next step? I needed to learn more about her, and the only way I could think of was to read about her sister. I'd get my ass back to work, and while the coffee beans heated, I could read the backstory on social media and buy a subscription to the magazine she writes for. Something about women? The Insta posts had mentioned the name of the magazine, which brought me back to social media as a first step.

Determined to solve my problem, I

abandoned the bench, rolled my shoulders back, and marched to the shop. Armed with a plan, direction, I felt better. And for a few minutes, I allowed myself to savor the excitement and anticipation of a new relationship.

◍

Late in the afternoon, I headed upstairs for a break. The crowd I had expected turned up, nearly wiped out our inventory, and, oddly, snapped pictures of their food, retail bags of coffee, and anything else drawing their attention.

I needed to start a notebook on the strange events in the shop. It wasn't lost on me that mystery woman and her sister were usually involved on some level, leading me to believe the rush of customers and pictures were another part of their magic. God bless them. Even though I walked around in a state of confusion, the sisters made my life better.

In my apartment, I plopped on the couch with a grunt of appreciation. My place was perfect, from the exposed brick walls and tall windows to the gigantic grey couch and overstuffed red chairs. Everything I'd chosen was comfortable and functional. The recently remodeled kitchen held large and small appliances making cooking easy, and when I had spare time, I prepared the comfort food my mom always served. Tonight, I might treat myself to beef stew with carrots, onions, and potatoes.

But first, I had some digging to do.

I slid my laptop from the end table and opened it. After pulling up my Insta account, I found the Random Husband posts and read long enough to learn two things: Yes, the sisters were responsible for the busy day, and the name of the magazine was *Women First*. I went to the magazine's page and bought a subscription, where I found the articles I needed. Since I wanted information, I was gratified to see a string of articles by Abby about Random Husband. Somewhere in these words I might find clues about the woman I couldn't get out of my head.

The first story explained the basic premise: Marriage is based on little more than a minimal level of mutual attraction, similarities, and availability. Over time, mutual attraction becomes less important, explaining why partners remain devoted in sickness and after accidents causing physical deformity. With acceptance, kindness, and work, nearly any two people should be able to build a successful marriage.

Soulmates don't exist.

At first the idea sounded cold. But the more I considered it, the more I questioned my own views about what brings people together. I believe in God, but I'm not convinced He micromanages our lives to such an extent. Maybe karma or fate ultimately made sense of turmoil, molding our destinies with some cosmic purpose. No matter what you called it, the romantic notion relied on someone or something besides us in charge, and I sure hoped that was true, because I sucked at relationships.

But did I believe in soulmates?

I pictured Zoe and had to admit I wouldn't have considered her my soulmate even when I was ring shopping.

I kept reading.

Abby reflected more on the idea of a soulmate. Did everyone have to find their "one" in *all* the eligible people of the world? The sheer probability of locating a needle in a thousand haystacks was staggering. And what if we found a needle in the first haystack, but it wasn't the right one? Did soulmates give people a free pass when the right one came along? *Sorry, honey, but it turns out my sexy young secretary is the "one" for me.*

The article raised some interesting questions, and I could see why people followed the story. The personal angle added more weight to her musings. Abby was going a huge step beyond the general premise to test her theory, and I couldn't believe she was willing to marry a man she didn't know. Marriage seemed so final. But as she explained in her article, in today's world, marriage isn't final. At all. Again, I grudgingly agreed with her. I couldn't help but see her point: Marriage to someone sure as hell meant they'd spend time together, and since togetherness was a crucial element of attraction, it could work.

My stomach growled. I'd have to eat something before continuing, and I definitely wanted to read more.

Abby seemed bright, and I wanted to get to know her better. Although I wasn't attracted to her, I thought we could be friends, especially if I could make some progress with her sister.-For some reason, it was tough to picture the mom-ish woman conducting interviews as the same woman who wrote the commentary. While I settled for a peanut-butter sandwich, I tried to adjust my perception of Abby to fit the person who wrote these probing words and soon would march down the aisle. It was a hard sell when my brain conjured up images of a kitchen full of kids and warm baked goods.

Yeah, I recognized it was sexist.

Back on my couch, I wolfed down the sandwich and continued reading. The next article laid out the plan, including the rules for applicants and a caution about a complete lack of privacy. For the sake of a story, I could see the need for a warning. There wasn't a story if Abby couldn't share her experiences.

Even though I balked at no confidentiality, it seemed many men were okay with fame. Look at reality TV shows. I'd never seen one, but I'd heard enough to know some people loved them—

participating or watching, whichever they could get. Reality shows often made people seem like complete dumbasses, or maybe they revealed the truth, but no one seemed to mind, least of all the poor fools. The idea made me cringe.

How would Abby tell the truth without making the guys seem stupid and needy? Then again, if they'd signed off on it, they might be fine with any notoriety she would offer them, making them either famous or infamous.

The third article satisfied my curiosity. I read the opening paragraph four times and couldn't find anything I'd consider cruel.

Five hundred seventy-nine applications! I want to take this space to thank you for the compliment and the courage it takes to participate in life. Everyone who applied should feel proud of attempting to guide your own destiny and find a happily ever after, or at least as long as a marriage lasts in this confusing world of relationships. I can only assume each of you knows what it feels like to live through a broken promise, a failed wish, or a crush who let you down, but please know your experience makes you part of the human condition. You cared. As long as you stay open to happiness, you will find it, I promise. Keep being kind and positive and adventurous in your life. Participate!

The rest of the story hinted at the wide variety of applicants, finding dozens of details to compliment, from "great smile" to "fascinating interests." Although I hadn't applied, I ended up feeling proud of the men who did. Good for them. It wasn't lost on me that Abby urged them to participate, and I wondered if there was a book somewhere read by every woman, teaching them to lift people up. Or maybe it was genetic. Either way, I liked Abby more with every word.

A few follow-up articles highlighted specific applicants, putting them on a pedestal for some attribute or another, and explained the next steps.

I was surprised and grateful to see the advertisement for Historic Coffee Roasters—advertisement I hadn't paid for. The magazine probably earned the bulk of its income from ads, and the pages were littered with discounts from wedding venues, florists, caterers, and dress shops. Once again, I had to hand it to Abby; her project promised a flood of revenue. The clipboard-holding, mom-vibe woman might be a genius. The only questionable part was her willingness to sacrifice her marital future for the sake of an article. Still, if her theory was right, she might be orchestrating her own happiness.

I don't know why it mattered to me, maybe it was the kindness and intelligence in her writing, but I wished her well.

Although my stomach loudly demanded more food, I couldn't stop reading. I had to laugh at my interest in what amounted to a reality show, and I tried to tell myself the topic was silly. But the way Abby wrote made me think about love and marriage at a time in my life when they mattered.

Good lord, was I hooked on an "influencer?"

Still shaking my head at how ridiculous I was, I opened the page for Insta posts on Random Husband. The easiest approach was to start with the most recent post, which I was interested to see was sweaty guy. Abby moved fast! The interview happened only this morning, and she had already reported details. The picture showed an avatar of sweaty guy, a fair likeness that wouldn't give away his identity unless someone had watched the interview, and she called him Brandon, which I assumed was a fake name.

I could spare three minutes for another sandwich and a beer while I read about "Brandon." At this rate I'd never cook a real dinner, opting instead to follow Random Husband like an unemployed schlub who needed to know other people's drama. I reminded myself my mission was to search for clues about mystery woman and maybe get a peek at references to the coffee shop.

But now I also wanted to know the sister's story.

I sat at the kitchen counter and devoured my

sandwich while opening the latest post. With an avatar of sweaty guy on the screen, Abby spoke a voiceover.

Today I had the pleasure of meeting Brandon, a handsome man with a strong jaw and deep brown eyes, both of which take a back seat to his impressive physique. Brandon's broad shoulders and six-pack abs make him stand out among other applicants. Admittedly, he's the only man who submitted a picture naked from the waist up, but hey, kudos to people who show off their best assets!

Now for the human side and my advice to Brandon. You have so many great qualities. Remember your beauty and your worth when you feel nervous, and until you reach your goal, carry a towel to blot sweat. It's okay. We all struggle with something—most of us struggle with a whole bucket of somethings! My second piece of advice is to allow yourself to be vulnerable.   Confidence is great in moderation, but avoid being so confident that you mansplain to people, especially women, who have to hear the approach far too often in their lives.

Finally, here's my random guess at your perfect match. I see you with a beautiful, fit woman you meet at the gym, where you obviously spend a lot of time and where everybody should sweat. The next time you're working out, look around for her, be bold and confident, but let her talk. And above everything else, be kind. Women like kindness in a man. I wish you luck, happiness, and a successful marriage.

Oddly, or maybe not so odd, an ad for antiperspirant urged followers to control excessive sweating and smell like an ocean breeze. Abby probably had no control over ad placement.

I read the posts back through time, where most of what she wrote was a shorter version of the magazine articles. Maybe because she had conducted only one interview, most of the posts reflected on relationships, love, and marriage, chronicling the writer's thoughts. It made sense to post often to keep people engaged in the story. Given how fast Abby could turn around an event like meeting sweaty guy, her followers wouldn't be disappointed as the interviews continued.

While I skimmed older posts, a new message popped up. Abby would interview men tomorrow between ten and two at my shop. I wasn't sure if I should overstock the cases again, but I'd better plan to have plenty of coffee and at least check the food inventory. I drank the last of my beer and headed down to the darkened store, hoping I'd see mystery woman again tomorrow.

Days passed with no sighting, and once again I had to wonder if I'd see her again. The sister settled into the shop, bringing enough customer traffic to keep us busy, and somehow, she managed to disappear before I could be a pain in the ass about her sister. I considered responding to one of her posts with the question, "Who is your sister, and how do I find her?" But I'm an adult man, and I do have some pride. I was willing to follow the story, but I wasn't willing to participate.

By the end of the second day, I convinced myself I'd still be a man if I cornered the sister during interviews. The uneasy feeling was tied to the crowd of people who obviously watched the drama unfold, and as soon as I approached the writer, I'd be part of the show. Mornings before work and evenings after work, I read posts and any new stories in *Women First*. Mostly the evening posts reviewed the men interviewed during the day, always honest but kind. That kindness and intelligence sold me on approaching the sister the next day.

After tangling myself in the sheets all night, slogging through dreams of biking my old paper route but tossing papers from the week before, I opened my eyes to a pitch-black room. Awake again. My hand reached for the phone while I told myself not to look at the time. Four o'clock. No matter how hard I crunched my eyes closed, they popped open as though searching for a threat in the darkness. I yanked a pillow over my head, pressing my eyelids down for the count, and dragged deep breaths down to my stomach. Instead of quieting, my mind raced through Abby's articles and posts, creating a word cloud of love, husband, and marriage.

I smashed my lips together and groaned. Tossing back the covers, I sat on the edge of the bed, pissed off because my mind wouldn't shut up already. After watching hope die for another minute, I plodded to the kitchen for coffee. The shop wouldn't open for another three hours, the gym was closed, and most of the city slept a hell of a lot better than I did. Thank goodness my coffee prowess took a while, from grinding beans and boiling water to staring at the French press. By the time I held the filled-to-the-brim mug, I had only two hours and fifty-one minutes to kill.

I stretched out on my couch and sipped hot coffee, closing my eyes to focus entirely on the experience. Since coffee was my world, I limited myself to one cup in the morning. Today, maybe two.

Two hours and forty-eight minutes to kill.

I dragged my phone into my lap and scanned through stand-up comedy routines, knowing Bill Burr or Kevin Hart would help me pass the time, but I'd already heard the shows.

Who was I kidding? What I wanted to read was Random Husband.

I searched for new posts and came up empty,

wallowing in self-pity over not sleeping and finding no entertainment either. I dragged my laptop toward me, telling myself I could check email.

In a defiant turn, my fingers opened *Women First*. Nothing. I slammed the laptop shut, frustrated with the lack of sleep, elusive mystery woman, and no new information on Random Husband.

Little did I know, the next story would be a nightmare.

CHAPTER 15—ABBY

Karen met with applicants, and I forced myself to stay away because ninety-five percent of my mind ruminated over the barista. I pictured him there, roasting beans, making coffee, serving customers. In my fantasies, he worked behind the counter, bare chested, his intense blue eyes scanning the room. Of course, I had no idea what his chest looked like, but the muscles I'd felt gave me a good indication. Each day, by noon, I had to talk myself out of popping by to check on Karen.

She might need me.

Only she didn't, and she'd see right through my visit, guaranteeing a round of well-deserved teasing.

I opted to stay busy, as usual. From ten o'clock to two, meetings with caterers, florists, and Edith kept me running around town. Weddings usually last only a few minutes, but my editor wanted me to drag it out to at least an hour, which meant meeting with readers and the press while I got ready and hosting a pre-reception reception after we said "I do." The real reception would include the first dance and traditional cake cutting. Both receptions would need to be catered, which meant working through two menus. And both would need decorations, including flowers. I chose white roses and greenery for the events to keep things simple, and the decorators would work their magic with candles, trinkets, and whatever else a wedding required.

Edith insisted I work through the details. She acted like it was a favor to let the bride plan her wedding, but I suspected she didn't want the hassle. I wasn't surprised when she told me the magazine would need to approve my choices and expenses before they'd finalize any decisions. I suppose her demand was fair given they were paying for the parts not donated by our sponsors.

Her only concession was the wedding gown. She decided I could choose my dress, as long as it was white, full-length, and had a train. With a remarkable force of will, I'd stopped my eyes from rolling toward the ceiling.

While Karen interviewed, I focused on the gown, knowing the task would hold my attention. The designer met with me at his shop, a modest space with floor-to-ceiling windows tucked away in an otherwise deserted strip mall. After bowing and introducing himself as Hao, the designer invited me to sit in an elegant red chair. Around me, yards of silk and lace, brilliant tiaras, and design books gleamed under recessed lighting. Hao sat across from me in a tailored gray suit with a red tie and pocket square. His erect posture and subdued movements telegraphed success, which was reflected in the Chinese-inspired furniture and rich red walls. Even the incense wafting from the corner smelled exotic.

I wasn't a princess-skirt, tiara sort of bride, but I had no idea what might appeal to me. Hao quietly explained the shapes of gowns, bodices, and necklines. I had to lean forward to hear him well, letting his gentle cadence flow over me like warm water. If he hadn't been such a fantastic designer, I'd have sworn he missed his calling as a meditation instructor.

In his euphonious voice, he said, "First, I will learn of your essence. You will tell me about yourself, your life, your dreams. Second, I will learn of your body. You will stand and allow me to measure. Third, I will design. You will wear the dress that suits your person, both body and soul." Then he opened his hands in front of him as though displaying his world to me.

I wasn't sure if the gesture meant I should talk, stand, or moonwalk across the room, so I settled for staying quiet. The silence stretched for what seemed like ten minutes but was probably more like fifteen seconds before I smiled under his watchful eye.

He waited.

I blinked.

Unable to sustain the silence, I said, "About

me. I have a wonderful life with a great family. My sister and brother-in-law raised me through teenage years because my mom died, and my father left long before I could remember him. My sister is my best friend." Under Hao's watchful gaze, my eyes unexpectedly filled with tears. I don't know why talking about my family felt poignant, but it did. I shook my head a little to get back on track. "In my dreams, I want to make a difference in my little corner of the world. Not just a difference, but a positive influence."

My confidant spoke softly. "This is what you do with your writing?"

Maybe. "If I'm lucky. The dream is to empower women in some way, urge them to take control of their lives, whether it's in a relationship or what they look like or how they come to accept themselves. Along the way, I try to ask challenging questions and get people to examine their beliefs."

Hao nodded slowly. "This is why you marry a man you do not know?"

Clearly, my designer had done his homework. And now he was asking *me* the challenging questions. "Yes, that's part of it. If people want something, they should take control or at least encourage luck by participating. Especially women. We're taught to wait for Mr. Right to come along, ask us out, and propose. So much of the process is out of our hands—or so we're taught."

"And the other part?"

Oh, he was good. I thought he'd let me get away with the one part, but I should have known better. "The other part is loneliness. I love my sister, my family, beyond words, but I also want a partner, a lover, someone I come home to every night, plan weekend getaways with, and spend pajama Sunday snuggling on the couch. Sometimes my heart breaks from missing him, and we haven't even met." Tears filled my eyes again. Where was this coming from?

Hao pulled a tissue from his general vicinity and handed it to me. "Stand." He stood to demonstrate the required action. Taking me by the hand, he led me onto an elevated platform in front of a huge, ornate mirror. With a swirl of his finger, he directed me to turn in a circle while he scrutinized me. A tape measure appeared in his hand, and he measured more parts than I thought should matter, writing down nothing as he memorized my form.

"Yes." The tape measure vanished as quickly as it had appeared. "Yes. You come back one week before the wedding to fit."

Wait. Was I dismissed? What about the design? "Um—" My single syllable was meant as a question, but he simply stared with his gentle smile. I tried more words. "What do you have in mind for the dress?"

He stepped back and studied my figure as though already envisioning his creation. Almost a whisper, he said, "You trust me."

Damn it, I did. There was nothing more to say. He held my hand as I stepped from the platform, where he paused to bow deeply. When he released my hand, I tiptoed out of the shop as though leaving a church after communion.

⊕

In the afternoons, Karen turned over video of her interviews, and I spent the rest of the day reviewing, creating avatars of each candidate, and writing posts for Karen to record over the pictures. In the evenings, when the kids were tucked away in bed and Ricky was tucked away in front of the TV, we finalized the posts. Although it was time-consuming work, the week would pass quickly, and we'd move on to a less intense phase. I tempted Karen with a day of tasting wedding cakes as a reward.

"What about the dress?" she asked. Ricky's TV show droned from the living room.

I downed half of my water before filling her in on my surreal experience with Hao. I didn't blame her for the shocked face when I admitted I had no idea what the designer had planned and was okay with being in the dark.

She choked on her tea. "You know *nothing* about the dress?"

"Nope."

"At all?"

"Nada."

"You're going to marry a stranger in a dress

you didn't pick?" She sipped her tea again and shrugged one shoulder. "That tracks." She massaged the small of her back. "Tomorrow is my last day of interviews."

"Have you seen sexy guy making coffee?" I knew I shouldn't ask, but I also knew she'd tell me, feeding my curiosity about the man. Although I also wanted to ask what he wore and how he looked, I held back.

"Yep. I notice him around, but I stay busy. I've been shocked by how many people hang out to watch the interviews, but I guess Edith wanted the hype to drum up interest. Only a few people stay the entire time, but most people stop by for a while and stare. I don't know if they're following the story or notice the camera."

"What was he wearing today?" Damn. The question slipped right out. But as long as it was on the table…

Karen rewarded me with a long-suffering sigh. "I'm going to guess an apron." I gave up when she changed the subject. "Soon you can pick your top five for *husband*."

Leave it to my sister to redirect me. Because she was right, I let her adjust the conversation, although I couldn't as easily adjust my thoughts. "Sure, sure, I'll narrow it down to five and set up meetings." Based on the interview videos, a few applicants stood out, which would make my job easier. "I should find my husband in, say, a week?" As the words left my mouth, I realized how strange they sounded.

I'd spent more time picking out my prom dress.

⚭

For most of the night, I worked on a *Women First* article focusing on the effort of maintaining a marriage. The subtext of the article was a salute to my sister and her husband, a surprise she'd try to talk me out of if I told her. Sometimes she was too humble. I also wanted to publicly thank her for her role in the project and give readers a peek into my family life, a blessing I always felt thankful for.

The story flowed so well I couldn't sleep and ended up staying awake until I sent it to Edith in the darkest hours of the morning. The woman never slept, and I trusted she'd either make the article public or tell me to start over. My phone dinged at three, letting me know the article went live. I tucked two pillows under my head and reviewed the story, a habit used to help me catch a typo in time to avoid embarrassment. I often wanted to change a few words, but mostly I felt proud. Something about a finished product out in the world thrilled me, and I have to believe most writers have the same experience.

I reread my gift to Karen.

What I know about love and marriage comes from my sister. I'll call her K, for kind. At the age of twenty-four, she married the rock of our family. I'll call him R, for rock. Seven years older than her, R devoted himself to meeting K's every need, including letting his sister-in-law live with them. Of course, the sister is me, and this article is a tribute from me to my beloved K and R.

My sister is beautiful and independent, living a full life, but at the end of each day, she returns to her little family and offers the care and nurturing that help define Southern women. She adores her husband. When I asked her if R was her soulmate, she didn't hesitate in her answer. "Yes." Although I don't believe in the universe secreting away a Mr. Right or the perfect "one" for each of us, I do believe my sister is married to her soulmate.

Let me explain.

These two lovely people lived in the same city, which increased the probability she'd work in Savannah, where R searched for a receptionist. He needed someone to field calls and schedule appointments so he could concentrate on the hands-on work of his business. K applied, and he hired her. I like to believe he fell for her at first sight, but he's a quiet guy who would save those mushy details for my sister's ears alone. Either way, this beautiful, kind young woman became his partner, in a sense, before they ever got married. Over a few months, she became his confidant, friend, and lover. No one was surprised when they married at the justice of the peace four months after they met.

Being part of the family, I can tell you they had some rough times along the way. The marriage wasn't always easy, and I doubt she'd want me to write otherwise. Sometimes they broke the tired old rule of never going to bed angry and woke up still in the throes of their argument. But on those tense mornings, I'd catch R watching K with adoration in his eyes as she cooked breakfast and plopped a full plate in front of him with extreme prejudice. As she walked away, leaving him to find pieces of toast strewn across the table, I saw her stifle a giggle. Like a couple of children, they'd move from aggressive silence to teasing banter to a bear hug initiated by R and accepted by K with only a token push away.

I saw their brief courtship and the arguments of early marriage. I watched as they struggled to learn what it meant to be married to each other, with their flaws and their needs. They adjusted over time, focusing on the best parts and working toward minimizing the inevitable bad parts. They persevered. And over time, they stopped looking like a jigsaw puzzle with pieces crammed into the wrong spots, forced to fit by a child's frustrated hand. K and R, my sister and my brother-in-law, now treasure each other and their marriage. They treasure their children. Every decision is based on what's best for the family, from the food they eat to the least stressful vacations.

I still claim you shouldn't waste time searching for the "one" person out there set aside for you. Don't assume the universe will steer your path toward a soulmate. But K and R taught me something new. The best marriages create soulmates. Through love, commitment, and resilience, the "one" will emerge right in your own home. One day, your hard work and perseverance —your participation—will manifest your soulmate. He's not the man at the end of the bar or the guy on a dating app. He's your husband.

I rested the phone on my chest. My sister and Ricky would like the article. I was proud of it, and I was proud of them for what they'd created. Secure in the belief the article celebrated their love, I finally slept. I don't think I moved for five hours, and when I woke up, I felt more rested than I had since starting the Random Husband project. I read the article again (don't judge— every writer does it) before taking a long bath and cleaning the house.

By noon, I was hungry, and my fridge held only Karen's lasagna, which I'd eaten for the past three days, and a bottle of kombucha I couldn't bring myself to drink. I perused the pantry, and my eyes skipped over a can of corn, some olive oil, and a jar of peanut butter I could rely on to sustain my life in a pinch. What I really wanted was a chicken-salad sandwich on thick, homemade bread. And a cup of coffee. Fantastic coffee.

My stomach growled. I glanced down at my sweatpants and faded shirt, noting I felt very comfortable and looked like crap. Without allowing too much mental input, I ran upstairs like I had a purpose (even though I didn't!) and pulled on some skinny jeans and an adorable sleeveless shirt I'd picked up at a thrift store. I tamed my hair with damp hands while examining myself in the mirror. Still for no reason whatsoever, I applied a mere touch of eyeliner and mascara...a dab of caramel-colored lipstick. People should dress their best when they go out in public, a philosophy I planned to adopt starting now.

Downstairs, I slipped my feet into flipflops and grabbed a baseball hat and purple glasses. I marched to my car, well aware of my destination: Historic Coffee Roasters. Can't a woman pop into her favorite coffee shop without making a federal case of it? No big deal. I'd order a coffee and sandwich to go and only be in the place five minutes. I wouldn't try to see who's there other than my sister.

My hand shook a little when I opened the shop door, or maybe the jittery feeling was only in my stomach. Karen had set up on the right side of the store, with the camera behind her shoulder. A blond-haired man faced her, but I could only see the back of his head. My sister seemed engrossed in the conversation, which probably meant the interview was going well. Most of the surrounding tables held one or two people each, and they made no effort to hide their interest in Karen and the man she now smiled at.

My eyes wandered, searching for nothing in particular. At the back counter, two servers prepared coffee, and one of the women looked familiar. The roasting room stood empty, not that it mattered to me—I was here for lunch and a coffee to go.

I approached the counter, where the familiar woman wore a nametag with "Anuli" in elaborate cursive. With my best attempt at a winning smile, I asked for a latte with Splenda and a chicken-salad sandwich.

She nodded, already starting on the sandwich. "Will your order be here or to go?"

"Here please." I didn't want the sandwich to get soggy on the ride home.

And the coffee might get cold.

The other woman behind the counter walked

away, leaving me alone with Anuli. I glanced behind her at the roasting area and told myself not to dare think of steamy kissing and the feel of —.

"Lettuce?" Anuli brought me back to the present.

"Yes, please." But I realized more words would bubble out a second before it happened. "Um, I think you have a guy who works here. I've seen him sometimes. He makes a great cup of coffee." I sounded like a vapor trail with legs, and Anuli's stare didn't help. When I stopped talking, she raised her eyebrows in question. I soldiered on. "So, yeah, I was wondering what his name is."

She pressed her lips together, but I could still see the grin. "We have four male employees." Anuli went back to making my sandwich as though she didn't see the heart pumping on my sleeve.

"Oh, um, he has dark hair."

One side of her mouth quirked up before she got it back under control. "That rules out one. Three left."

Shit. "He's big." I touched my shoulders to show what I meant.

"That rules out another one." She cut my sandwich in half and reached for a coffee cup. "Can you describe him more?"

He's sexy. But I had at least some pride left. "Blue eyes. And he works over there sometimes." I gestured toward the roasting room.

"Oh! Max. You're describing Max." She turned around to make my coffee, but I caught a glimpse of her smile. Was this woman messing with me?

Two men walked up to the counter, and while they waited for their turn, they talked about the interviews. Apparently, both had applied to Random Husband, and one had recently finished his meeting with my sister. I was grateful they kept the conversation light, turning their attention to what they would order.

Anuli returned with my coffee. She picked up a black marker and poised it over the cup. "I need to grab some Splenda from the back. What's your name so I can call you when it's ready?"

I felt the men's presence behind me. In the silence, I panicked and said the first name I thought of. "Karen."

She wrote it on the cup and excused herself. Her coworker came out of the kitchen and poured two drip coffees for the men. I stood to the side, hoping to get my lunch before Anuli could shout out my sister's name and create any more confusion.

⚭

After getting "Karen's" lunch, I found an open table outside, finally allowing disappointment to roll through me. He wasn't here. What had I planned to say if I'd found him? *Hi, I was hoping we could pick up where we left off the other day.* Which was ridiculous given my sister was in the process of finding my husband, and he definitely wouldn't be Max.

Max. What a great name. And it suited him. I wanted to kiss Max until the throbbing heat started, which, if memory served, would be about two seconds into the kiss. No, wait. I felt the throbbing already, so the anticipation obviously was enough to get me going. Max. With his beard stubble and messy hair and those blue eyes…

"Hey." Like magic, Max appeared in front of me wearing shorts and a T-shirt and holding a gym bag. My heart reacted like I'd been tasered—or at least what I imagined tasers would do after watching cop shows.

I silently cursed the table for separating us. "Good morning!" I said too loudly.

He barely made eye contact. "Morning." Shifting his bag to the other hand, he turned toward the front door. "Well, I'd better get to work."

He was leaving? No banter or smile? He acted like our steamy kiss never happened. His dismissal made no sense, and to be honest, the rejection stung. Maybe I misread his attitude. "Want some company?" I smiled, trying to remind him how adorable I was.

Max faced me again. "We'd better not." The corner of the building seemed to hold his attention more than me because he stared at it when he said, "I need to apologize for kissing you the other day. I'm not that kind of person."

"Not the kind of person who kisses?" I teased. "Or does your religion tell you kissing before marriage is a sin?"

His head snapped back to me, reminding me of his intense gaze. "No, kissing *after* marriage is a sin." The anger on his face took me completely by surprise. Since when did flirty banter become accusatory?

"Uh, yeah, I guess, unless it's your spouse." What conversation were we having? Either I was missing something, or he wasn't as mentally stable as I'd assumed. I stood and matched his stare. "And just to refresh your memory, I kissed you first."

He leaned across the table toward me, and I leaned in at the same time, bringing our faces within a few inches. I could see his jaw clenching and unclenching. "Yeah, you did." He glanced at my lips. "No matter how tempting you are, it won't happen again."

What the hell? This moodiness was not attractive. I wrapped my hand around his bicep as far as my fingers would reach, intent on making a physical connection and breaking through his defensiveness. He glanced down at my hand and then back at me, his expression of disapproval shocking me into jerking away. I laughed, but the sound was too high-pitched. My chest hurt like it did when I wasn't picked for kickball in middle school. Sharp little waves of pain radiated from my heart. I must have been *way* off base about this man. Max.

I sat back down and examined my sandwich. The sting of tears behind my eyes nearly sent me running down the street, getting as far away from him as possible. I settled for grinding my teeth together and telling myself to focus on breathing. No way would I make a fool of myself over a man I barely knew.

With a mumbled, "Anyway, I'm sorry," he walked away.

I counted to ten. With Herculean effort, I picked up my sandwich and tasted it, but my stomach had other ideas. I snatched a napkin from the table and spit out my food in a way that would have made Martha Stewart proud. So much for acting like today was a plain old enjoy-the-sunshine kind of day. It's almost shocking how quickly a negative interaction can screw up a mood. We can tell ourselves to get over it, to not give the other person power over us, but that's bullshit. Our minds will review and revise until we're making up things we might have said, sometimes creating entire fake conversations in our heads. Or we ruminate and try to justify our own perspective.

All I felt was confusion.

I found a trash can and dumped my lunch.

CHAPTER 16—MAX

I was a homewrecker. Mom would be so proud. In the darkest hours of the morning, I had read and reread (and a third time) Abby's tribute to her sister's marriage. What a sham. Did the writer know anything about her sister? Her sister, who she'd called K for kindness, for god's sake, seemed eager to get down and dirty with me while her loyal husband waited in the wings. Hell, she had *kids*! I wouldn't have known by the way she looked. I'd assumed she was in her mid-twenties, but clearly, I was way off. Or maybe she'd been a child bride and wanted out of the marriage, a fact her sister didn't know. The husband might not be wonderful behind closed doors, and K was trying to find a way out.

No.

Full stop.

I wouldn't rewrite her story to make her look better and say she might need me. I paced behind the counter. Abby had written about her sister's successful marriage, great husband, and happy kids. K's behavior was unforgivable. I hadn't known she was married when I stuck my tongue down her throat, but I held myself responsible for making out with a married woman. As far as

I knew, I'd never done it before.

I couldn't decide which was worse, the shame or the disappointment. Right this minute, I still wanted her. I wanted the sweetness, fake or not, I'd felt when she touched me. If she stood in front of me right now, I can't say I would ask her to leave. I'd want to talk to her, sure, but I also wanted to do other things with her. The shame I felt wasn't dedicated only to what I'd done, but what I still wanted to do.

My only option was to stay away from her.

Hell, I'd abandoned the shop, distracting myself with a harsh workout. By the time I'd made it back to work, my mind felt clearer. I'd fully intended to avoid K until I could get myself together, which meant letting go of the attraction.

But there she'd sat, looking young, sexy, and unattached. And damn, she was pretty sitting in the sun with a big smile and bare shoulders. It had hurt to see her and know my fantasies would never be real. My roller-coaster mood dipped into defeat.

Righteous indignation won out among the other emotions of the day, nudging me to confront her about being married and making a pass at me. Yeah, I was thinking like a virginal Elizabethan woman, but I felt like she'd lied to me by hiding her true identity. Shit, now I acted like she was a superhero, pretending to be a mild-mannered citizen until she tore off her clothes and revealed a big "S" on her chest...more like a scarlet "A."

By the time I'd reached her table, my jumbled thoughts strangled out one word. "Hey."

Brilliant.

That'd teach her.

I still couldn't believe she'd been so cheerful, leaving me practically speechless while part of me—a deep part—wanted to rant. I needed to get away from her before I begged her to tell me she had no husband or kids, losing my pride while I asked for something I couldn't have.

Damn it, she'd kept trying to make cheerful conversation, breaking my heart for pushing her away. She'd left me no choice but to face the damage and apologize for kissing her. I imagined she'd also apologize, but she skipped down a different road—more innocent teasing until she'd read my body language and given up.

I don't know why it'd been so important she freely tell me the truth, other than it would have redeemed her a little. I wanted to think the best of her—at least as much as I could under the circumstances. Instead, she'd stood up and challenged me, sort of like a superhero might do.

When she'd squeezed my arm like a child asking a parent not to be mad, her touch tormented me, and I don't know why. I'm almost ashamed to admit I'd wanted to march around the table and grab her against my chest, stroke her soft hair, and tell her everything was okay.

But everything was not okay. Rip off the bandage and take the pain in one go.

She'd pulled her hand away and laughed, but it wasn't a satisfied or taunting laugh. It was an uncomfortable, I-don't-know-what-to-do laugh.

My heart ached for her. And for me.

I swear I'd seen tears in her eyes before I left, but what could I say? "I'm sorry."

Φ

Thirty minutes later, showered and still in a foul mood, I returned to the shop floor. K was gone, as far as I could tell from the back of the room, and her sister continued to interview potential husbands. The woman seemed like a saint compared to her two-timing sister, but I sure as hell wouldn't be the one to educate her.

When I went behind the counter, Anuli hooked a finger at me like she had a secret to share. I followed her to the end of the counter. "What's up?"

She grinned. "I got her name."

"Who's name?"

"The woman with the purple glasses."

Oh. Well, I *had* asked, and letting this play out would be easier than explaining the mess to Anuli. "What's her name?"

"Karen." The grin widened to a smile. "I pretended I had to go get Splenda, then I asked for her name to call when the coffee was ready." My manager was proud of herself, and I couldn't burst her bubble.

"Thank you." I turned, hoping to end the conversation. It occurred to me the name "Karen" didn't suit mystery woman, but maybe I'd have to shift the name into a sexy category with Selena and Lenore.

"And Max," she whispered. "She asked for your name. The woman went on and on about how handsome you are!"

Anuli tended to exaggerate, but I liked knowing Karen had asked about me. Either way, it didn't matter now, other than making me miss her again—miss the idea of her, anyway. Anuli waited for a reaction, so I nodded and smiled. "Thanks again." Those words seemed to satisfy her, releasing me from yet another reminder of the woman I'd never have.

As I walked away, I thought again of going home for a visit. I needed the grounding my family offered, especially mom. Most people find the best version of themselves when they return to their roots, where childhood routines bring comfort, and family gushes unconditional love. Sure, mom would offer advice, but more importantly, she'd remind me she'd raised a good person, someone who knows right from wrong and chooses the best path even when it's the most difficult.

From the door of the roasting room, I turned back to Anuli. "Hey, I'm thinking of taking a few days off to visit my family. Think you can handle the place without me?"

"*Really*?" She did a happy dance with her arms in the air. "Definitely, boss! I got this!"

For the first time since I woke up too early this morning, I smiled.

CHAPTER 17—ABBY

After Max soundly rejected me, I tucked tail and drove home. In my backyard, an oasis surrounded by magnolia trees and crepe myrtles, I stretched out on a lounge chair and lifted my face to the sun. A few minutes of sunshine always eased my mood. A few margaritas and a dozen donuts would have served the same purpose, but soon Karen would bring me the final videos.

The next couple of days would be too busy for me to think about Max's rejection. Unfortunately, I had at least one empty hour to ruminate. I pulled out my phone and read article comments, a flood of support for the project and thankful comments toward K and R. Karen would see the comments this afternoon. I smiled. Karen's happiness was one of my core values, right below God and country but above kindness and trying to stay healthy. I had to put kindness below Karen because if anyone hurt her, I would *not* be kind. As for healthy living, refer to my prior comment about margaritas and donuts.

I read more responses to my article, feeling better by the minute. With Max out of the picture, my heart would be entirely on the project again, and I vowed to keep it there. I truly believed a perfectly adequate husband would be found in the final five candidates—a man who would be more than adequate with time and commitment. Public support didn't hurt either; I was fortunate to have kind followers. So many people read *Women First* and the social media posts, and the more people talked about it, the more the story spread, until it seemed like most people on social media would have tripped across a post by now.

Shit!

I got a frozen feeling like when I accidentally included someone in a text group who shouldn't read the message, but it was too late to pull it back—the don't-move, don't-breathe clench immediately followed by my face and body flooding with heat. Out of nowhere, it occurred to me Max might know I'm searching for a husband and had lip-locked him anyway. *Damn.* The kiss in the middle of Random Husband made me a floozy. Or a tramp, but that label sounded like a cute word for a cartoon dog.

My brain raced through ways out. No, he had kissed me back and initiated a second kiss. My mind tried to linger over the sexy memory, but I shut it down. Maybe that's why he'd apologized, knowing it was wrong. Or maybe he'd heard about Random Husband after the kiss. He had several days to learn the details. I was careful to blur my identity by using an avatar, but still he could have figured it out when I hovered in the background of interviews.

The more I thought about it, the more my epiphany made sense. I groaned out loud, my mind struggling through ways to fix the problem. And yes, it was a problem. My path wouldn't lead back to Max, but I cared what he thought. The poor man had apologized to me, when I should have been the one asking forgiveness. I resolved to eat crow tomorrow.

⚭

Early the next morning, I felt in control of my life again. After watching the remaining interview videos, I'd written copy for avatars and taken everything to Karen for voiceovers. By late evening, every review was posted, and I left my exhausted sister to her husband. I wouldn't sleep, so I headed home to keep working.

By the time midnight rolled around, I had a cup of hot green tea on the living-room desk and my laptop open to the candidate files and notes. Whenever my brain returned to Max, I refocused on the files. When stern self-control didn't work, I wrote myself a note saying I'd apologize in the morning and stuck it to my desk. I'd learned the strategy years ago to stop the Zeigarnik effect, an endless loop of worry when a situation has no closure, no plan.

With some effort, I dove back into the files.

Page after page of notes accumulated on my

legal pad while I reviewed interviews, pictures, and shared interests. The files began to blur together because most men had the same responses. For the most part, the applicants played it safe. What became more important than interests we shared were the ones we didn't have in common. I omitted six candidates for their devotion to extreme sports. Likely they wanted to seem manly, but the idea of spending weekends risking our lives didn't appeal to me. I prefer a quiet weekend with walks, books, and outings like taking pictures in an ancient cemetery. It wasn't lost on me that judges ended up omitting options to whittle down their work rather than simply trying to find the best quality. I had to get the pile down to a workable number.

Thank goodness I'd already seen videos of three men who caught my eye. The three seemed confident, intelligent, and open. Their kind interactions with my sister won me over too. And, well, I was attracted to them as much as someone can be without face-to-face interaction. When I tried to envision our married life, I couldn't quite get there, but I'd meet each one soon. After reviewing their files, they stayed on my top-five list.

Choosing the final two men kept me up until three. Every time I thought I'd narrowed down the list, I'd see another candidate who seemed like a solid choice, and I had to go back through the list. After six cups of tea and three urgent trips to the bathroom, I finished my daunting task. A fresh piece of paper held the five names and clues to help me remember them.

> *Rob—black hair and brown eyes, great smile, accountant*
> *Kadeem—strong, silent type, mysterious, lawyer*
> *Trent—blond, easy going, entrepreneur (local gym franchise)*
> *Ashton—red hair, blue eyes, programmer (Apricot Industries)*
> *Luis—beautiful skin, very friendly, college professor (history)*

My next step was to call tomorrow—today—and schedule interviews. An in-person meeting might help me choose a husband. Oye, my stomach clenched.

Probably too much tea.

I stretched out on the couch and fell asleep clutching the list, waking only when the sun speared my eye. I loved the openness of the house, but the downstairs wasn't conducive to sleeping late, a luxury I needed after the long night. When I saw the husband list on the floor, sleep abandoned me. It was too early to call anyone, but I could pace the floor for a couple of hours, watching the clock and drinking too much coffee.

What if I'd missed a valuable candidate? I

glanced over at my desk.

Stop, just stop, I reprimanded myself.

It's always tough to know when a job is done because something inside of us questions the work. Could it be better? Is it the absolute best it can be? Long ago I'd come to terms with the voice and dealt with it harshly. I always did the best I could do and then moved on, which was exactly my plan this morning.

The prep work was done. The day was planned. First, I'd go apologize to Max for kissing him when I should've focused on my near-future husband. My stomach flipped painfully, and I didn't know whether to blame the looming apology or the impending meeting with Max, especially after his thorough rejection.

Probably both.

Next, I'd schedule candidate meetings at a different coffee shop. I doubted Max wanted to see me again, and after humbling myself today, the feeling would be mutual. If the five finalists were willing to meet with me right away, I could move on to the next phase. The magazine would work with my future husband to invite family, arrange travel, and incorporate his preferences into the wedding ceremony. Of course, he'd sign a non-disclosure agreement about my full name and any other private information he learned about me through this process. Even to me, the arrangement sounded one-sided, but every candidate knew the deal when he applied. The best I could offer was to honor my promise to the magazine and still be kind and supportive of my husband. After three months, we would either end the marriage or continue as a typical couple, with no more posts to the world.

At three months, the marriage would become real.

Edith had hinted the marriage license wouldn't be filed until three months had passed, as though waiting changed anything. Without filing, the marriage would still be binding. The magazine planned to keep my real name out of the press by stalling, and I had to agree, writing under a pen name offered more freedom. It might seem like overkill, but fans can be more resourceful than stable, and I'd rather not worry about a stalker in my garden or my sister's house.

When I personally interviewed the final five, my avatar identity would be lost, an inevitable outcome, since in September, I'd stand in front of hundreds of fans in Forsyth Park. In fact, this afternoon I'd post the time and location of interviews. So much for my anonymity. Edith wanted to continue the hype, and it's what I'd signed on for, leaving me no room to complain. I could hear her now. "This is business, and there's no business without customers."

⊕

After a long bath where I nearly fell asleep, I dressed slowly to kill time until eight, when I figured Max would be working. I tried on six outfits and settled on a white sundress with spaghetti straps and a full skirt to my knees. Taupe wedges promised to sprain an ankle if I walked further than two blocks, but hey, they looked good, and today I needed the confidence boost. I picked dangling ruby earrings, an extravagance courtesy of the lottery, knowing they would sparkle in the sunlight.

Out of habit, I picked up the purple sunglasses on my way out, but then I remembered the incognito part was pretty much over. Leaving them on the passenger seat, I drove to the coffee shop and found a parking spot around the corner. I said a little "thank you" to the universe, convincing myself the good fortune boded well for seeing Max. The short walk couldn't be blamed for my pounding heart, an affliction I attributed to admitting fault.

I opened the door with a flourish, pretending to myself Max would accept my apology and see me as a good person. Or at least a slightly better person. Frankly, no matter what I said now, I *had* attacked him with my mouth while searching for a husband elsewhere.

With a march of confidence I almost felt, I crossed the floor and approached the counter, where Anuli handed a sandwich to a customer.

When she saw me, she smiled like we were friends, and again, I thanked the universe for good vibes. She reached for a cup and asked, "Your usual?"

I returned the smile. Why not enjoy a coffee and grovel at the same time? "Yes, please." While she worked her magic, I fumbled for words. Too bad I couldn't write them down first. "Um, is Max around?"

"Oh gosh, no, I'm so sorry." She said it with gentle pity. "He's gone to visit his parents for a while."

Deflated, I accepted the coffee she handed me and paid. Damn. I needed to modify my plan for the day. The apology would hang over my head like the sword of Damocles for an unknown stretch of time.

Damn.

Anuli continued to appraise me with puppy-dog sad eyes. I wasn't sure what to say, but I could tell she expected something. "Okay, thanks anyway."

"He should return in a few days, I think."

I backed away. "Okay, yeah, okay." After nodding to communicate all was well, I turned to the side and sort of crab-walked further away. "Thank you." A salute with my coffee cup. "Good coffee." Then, because she kept staring and feeling sorry for me, I gifted her with a laugh high-pitched enough to surprise us both.

Ⓜ

My sister and I always say, "When life gives you lemons, it'll make a great story." I headed to her house to bring her up to date and reveal my short list. Her warm kitchen offered sanctuary.

173

I rang the bell twice to let her know I had arrived and would unlock the door without an invitation. The worst I'd ever seen during an unannounced visit was Ricky in his saggy boxers, but the sight had stopped shocking me long ago. God bless those skinny white legs.

In the kitchen, Karen dried dishes and hummed along with The Beatles.

I hugged her. "Love you."

She drew back and examined my face. "What brought this on? Is something wrong?"

I had to laugh. "What could be wrong?" I plopped into my usual spot at the table. "I've narrowed the list down to five."

"*What*?" She dropped the towel on the counter and sat with me. "Tell me everything!"

After handing her my one-page list, I opened my computer and clicked into the files. "Here are the names, and I have the files open if you want to see them. I'm going to call and try to schedule meetings for tomorrow."

She read the list, nodding approval of my choices. "Are you still planning to use a different coffee shop?"

"No need. I won't be distracted by Max because he's out of town."

"*Max*, is it?" She waggled her eyebrows.

My cheeks burned a little, so I squinted at the computer to show how hard I was concentrating. "I just need to pull their phone numbers...phone...numbers...numbers...I know they're here somewhere..." I pulled the page from Karen's hands and filled in the numbers. When I glanced up again, her arms were folded across her chest.

She squinted at me to show how hard she was concentrating. Well played, sis. With a chuckle, she said, "Not much longer now. Are you excited? Nervous? Still committed to the plan?"

"Of course!" Okay, a little too cheerful for the occasion, but I never claimed to be an actress. "Really! Any of these five would make a great husband. I'm hoping for a definitive 'this one' when I talk to them."

I had no way of knowing how truly difficult —and temporary—the choice would be.

CHAPTER 18—MAX

After a boring drive on Interstate 16, I pulled into my parents' driveway. Mom opened the front door immediately, leading me to believe she'd been standing by the window watching for me. Typical mom. She met me on the front steps and hugged my waist. "Welcome home!"

I followed her inside, where dazzling scents of turkey and cobbler filled the house. A few years ago, they had downsized to a three-bedroom, two-bathroom ranch in a quiet old neighborhood. It had once been their only foray into rental properties, but dad quickly realized he wasn't cut out to be a landlord. He told stories about the tenants demanding him to change lightbulbs, snake a clogged toilet, and roll the trash can to the curb. Since then, my mom had renovated the house, including a new kitchen, refinished wood floors, and fresh paint both inside and out. The walls were painted coordinating hues of soft orange reminding me of an Arizona sunset, which served as a backdrop to comfortable brown couches and leather recliners. Brightly colored Moroccan area rugs reflected mom's taste. The kitchen sported new stainless-steel appliances and grey cabinets held a lifetime of plates, mugs, and gadgets used by mom exactly once.

I dropped my backpack inside the front door and surveyed the room, grateful to be home. New quilts draped across the furniture. "The house looks great, mom."

She waved away my comment. "Looks the same as always." A few steps away, she entered the kitchen. "Are you hungry?"

At home, I was always hungry. "Yes ma'am. I could eat."

More than complimenting her decorating skills, my willingness to eat put a smile on her face. The woman was a caretaker to the core, a beautiful quality in many Southern women and one my father bragged about at length. According to him, he came to Georgia for the work but stayed for the wonderful women. Detroit would always be where he was from, but he'd never leave the warmth—literally and figuratively—of the South.

She scooped peach cobbler from a dish on the stove and plopped vanilla ice-cream on top before putting it on the table. "Sit, sit!" Then she bustled (yes, she bustled) around, cleaning already clean surfaces. After a few minutes, she perched on the edge of a chair next to me like she wouldn't be able to stay long. "What's going on? Why are you home? Is something wrong?"

A huge spoonful of cobbler and melting ice-cream came within an inch of my open mouth.

I put it back in the bowl. "Nothing's wrong. Business is good. Coffee's selling, and—"

She waved my answer away, and I wondered when she'd picked up the annoying habit of seeing through me. "*Psh*. I know you're a great businessman. I meant your personal life. You know, the ladies, the women. Zoe?"

I decided to take a bite. "Delicious," I said around the mouthful.

Like a mom, she waited.

I swallowed the buttery sweetness. "Well, Zoe and I broke up."

You'd think I'd told her dad ran off with his eighty-year-old secretary. "Broke up?" She reached an arm around my shoulders and leaned her head on the closest one. "I'm so sorry, Max. Did she break your heart?"

"What makes you think she broke up with me?"

"Oh! Did you break up with her?"

"No, but...I could have." I shoved another bite in my mouth, swallowed. "But I didn't. She said I had too many flaws." I laughed to ease my discomfort.

"Fuck her."

Mom's blunt response always surprised me, but her words meant Zoe was forgotten, summarily dismissed from our lives forever. Crossing a member of the family meant being ostracized. Around another mouthful of homespun goodness, I mumbled, "I figured you'd say that."

"Onward and upward. Any new woman on the horizon?"

An image of Karen popped into my mind. "No, not really."

Mom, being an intelligent person, eyed me like she had when cookies went missing and I was caught hiding in the closet with chocolate on my five-year-old face. To her credit, she didn't push.

I should have come home sooner.

CHAPTER 19—ABBY

All five applicants agreed to meet the next day. Karen offered to sit beside me and provide moral support, but she wouldn't be there during my marriage, so I might as well forge ahead alone at this point.

That night, I slept and dreamed of Max.

The next morning, I dressed in gray slacks, a blue silk blouse, and short heels. My hair wouldn't cooperate, leaving me to pull it back in a severe bun at the base of my neck. The big question was which earrings to wear, but eventually I settled for fake sapphire studs surrounded by cubic zirconia.

When I arrived at the coffee shop, I ordered a latte and, out of habit, I scanned the room for Max and tried not to feel deflated he wasn't there. I settled at a small table near the middle of the room and pulled out my notepad to jot down impressions after each interview. It was nine o'clock, an hour before Kadeem would arrive. While I waited, the room began to fill until every chair was taken, and onlookers leaned against the retail racks and lounged along the wall, with most of them trying to appear busy on their phones but glancing at me every few seconds.

Promptly at ten, Kadeem walked through the door and scanned the room, finally settling on me smiling and waving him over. I'd have to say he strutted toward me, but my perception might have been influenced by the suit, vest, shirt, and tie, too many layers for the Georgia heat. He scraped the chair loudly across the floor and winced. As it turned out, his wince was the only facial expression I'd see from him during our fifteen minutes together. I had no interview items, opting instead for an easy-going chat between two people who may or may not get married.

"Good morning, Kadeem." I reached across the table and shook his hand. "Thank you for meeting with me on such short notice. I'm sure your law practice keeps you busy."

He nodded once. "I did have some clients this morning."

What could I say? "Oh, well thank you."

Kadeem nodded again, offering no information other than, "Uh-huh."

His mildly hostile reaction shook me, but I pressed on. "I wanted to meet and get to know you a bit personally. You interviewed with my assistant, who also happens to be my sister, but I thought it was important for us to meet face-to-face." He stared. "I mean, we might get married, which is a pretty big deal."

He leaned back and folded his arms across his chest. "It's a legally binding contract."

I'd made a terrible mistake.

Not in my wildest dreams could I imagine marrying this man.

I nearly giggled when I pictured what sex might be like—a silent, cold, efficient coupling sure to leave me unsatisfied but probably not out of breath. This morning, my polite upbringing required fifteen minutes of conversation, and it didn't matter if the only effort came from me.

I made it to twelve minutes.

Exhausted, I stood and extended my hand. "I don't want to keep you from your clients. Thank you again, Kadeem."

His slight frown told me he knew how badly he'd interviewed, but I'd also have figured it out when he stomped away without a word of goodbye. I heard murmurs around the room, and I'll admit I didn't have the self-control to focus on my notepad. With a glance to my right and left, I saw people chatting with each other and shaking their heads. Later I'd have to write about this interaction and find nice words to describe him.

Tough one.

I jotted down a few notes, turned them face down on the table, and went to order a breakfast sandwich. With nearly an hour to kill before Trent arrived, I needed to stay busy and dissuade fans' questions. Ten minutes to eat outside, a trip to the bathroom, and a phone call to Karen brought me to eleven o'clock and my second chance at marital bliss.

Trent entered with a smile and a loping gait matching his casual chinos and black T-shirt. He also wore tennis shoes, and I assumed he'd come from his gym or was headed there afterward. I waved and grinned, happy to see the polar opposite of Kadeem.

In one fluid motion, Trent sat across from me, briefly touched the back of my hand, and said, "You must be Abby. At last!"

"Yes, I'm Abby. It's nice to meet you, Trent." I shook his hand across the table, but he grabbed only my fingertips, leading to an awkward exchange.

"When I met the other lady, I thought it was you, and I was like, 'No way, Jose,' Abby's supposed to be way hotter than this." He grinned and examined my chest before returning to my eyes. I'd have been more offended if he didn't remind me of Eli or some other eager boy. Life hadn't yet worn the rough edges from his character.

"Before you say anything else, I should tell you the other woman who interviewed you was my sister."

Trent covered his mouth with a hand, eyes wide. He laughed loudly. "Hey-oh! But you're super hot, so we're good."

Scratch the similarity with Eli. My nephew had better manners than Trent. I couldn't make myself say the line about getting to know each other because we might get married. Obviously, he wouldn't be my first choice. Or my second. But I did have to write a post about him, which meant we had to interact. Through a series of questions, I learned he wanted to open two more gym franchises and focus on a week of personal training for new members to get them started. It wasn't a bad idea, and I told him so. He beamed at the compliment, and I could almost see him as a viable candidate again—way in the shadows of my peripheral vision.

After fifteen minutes of small talk, I stood and extended my hand. Trent recognized the not-so-subtle hint and got up, but he squeezed the tips of my fingers rather than press palm to palm. I knew the advice I'd offer him in my post. Most women are quite capable of a real handshake.

With time on my hands again, I walked outside for some fresh air and pretended to make calls. Careful to avoid eye contact with the lurkers, I returned to my interview table and reviewed my notes. At ten after twelve, I assumed Ashton wouldn't show, but he rushed in and scurried to my table. His wrinkled cargo pants, T-shirt, and flip flops let me know he wasn't a big fan of fashion. Heavy black glasses covered half his face.

"Hi, Ashton, my name's Abby. Thank you for coming." I smiled and reached my hand across the table to shake his.

"We don't need to shake." He stared at my

hand with something akin to horror, and I pulled back to my own space. "I opened the front door and haven't washed my hands." With a little shrug, he held his hands under the table.

O-kay... Aloud, I asked, "What's it like to be a programmer?"

Ashton's eyes lit up. Apparently, I had asked the key question, because words flowed as fast as I imagined he could type code. "It's great! I get to spend all day working on my computer, solving problems for the team and creating apps to help the industry. *And* I work from home, which means I don't have to deal with people. I prefer working at home where I can make sure everything stays clean and sanitized. Out in the world, you never know what you've touched. Did you know they've done studies about it, and your phone and keyboard are two of the dirtiest places in your life? Clean, clean, clean is why I like to work at home and why I sanitize my phone and computer at least three times a day. Four if I work more than twelve hours."

He paused to inhale and started up again, peering at my notepad and frowning every minute or so. The notes were face down; he couldn't read anything. The mystery was solved when one hand lifted from below the table and centered my pad in front of me. When he met my eyes again, he apologized. "Sorry, sorry, I'm more comfortable with order. I guess it's because I'm a coder, which means I worship order.

Otherwise, it's gibberish. Madness." I wanted to tell him I had run my fingers along the outside of the building and then touched the pad, likely smothering it with germs, but he might have a heart attack. Besides, I couldn't sneak a word into his monologue.

And on it went until forty-five minutes had passed. I never gave another word of encouragement, but Ashton didn't need my help.

I made a production of reading my watch, hoping my companion would take the hint. Not a chance. I stood and remembered not to extend my hand. "It was nice to meet you. Thank you for coming."

"Is it because I have red hair?"

"What?"

"You're sending me away because I have red hair."

"No, I—" His hurt tone worried me. "I think your hair looks nice. But I have another meeting in a few minutes."

He pushed back his chair, knocking it over in the process. When he fumbled to pick it up, the noise level of the room increased, and I understood observers' opinions without hearing distinct words. Ashton smoothed the short hair on top of his head and murmured, "Pick me." With that, he stutter-stepped away like a bride walking down the aisle. As he approached the door to leave, Luis, my next interview, opened it, and Ashton scooted out sideways with no contact. Luis looked after him for a second before turning his attention to the room and finding me smiling with a wave.

Three down, two to go. *Please send me a good one.* I crossed my fingers and pressed the hand to my lap.

Luis was one of my top choices, and I had high hopes for this meeting. He'd nailed the right amount of casual in his khakis and blue button-down shirt with the sleeves folded up twice. Surely he wouldn't raise any red flags. If I didn't find a potential husband in the final five, I wasn't entirely certain what I'd do next. He pulled out the chair and sat, shaking my hand when I offered it, and smiled a hello. "I've been looking forward to meeting you, Abby. Your avatar doesn't do you justice."

If we continued down the flattery path, eventually I'd blush. I thanked him and changed the subject. "I appreciate you meeting me on short notice. I'm sure you're busy."

"Not a problem. My grad student is teaching my class, and I'll be back in time for the others. We need to get to know each other in case we end up married." He laughed and leaned forward on his elbows. "What questions do you have for me? And will you tell me more about you?"

His skin was the color of dark-roast coffee, and for the life of me, I could see no flaw on his face. Add his perfect complexion to a PhD, easy conversation, and a killer smile, and he was the whole package. A tiny blossom of faith began to grow, bringing with it a tingle in my gut. The sun outside grew brighter, the coffee smelled richer, and I let out a breath I'd been holding.

Suddenly I realized I was staring. I hurried to say something intelligent. "Do you enjoy working at the university? How are your students?"

For almost an hour, we shared our stories. He told me about the challenges and pleasures of teaching and writing textbooks, and I explained what I wanted to achieve from my writing. I didn't say aloud my vision of us working at home, sharing ideas and pieces of our work, getting input on what we wrote. It was a cozy image. While I fantasized, we talked about our most recent vacations, what we did to relax, and the importance of healthy living. He considered himself a good cook and promised to make chicken cordon bleu for me.

I'd found my husband.

Near the end of the hour, he looked at his watch and stood, extending his hand. "I know you have another meeting, so I'll get out of your way. It was a pleasure to meet you, Abby. If I'm not your first choice, I'd still love to make dinner for you." Then, with a smile that should have twinkled like the teeth of every Disney hero, he turned and walked away.

Enter Rob.

His beige slacks, untucked green shirt, and

brown shoes sent the message he'd dressed for the occasion but had a fun, comfortable side. A radiant smile sent the same message. When he sat across from me, his deep brown eyes drew my attention almost as much as the black wavy hair tumbling over his collar, with a curl falling across his brow. I extended my hand, which he shook with a we're-equals firm grip. I liked him immediately.

We both settled into our meeting, leaning forward slightly and exchanging grins as he nodded his head toward our audience. I enjoyed his self-deprecating sense of humor—the kind with gestures and comments revealing he didn't take himself too seriously. If we don't laugh at ourselves, everybody else will.

He seemed to be waiting for me to take the lead, so I did. "Thank you for meeting with me today. I'm sure you're a busy man."

"My pleasure." With a shrug and a smile, he added, "I work with numbers, and numbers can always wait when there's something more important." He gestured toward me. "Like you."

"Thank you, Rob. I guess we should dive right in." I rested both elbows on the table, bringing me slightly closer to him. "What do you do for fun?"

"I guess I'm too young to have a bucket list, but I like to try new experiences. Last month I signed up for pottery classes and learned I can't even make a pencil cup." He laughed at himself and shrugged. "This month I'm working with stained glass. My goal is to finish a table to sit beside my lawn chair."

"I love it! Let me write those down." I scribbled and met his gaze again. "I like to work with my hands."

"Me too." Did I read a sexy message in those brown eyes? He grinned with one side of his mouth, letting the silence stretch between us.

The blush crept into my cheeks before I could stop it, but I pretended not to notice, hoping he wouldn't mention it. I filled the silence by asking, "What about next month?"

"Next month I'm getting married." Rob held a deadpan expression for a few seconds before laughing to let me know he was teasing. "Or getting a puppy." He held up his hands as though weighing options. "One or the other, for sure."

I had to laugh—and change the subject to ease the heat from my face. "What about base jumping?"

"Not for me, thanks. I want to have fun, not die." He rolled his eyes to the ceiling. "Life is full of thrills without physical danger." With a grin, he said, "Like taking a great picture, traveling the world, and curling up with someone special." Again he gave me an intimate look I could get used to.

Based on the increased noise level in the room, our admirers must have seen the look too. They approved, and so did I. Spending time with

Rob would be a blast, and I enjoyed the mix of curiosity, humor, and sexuality I saw in him. Yeah, I could get used to this.

With a smooth segue, Rob turned the subject to me, asking about my writing, family, and hobbies. He seemed interested in every pastime I mentioned, and for a minute I wondered if his responses were entirely honest, until I mentioned jigsaw puzzles.

He held up a hand in a "stop" motion. "I suck at jigsaw puzzles almost as much as I sucked at throwing clay." With a smile, he shrugged. "But, hey, with a couple of beers, I might help you find a corner piece."

We talked for well over an hour, and I think we'd have continued except I was starting to feel awkward after so many hours in the spotlight. "I hate to say this, but we'd better wrap up our meeting. I've had so much fun."

Without hesitation, he stood and reached across the table for another of those perfect handshakes. "Me too. Is it okay to say I hope we meet again?"

"Yes, more than okay. Great, actually." I don't think my smile could have been any wider, but I wanted to communicate my interest in the only way I could across a table in front of dozens of people.

I watched him walk away. The man had a great butt on top of everything else. Maybe marriage to him would take my mind off Max.

Damn it. Where had Max come from?

Rob, or Luis, for that matter, seemed wonderful, and hell, I knew them better than I knew Max. I chalked it up to pre-wedding jitters because I'd ask one of the final two candidates to be my husband.

Rather than see the restless audience in my periphery, I heard snippets of conversations, many of which indicated they were headed my way with questions. It seemed unlikely I'd avoid them altogether, and they had been patient through interviews, so I scanned the room with an open expression meant to serve as an invitation. For the next two hours, I listened to advice about who I should pick and why, what my next story should focus on, and how to let four of the men down gently.

In a continued effort to put good out into the world, I listened and nodded. They meant well. But in the end, I had to pick my own husband, and I definitely would be gentle with the others.

Eventually the last fan waved goodbye, and I sat back, worn out.

Tonight, I would let Karen know who I'd marry, and she'd probably insist on celebrating with coconut cake and cold almond milk, a substitute for champagne. Truthfully, if she wasn't pregnant and the kids weren't at the party, my sister would probably add champagne to the menu.

But first, I needed to get Max out of my mind

once and for all.

I was glad to see Anuli behind the counter. I felt we'd made a connection over her sharing Max's name with someone who obviously had a crush.

Past tense.

Had a crush.

I practiced deep breathing while approaching the counter. *In* (one...two...three), *out* (one...two...three). What was I nervous about? Max wasn't here.

"Hi, Anuli." I smiled to let her know I was harmless. "Can you please give Max a message from me? I can write it down, if it's easier." Well, writing would be easier for me, and I assumed she'd agree.

Instead, she grinned. "No need. I have an excellent memory."

Crap. I didn't want my humble apology floating around in the world without a home. "Well, I guess first I should ask if he's for sure coming back. I imagine a roast-master can work in any coffee shop."

Anuli frowned. "He'd better come back. He owns the place."

CHAPTER 20—MAX

After four days eating a copious amount of food, drinking beer every night with my dad and brothers, and sitting on the couch with my phone, I was ready to get back to work. The mornings offered too many leisure hours, with Random Husband my only entertainment, but the many posts and comments didn't swallow enough time. My main goal was to avoid thinking of Karen, with her silly purple glasses, soft lips, and hurt expression the last time I'd seen her. Why did I feel like such an ass for hurting her feelings? Basically, she'd cheated on her husband, and I'd been more than ready to take our kisses to my bed.

If I felt like crap now, I could only imagine how I'd have felt if I'd slept with her and then learned about her husband—and *kids*.

My trip to Macon was supposed to recalibrate my life, remind me what kind of person I am, and purge thoughts of Karen naked. I'd have to settle for two out of three. My body still wanted mystery woman, with her sweet pink tongue and little moans of encouragement.

Work might offer a distraction, and if work didn't do the trick, I'd dive into something else.

Eventually Karen would be a distant memory.

The next morning, I kissed mom goodbye and allowed I-16 to hypnotize me on the drive home. I barely made it in the front door of the shop before Anuli pulled me to the back of the store.

In her best I-have-gossip voice, she said, "The Karen woman came in and said to tell you she's sorry. She said you'd know what she meant." Nearly on tiptoes, she waited for an explanation.

"How was business?" I walked toward the steps to my apartment for a quick exit. "Everything go okay?"

"No problems." As she scrambled to keep up, she dropped a bombshell. "Don't get mad, but I had to order paper products, so I called Zoe."

I stopped, and Anuli ran into my back. "Did she give you a different contact? What did she say?"

From the apartment-steps alcove, Zoe's voice purred, "I said I'd be over right away." She came forward and kissed my cheek. "My Maxie needed me."

She'd dumped me, and here she was calling me Maxie, a pet name I hated. But I had to admit she looked great. A low-cut pink shirt showed off an obvious pair of assets, and tight black jeans stretched across curvy hips. She saw me staring and smirked. Even her lips looked good in dark pink lipstick I'd had smeared on more than one body part when we dated.

I felt Anuli watching and forced myself to smile. "Zoe, would you come with me, please?" We walked to the kitchen before I faced her. "I'm not sure what your game is, but you know I don't need you. I need paper products, sure, but not from you."

She pouted, and if I was a different sort of man, I'd have told her how ridiculous she looked. Not one to give up easily, she grabbed my hand and pressed it to her chest before pleading, "Maxie, don't be mad. I'm here to help." While she rubbed my hand against one full breast, she continued to pout. "I've missed you."

Instead of jerking my hand away, I pulled it back to my side slowly and gently. Anger simmered below the surface. Maybe she'd earned my resentment, or maybe I still felt generally unhappy with my love life right now, but either way, she would have to carry it since she'd barged back into my life. "Zoe, I need supplies. Only supplies. And there are plenty of other companies to satisfy my needs." *Read the subtext, sunshine.*

Her face previewed the attack before she spoke. "You have a lot of nerve. After months of trying to get close to you and failing, I let you go. What choice did I have? You were closed off, in your own head, and living your best life without making room for me."

Well played. When in doubt, take the offense. It was a strategy I understood and could respect from time to time.

We stood close—close enough that I had to stare down at her. Probably by intention, she let her eyes soften, opening herself up to whatever I wanted from her. It was the closest she'd ever come to giving me the upper hand. Mom's directive to "participate" filtered through the smell of Zoe's flowery perfume, and I closed my eyes to enjoy the scent. I can't say which one of us kissed the other; I only know we kissed. She tasted like minty citrus. My mind wasn't a hundred percent on board, but my body was, spurred on by her hips grinding against me.

God, it felt good. I was lonely, confused, and ready to take what she offered.

With a giggle I assume she'd perfected at home, she reached down and stroked me until I thought I'd come right there in my health-inspected kitchen. I snatched her hand, and the walk from the kitchen to my staircase alcove seemed to take an hour, with Anuli watching wide-eyed, and customers glancing in our direction. If they looked below my belt, they saw evidence of what was about to happen.

We made it upstairs, but we didn't make it to the bed, falling on the couch in a jumble of arms, legs, and discarded clothes. Zoe wrapped her legs around my back and lifted her hips, ready to claim me again. I pulled away and stood beside the couch, appreciating her flushed face, splayed hair, and fantastic body.

Then realization hit me.

Her body might have been under another guy last week.

I stepped back. "Hold on." Her shocked face almost made me laugh, but I was way too horny to stop. "Condom." In less than two minutes, I was sheathed, inside her, and ready to release weeks of pent-up hurt and confusion. Later I'd make way for shame, but for now I used her body like she asked me to, searching for my own pleasure and blocking out conscious thought.

She rocked her hips and urged me to go faster, harder, knowing I'd lose control at some point. I felt her hot breath in my ear. "Punish me, Max. Come hard." I granted her request and focused only on purging frustration from my body.

Sometimes women are too much work, but other times, they offer sanctuary. I felt grateful and lighter than I had in a while. When Zoe wanted to cuddle afterward, tucking herself against my chest, I hugged her as quid pro quo—one desire in exchange for another. I convinced myself we might have a future; we could pick up where we left off. After all, I had planned to marry her, and if Abby was right, there was no soulmate waiting around the next corner.

Relaxed, I enjoyed the heaviness of my body near her soft one. "Zoe, why are you here?"

She giggled. "I think it's obvious."

"Sex? Okay, I can do that." I know I should

have been offended, but I'm a man, so I wasn't. Seemed like a win for me. I removed the condom and stretched over her to drop it in the wastebasket before laying down beside her again. "No strings attached."

"No!" She sat up halfway. "I'm here for you." And because Zoe loves to communicate *all* the time, she kept talking. "I've been reading *Women First*, and this woman named Abby has been writing about taking control of her own love life and finding a husband. I know understanding women isn't your thing—"

There was the critical Zoe from my not-so-distant past. And did she say "husband?" I kept quiet and let her ramble on.

"—but this Random Husband series is fantastic. Abby invited people to apply to be her husband, and she's picking her favorite! Talk about a gutsy move. I'm in awe of this woman, and I figured I'd take control of my own life." She laid back down and pressed her face to my chest. "I'm 'interviewing' men I think are husband material and will pick my favorite."

What the hell? I couldn't be hearing this right. Zoe, who had dumped me, was now screwing men and deciding which guy she'd marry? Including me.

Thank god I'd worn a condom.

I wanted to address her take on Random Husband, but I wasn't willing to tell her anything else about me. With carefully chosen words, I tried to make a point. "Did the writer let people apply, or did she include people without their consent?"

My point was lost on Zoe. She smacked my arm. "Silly, she let them apply. They realized what they were getting into every step of the way."

"Exactly." I waited. Had she always been this slow on the uptake?

"Exactly, what?" Leaning away, she stared at me blankly. When I didn't answer, she talked more, big surprise. "Anyhoo, you're my third candidate, and my goal is to have ten to choose from."

This woman was crazy. "Remember how you told me I didn't want to commit? How would you make a husband out of me?"

"Maxie, you only have a ten percent chance of being my choice." She was cheerful and matter-of-fact. And bat-shit crazy. "But if you win, I'm confident we could work through your issues and get you fixed up. You'd be begging me to marry you within six months." Pushing herself off the couch, she looked down at me, stretching her arms wide. "I mean, look at me."

I stared.

The chaos I had purged filled me up again, and the shame I'd anticipated felt worse than expected. Without a doubt, a few minutes inside her weren't worth the price of feeling like a used, shallow, dumb piece of crap. I thought about telling her off, and maybe I'd have enjoyed vomiting words on her, but I doubt she'd have heard me. And piling one bad decision on top of another never solved anybody's problems.

Right now, I needed this bat-shit crazy woman to leave. I'd take a shower, change my paper supplier, and maybe become a monk.

Thankfully, Zoe was no more interested in spending time together than I was. After pulling on her clothes, she nearly skipped her way out of my apartment, tossing back over her shoulder, "See you after number ten, lover!"

Not if I could help it. I locked the door behind her and saw the rumpled couch.

Maybe two showers.

CHAPTER 21—ABBY

For the tenth time, my sister broached the touchy "Max" subject. "So he owns the coffee shop." She leaned against the kitchen counter and folded her arms. "Unless you see a solution, you have to stop moping about it."

Was I moping?

My stomach churned with an emotion I couldn't name. I'd say anger, but what could I be angry about? Maybe disappointment because I'd written him off as a viable candidate, although I had to admit the biggest stumbling block was that he hadn't applied to Random Husband. *Hello*! Max was never an option, and I needed to let it go, already.

I rested my head on the kitchen table, feeling the cool surface against my forehead. "Yeah, and I know, it wouldn't have made a difference anyway."

"Do you want to continue with the project? You don't have to, you know. It's your life." She stroked my hair once, and I lifted my head.

"I'm a big girl. I'll get over it." Max had utterly rejected me the last time I saw him, and although I assumed he knew I'd be married soon, I couldn't be sure. I saw, without a doubt, his lack of interest. Was I planning to follow him around like a puppy, hoping one day he'd feel sorry for me and give me some attention? Not a chance. I sat up straighter and set my mind on the future. "Karen, two of the final five were incredible, and I think I've decided which one I want to marry."

"Wow! Exciting news! Tell me about the lucky man." She held up a finger. "Wait. Was it Trent, the guy with the gym?"

"No! You probably liked him because he reminded you of Eli." I chuckled, and she didn't disagree. "He's a distant third choice, but not completely off the table. Want to guess again?"

"Hmm, I know it's not Kadeem because you told me when you called this morning. Ashton seemed nice enough, but he's not exactly your type." She leaned back and studied the ceiling. With a snap of her fingers, she refocused on me. "Rob!"

"Bingo. We had so much in common, and we talked for over an hour before I realized how late it was." I smiled at the memory. "As an added bonus, he's a sexy man."

"What about Luis?"

"He was wonderful too, but Rob nudged him out at the end. I'd say Rob first, then Luis, then maybe Trent." Surely Rob or Luis would say "yes," and I'd never have to consider Trent.

"How will you propose? On one knee at a romantic dinner?" Karen giggled at the image.

"I might have, but Edith said the magazine

will take it from here. I submit the top three, and the magazine's legal team will meet with them to get an answer and have them sign an NDA, including not sharing my name, address..." I bit my lip before admitting, "Technically, the magazine could require me to marry any of the three men, but I'm telling myself Edith will honor the order of my choices."

Karen shook her head. "When will you know which one you'll marry? His name has to be on the marriage license."

"That's where you come in." I watched her wary expression. "Can you set up an appointment at the courthouse for a license? After the two o'clock commitment ceremony in the park, he and I will both have to attend the meeting to get a license. At the smaller reception, a minister will take three minutes to marry us in the dressing room."

"So the ceremony in the park is a fake?"

"It's a real commitment ceremony, just not a real wedding."

My sister still frowned. "Why not get the license earlier and have a real wedding in the park?"

"Great question." I cringed at what I had to tell her. "But if Rob bails, the magazine expects me to marry Luis. If Luis gets cold feet, it's on to Trent. And remember, the specific order happens only if Edith honors my wishes." With one eye open, I watched her face.

"But… But it seems so *random*." I opened both eyes and stared deadpan, waiting. Three seconds later, she saw it. "Oh, right." In a monotone, she repeated the rules. "Three men similar to you who are reasonably attractive and aren't participating just for the cash."

"You got it. And I still believe the marriage will work. I prefer Rob or Luis, but even with Trent, I have no major complaints. And after the wedding, either of us can call it quits after three months; we're not stuck together forever."

"Okay, okay." I could almost see her mind adjusting to the wrinkle. "I'll make the appointment. How else can I help?"

"I need a few days to write copy for the final five posts, which I'll bring to you for voiceover. These guys deserve a little more detail since they got this far." Grabbing a napkin, I started a list. "Then I'll work on a longer magazine article about the details of what comes next, including the ceremony in the park."

Karen continued the to-do list on her fingers. "Finalize the dress, cake, catering, and flowers. What about a play list?"

"The magazine will take care of music, and they pretty much covered the rest too, right down to the fake officiant in the park and the minister at the reception."

"Dang, I went online and became a minister last night during a commercial." She gave me two thumbs up and a cheesy smile.

"Did you really?" I assumed she was teasing.

"Yep, I really did." She added, "Ricky said it couldn't be done, and I had to prove him wrong. I'll give him my framed ordination for Christmas."

"Actually, I was hoping you'd be my matron of honor." Before she could answer, I said, "I know this whole marriage thing is strange, but —"

"Hell yes! I'd love to!" She jumped up to hug me where I sat, kissing me on the top of the head. "Have you picked out my dress?"

"Nope, it's totally up to you. You'll be the only person up there with me, so any dress is fine." By now, I assumed she recognized what she was getting into. "Remember, you'll be in about two thousand pictures."

⊕

A week later, I had brought my readers and followers up-to-date. Karen and I focused our time and energy on wedding details—to be approved by the magazine, of course. For catering, I came up with a few snacks and bottled waters at Forsyth Park and a full dinner for the smaller reception. It took Edith three days to ditch plans for the park. Instead, the magazine wanted to invite dozens of food vendors who would set up tents and serve samples in return for free ad space. *Women First* would charge wedding "guests" twenty dollars for five tickets they could turn in for samples. Edith pointed out the plan offered a more festive event with great food and a healthy amount of revenue for the magazine. Once I gave it some thought, I had to agree.

When I told Edith I wanted only white flowers, she changed my order to red roses because they shouted "love" rather than whispered it. In a very un-Edith way, she sent me pictures of the bouquet and other flower arrangements, and once again, I had to admit they were beautiful.

I figured Edith would horn in on the wedding cake, but I'd promised Karen a cake tasting, and that's what she was going to get. We spent two hours at the Coastal Bakery, drinking sparkling cider and tasting red velvet, chocolate, key lime, maple pecan, and so many other cakes I lost track. My stomach cramped from the sugar, but Karen's giddy happiness was worth the scatological events sure to follow. We chose red velvet cake for the reception, and I asked Karen to cross her fingers while I texted Edith. My pacing lasted only a few steps before three dots appeared on my phone.

Maybe. Send me your top three choices.

Like the men.

I would choose the top three, and the magazine would decide from there.

I turned to my devoted sister and snapped like a brittle twig. "She wants my top three choices." I might have growled. "It's one thing to have them choose my husband, but this is a *wedding cake*. *Nothing* should be random about a *wedding cake*. I might not have a soulmate, but I *love* red velvet cake. No wishy-washy, most-cakes-are-fine, and I-can-make-it-work crap." I held up my index finger. "*One* choice! The *perfect* choice! Period!"

My head buzzed from breathing heavily. Karen's face blurred. From too far away, her voice reached my ears. "Abby, sit down."

A chair appeared behind me; I suppose an alarmed baker had raced to the rescue. I sat. In the fog of my head, the reaction seemed out of proportion, but the frustration was real.

Karen knelt in front of me and held my hands. "I'm guessing this isn't about cake." She squeezed my fingers. "We can talk about it later, if you want to. For now, know I will make damn sure you get the cake you want. I'll always have your back."

Like many people, when I'm upset and someone is nice to me, anger turns to tears. Well, that happened. Next thing I knew, I was sobbing and thanking Karen for being my best friend. She hugged me while I sat with my head bowed, tears running down my face and snot sneaking from my nose in a disgusting manner. Behind me, I heard the baker scamper from the room, probably praying no other customers would come in a see me sniveling near the cakes.

In a blur of self-pity persisting across town,

I ended up on my sister's couch with a fuzzy blanket and a tall glass of ginger ale.

Karen truly is my best friend.

⊕

For the next two weeks, I concentrated on moving forward with as little rumination as possible. Karen always said exactly the right thing in my hours—days—of need, but I saw the concern in her eyes. Her worry fed my worry. The best solution I could come up with was staying out of her kitchen, buying coffee from a different shop, and sharing the truth with my readers. I wrote articles about having cold feet and the self-inflicted demands of brides. Writing was therapy.

> *You'd think discarding the idea of soulmates would remove marriage anxiety. I still believe two similar people who are attracted to each other can sustain a successful marriage, but first you have to get down the aisle and say "I do." The flowers, food, wedding cake, and dress require countless decisions, all of which demand self-control.*
>
> *Hundreds of studies point to a finite repository of self-control that depletes with each decision, interaction, and daily demand, until, by the end of the day, there's nothing left in the tank. God help you if the evening requires more effort. The best a*

bride can do is try to spread out decisions across several days, tackling catering, for example, on a day when no other demand sucks away self-control. Or, and don't shoot the messenger, she can elope. The more I learn what's required for a wedding, the more I can see why people run away from family and friends for a quick "ceremony" with a Justice of the Peace.

As of today, I've finally wrapped up wedding decisions except my dress. I know you're thinking I could at least share the general design, the neckline and the skirt, but I can't. I'd love to, don't get me wrong, but my dressmaker is an artist who wants to reveal his masterpiece a week before the wedding. I'm not nervous about the dress, but I am curious. In a way, it's like waiting for Christmas morning so you can open your gifts. I want Christmas to get here, but the sweet anticipation feels good too. Fingers crossed the dress is the final piece of my wedding puzzle.

Well, there is also the groom. The man is not my soulmate, not Mr. Perfect, but my three top choices seem to be good people, and we have a lot in common. As for attraction, I can only speak for myself. Yes. My husband-to-be candidates are handsome and fit, with amazing smiles. I write this knowing you can't feel the spark *of interest from a simple description, but I can only offer words. In my mind, I accept any of the three men as a good husband, but...*

Today I admit to you I am nervous. No matter how hard I try, I can't pin down a reason to feel anxious, but there it is. This must be the "wedding jitters" or "cold feet" people talk about, and since the feeling isn't based on a valid concern, the wedding usually marches on, with only mom knowing the bride had a moment's hesitation. Marriage is one of those Big Decisions, even though, in reality, it's less permanent than your latest tattoo. So, based on the vision of marriage, the intention of permanence, rather than the reality of the contract, I'm nervous.

My plan is to focus on positive images of sharing my life with a great guy. We'll have coffee together, take long walks, share dreams. Sex isn't necessarily on the table, but I'll keep my mind open and the table cleared—just in case. We'll be fine. We might not be elected couple of the year, but we'll be fine. From today until the wedding next week, I intend to march on.

After rereading my latest write-up, I felt slightly better. It'll be fine. My top two choices would be good husbands, and the third choice would likely be okay. Sure, the thought of marrying Trent amped up my anxiety, but I refused to dwell on something that hadn't happened.

Ten days before the wedding, after I'd lost five pounds and still couldn't eat, Edith texted some good news. Rob had accepted their proposal on my behalf. With a weight lifted from my shoulders, I drove straight to Karen's house to share the news and eat whatever leftovers she had from last night's dinner.

Seven days till the wedding, Edith called while I was enjoying a morning soak before heading to the dressmaker. Edith rarely called. I dried my hands on a nearby towel and answered, my heart beating in my throat. "I hope it's good news."

"It's not."

My body went into fight-or-flight mode and chose flight. I stepped out of the tub, naked and vulnerable. "Hit me."

"Rob dropped out."

I closed my eyes, willing the disappointment to finish the journey down to my toes. I took a deep, cleansing, shaky breath. "Why?" It came out a squeak.

"His pregnant fiancé put the kibosh on it. Seems they needed the money, but his girlfriend got worried he'd leave her in the rearview mirror."

"O-kay." What else was I supposed to say? If

he'd been standing in front of me, I might have been tempted to punch him in the nose, but instead I dripped water on the floor.

Shit.

"Good news, though. Luis is a go." I heard her exhale and pictured smoke veiling her face. "Random husband, right? And something to write about." She paused, but I had nothing to add. "The magazine has contracted for a spread on the cake and catering, and I think the florist wants in for another spread. The project is a gold mine." Then she was gone.

I stared at the silent phone, shivering in the air conditioning. *Oh, good, the magazine is making money.* But it's fine. Luis is fine. I had spent a great deal of mental energy getting used to the idea of marrying Rob; now I'd aim my energy toward marrying Luis.

In seven days.

An hour later, Karen and I walked into the dressmaker's studio. Hao waited beside the platform holding a white dress, almost as though he'd predicted the exact second we would enter. "You will wear the dress?"

I assumed he meant right now, so I stepped forward and accepted the dress he handed over. Behind a curtain, I pulled on the smooth silk sheath, elegant but simple. When I stepped out, Hao buttoned, hooked, and adjusted before leading me to the platform, my back to the mirror so I faced Karen.

"Oh," she whispered. With one hand, she covered her mouth, and the other she pressed to her chest. Tears rolled down her cheeks. "It's perfect."

Beside me, Hao bowed slightly before turning me toward the mirror.

I've always been grateful for a pretty face, and I make an effort to stay in shape, but never until that moment had I felt truly beautiful. At first glance, the dress looked like a simple satin sheath, but a slight flaring at my knees reminded me of mermaids. A short, chapel-length train would form a bustle when I needed to walk freely. Across the top, the bodice felt secure with wisps of material across the shoulders plunging to my waist to reveal the inner curve of each breast. At the back, the silk formed an X, further securing the top. In this dress, I would display a dangerous amount of skin but know the bodice wouldn't shift out of place. I walked closer to the mirror and delighted in the tiny pearls along the edge of the dramatic V-neckline, the waist, and the thin straps across my back.

The dress felt like a perfect fit, but Hao gently pulled at the train and shifted the material. He stepped back and settled those peaceful eyes on mine. "You will wear the dress?"

Now it was my turn to tear up. Hao's work of art spoke quality and care, almost love, for the dress, if not the bride. "Yes, I will gratefully wear the dress." I must have said the right thing, because Hao bowed and grinned with pride.

When we left the shop, I lifted my face to the sun and smiled. In one week, I'd marry Luis, and damn, I'd look gorgeous. Too bad I couldn't walk around in my wedding dress every day. Maybe I'd pull it from the back of my closet each anniversary and dance around the living room with my husband. What a romantic notion.

I grabbed my sister's hand like I'd done as a kid. "You need a dress. Let's shop!"

She laughed and nodded. "Shopping is good."

For the rest of the afternoon, Karen tried on dresses while I took pictures and showed her how great she'd look in wedding photos. She settled on a salmon-colored sleeveless dress with a jewel neckline and an empire waist above her stomach, camouflaging a baby bump. The skirt was full, with soft material swishing around her knees when she walked. Humble Karen never saw her beauty, but I did, and my readers would too when I posted a picture of my matron of honor. She'd have to forgive me for putting her in the spotlight and gushing about how great she is.

CHAPTER 22—MAX

After a busy day in the store, I dropped onto my couch with a grilled-cheese sandwich. It had been a month since my stupid decision to sleep with Zoe. I hadn't heard from her, but since she's completely deranged, I couldn't be sure it was over. There was a high probability she'd pop up soon and say I was going to marry her, entice me to have sex (not going to happen), or let me know she'd picked someone else.

Fingers crossed on the last option.

I'd had plenty of time to think about sex. Okay, so I generally do spend plenty of time on the topic, but lately I thought a little deeper. Blame it on Random Husband and Abby making me rethink my beliefs about relationships. Even though Abby's stories reminded me of her sexy sister, and the memory still stung, I wanted to know if the mom-type I'd seen in the shop would find a good husband. Of course, she also challenged my assumptions in a way not nearly as painful as listening to Zoe criticize me, personally.

A month ago, when Zoe surprised me, I'd been a pushover when it came to sex. She wanted it, and I wanted it. No problem there, right?

Fifteen minutes—and I'm being generous with myself—of sex was followed by weeks of regret, and those fifteen minutes had erased my sexual energy for less than twelve hours. If releasing semen was the only goal, I could take care of it myself. It's no secret that every man regularly takes matters into his own hands. So, if it's not for ejaculation, what's the point of no-ties sex?

A different, meaningless woman every day won't fill a need I couldn't name.

Yet.

Having sex with someone important, a partner, felt different. When I'd been in relationships, including with Zoe, I still wanted sex often, but ejaculation wasn't the only goal. Sex, along with dinners and movies and talking, created intimacy and bonded us together; the intimate times became our partnership.

Good lord, I was becoming a woman.

It was too late for me to feign disinterest in Abby's quest, but I'm still a man, damn it. I stomped to the kitchen, grabbed a bottle of Makers Mark, and poured myself a double shot of bourbon. Neat, like a man. I tossed it back, savoring the burn. What would be my next manly demonstration? My gym bag sat by the front door, daring me to lift weights and get huge, like only a man can do. Sort of. But the logic worked for me when I needed it to. We tell ourselves whatever we need to hear in the moment, especially when we don't have a beautiful partner to do it for us.

Bottom line, what had I become? A sensitive, thoughtful gym rat who drank straight bourbon and masturbated for therapeutic purposes.

Yeah, I could live with that.

⊕

Three hours later, I'd lifted weights until my arms gave out, come home to shower, and released tension during self-imposed "therapy." I drank a glass of water and crawled into bed, enjoying the cool sheets and down comforter Zoe had once called "cozy." As a man, I called my bed comfortable. My nighttime ritual involved propping myself up on pillows and scanning posts about Random Husband. Tonight, the posts included pictures of a wedding dress resembling a negligee, if you judged based only on sex appeal, and it didn't seem to mesh with my image of Abby. Then again, I hadn't seen her or her sister for so long, Abby might look different. Don't get me wrong, by now Abby had grown attractive, if not beautiful, in my mind based on her stories, and I wanted her to find happily ever after.

Only one week to go.

Her article from a few days ago had surprised me. I guess I'd never thought about the work of a wedding; most grooms happily turn decisions over to the bride. Don't brides love planning a wedding, drinking champagne, and laughing with their friends? I'm pretty sure I saw it in a movie once. Come to think of it, the bridesmaids also had a pillow fight in teddies, reminding me fiction isn't real.

I reread the article. It was hard to believe Abby felt nervous. I'd always assumed it was the groom who got cold feet because he didn't want to be tied down, a sentiment I could understand. Besides, Abby had orchestrated the entire search to be exactly where she was now, near the finish line. She'd tried to calm her fears by writing how fleeting marriage could be, reminding herself many other life decisions last forever but don't give us pause. Then again, I would argue marriage is *supposed* to be forever, and she'd commit to marriage next week.

From what I'd read, Abby would be a loving, sensitive wife, making her husband a happy man. Love gurus always say men are simple; they argue we need only sex and food from a wife. Not true. A man, *everyone*, needs to be heard and respected, to lean on someone, to laugh, and a thousand other perks shared in a relationship. By now the experts should be teaching that people can't be reduced to their most visible needs. Hell, people can't even be reduced to male or female.

Now caught up, I thumbed through Instagram to kill time until I got sleepy, a luxury I'd lost over the past couple of months. A new post caught my attention. I felt a little less alone when I saw the picture of Abby in a pink dress. She looked happy, and I assumed she was past her pre-wedding jitters. I read the words superimposed on her image.

Behold Karen, my beautiful sister and matron of honor.

I bolted upright in bed, rigid and shattered at the same time, like a cartoon character hit with a hammer before crumbling into pieces. My mind raced to process the implications of the post.

Karen is the matron of honor.

Karen.

And this is Karen, the mom-type with the clipboard conducting the interviews and meeting potential husbands.

The first picture segued into Abby hugging Karen, both grinning at the camera, with a message appearing across the photo.

My best friend.

I let the post loop through the pictures over and over, squinting to examine every detail of Abby's face when it appeared.

Mystery woman, purple-glasses lady, writer, Abby.

My heart seemed to stop beating and then make up for lost time. Abby, the woman who awkwardly approached a guy on his computer and yelled, "I'll pay you!" as he sprinted to the door. It was Abby who watched over her sister's shoulder during the first interviews and told her to run away. I relived every detail, including Abby's touch on my bicep when she asked me to pass a note to her sister.

My chest ached.

Her cute smile and slight awkwardness had drawn me to her, and right now I could feel the attraction, all this time buried just below the surface.

Abby sneaking in to watch over her sister but instead kissing me in the roasting room. Her tongue in my mouth. She'd been single. She didn't have children. She didn't have a husband. Until next week. Oh god, I remembered the fear she'd shared in her latest article, and my chest tightened more. Abby, sweet, kind, intelligent, talented Abby, wasn't sure she wanted to go through with the plan but promised to soldier on anyway, keeping her promises.

I slogged through deep, aching regret that I hadn't applied to Random Husband and gotten to know her. I never had a chance.

No, that's not true.

I dragged both hands down my face. No. Abby did give me a chance. She'd kissed me first and urged me on when I returned the favor. And although I never applied to be a candidate, she'd waited for me outside in her pretty dress, a smile on her face, asking me to give her a second look.

Logically, I know people don't die from a broken heart, but physical pain shot through my chest like a sword. I had said I was sorry for kissing her. *Fuck me.* I said it would never happen again, and I wasn't that kind of guy. I'd rejected her without trying to make sense of her confusion.

I wondered if she'd suffered the same anguish I carried now.

I'd do anything to take back hurting Abby. Her dejected expression and quick exit would always haunt me. How long had she been gone? I hadn't seen her in the shop for weeks, but she was never far from my thoughts. Part of the reason I followed Random Husband was the prospect I'd read something about mystery woman. Little did I know, every word was from the woman I'd fallen for when I first saw her in the store, sitting there outside the roasting room trying to look approachable. Maybe as far back as the Porsche pictures, if I'm being honest.

A little voice in my head kept trying to get my attention, but for a while I was too busy feeling sorry for myself. After I ran out of painful memories, the message came through.

It's not too late. She's not married yet.

Maybe it *was* too late. What the hell could I do now? I didn't know Abby's last name or whether Abby was a pen name, and I sure didn't know Karen's last name. They'd stopped buying their coffee here. Dead ends. But the little voice was unrelenting, making me frantic to come up with a solution.

Abby worked at *Women First*, which had offices in Savannah. They weren't going to hand out personal information, but I could give them a message for her. What the hell would I say at this point?

Dear Abby,

I know I said I was sorry for kissing you, but I should have said I'm sorry for not kissing you more. I'm sorry for not applying to Random Husband. Although I don't know about being married, especially in an open-book situation, applying might have kept me closer to you somehow. Please come back and give me another chance.

Yours,
Max

In one week, Abby would have a husband. Did I have any right to interfere by throwing myself at her mercy? No, I'd missed my chance. And besides, what made me think I'd consider marrying a woman—even Abby— without knowing her better? Add simple logic to essentially living a marriage in public, and contacting Abby wasn't an option. But damn, I still wanted to try. I wanted my life to snap back into focus rather than stay this blurry half-life I'd been living since meeting her. I wanted to sleep again without dreaming about her and waking up at three in the morning.

I wanted to participate.

For the next few days, I paced the floor of the

shop, telling myself either Abby or Karen would stop by, and I'd be waiting. Anuli made a habit of watching me from the corner of her eye, like I'd become a different person, and in a way, I had.

Three days before the wedding, my diligence paid off. Karen burst through the door, marched up to the counter, and asked for coffee and cheesecake. She barely had time to finish her order before I stalked toward her with my heart in my throat. I was about to put myself on the line, and vulnerability was never my go-to move. Before I was close enough to accost her, Karen turned to me and said, "Do you have a minute?"

Did I have a minute? I had the rest of my life.

"Sure." I led her to the same table Abby had used on her first visit. We sat across from each other and both took a deep breath. Here sat the sister of the woman I needed in my life, and I wasn't going to play games by sitting quietly. "How's your sister?"

Karen pursed her lips and exhaled. "I'm glad you asked." She leaned forward, and I joined her in what felt like a conspiracy. "My sister is having a tough time. Have you heard of Random Husband?"

The old Max would've played dumb, pretending to have no clue about a magazine campaign to find a husband. No self-respecting man would say he followed every word like a ten-year-old waiting for the next installation of Spider Man. I nodded. "I've read every article and social-media post."

Smiling, Karen shook her head as if to say "life is funny." She picked up her coffee but put it back down again without a sip. "You know Abby is searching for a husband and agreed to marry a man in a few days."

"Yes, I know." I let Karen see my disappointment, but I didn't know what else to say.

"She does not want to marry this man. Which is why I'm here." She looked over my left shoulder and stared at the wall. "I know this will sound bizarre, but I have to ask. Are you interested?"

"Yes, I'm definitely interested." To put it mildly. I felt naked admitting my infatuation.

"Good. Because I know my sister, and my sister wants you. Based on what she's said and what I see on her face, you're more important to her than her fiancé." Karen glanced at me briefly then returned to study the wall. "Since she has to do this, I want her to have the best shot at happiness." Abby's sister and champion turned her coffee cup in circles, still avoiding my eyes.

Abby wanted me. Everything about the revelation felt good, and for a minute, I thanked the universe for the gift. Something went right today. "I want her too."

"Do you want her enough to marry her in four days?" It seemed to take effort for Karen to make eye contact with me again, and when she did, I saw the vulnerability on her face.

Marry Abby in four days. Four days. What I wanted was to date her, get to know each other, and find out if the connection I felt was real. I didn't want to dive into the deep end with marriage, regardless of whether the contract could be broken at any time. And I sure as hell didn't want to open my life, my marriage, to anyone who wanted a peek. The timing and the publicity together pulled an honest answer from me. "I don't think I can." My own words doomed me to suffer.

It was my turn to stare past Karen's shoulder and avoid seeing her disappointment. But I heard her clearly. "Well, someone can, and he'll become her husband and one of the luckiest people I know. I'm sorry it won't be you."

I didn't blame her for being pissed. But I did see marriage as forever, and this publicity stunt didn't feel like a forever deal. The pain I felt now would be nothing compared to the broken heart I'd suffer with a broken marriage. If only Abby would take a step back from Random Husband and let us get to know each other...and not report our every move to her fans.

Across the table, Karen stared at me, waiting, as though she thought I'd change my mind. In the silence, she handed me a scrap of paper with her phone number. I wouldn't be the first to leave the table, but I couldn't agree to her terms. She had every right to storm out and not look back, which is exactly what she did.

As I sat at the empty table, I made a pact with myself. I'd spend the next few days praying for Abby's happiness until I came to terms with the road she would take with someone else. I had no right to ask for more, and she had every right to be happy. As the culmination of my pact, I'd attend the wedding, welcoming the pain like biting into an aching tooth. If I couldn't have her in my life, I'd be one of her fans, supporting from the sidelines. It was the least I could do.

After the wedding, I'd head to Jamaica for a while and grieve without anybody watching. The Blue Mountain coffee would help ease the pain almost as much as whiskey, and I intended to drink plenty of both.

⊕

The day before the wedding, I ambled through Forsyth Park and watched restaurants pitch canopies and set up tables they'd use the next day. Abby's wedding would be held in the middle of the park on an elevated gazebo covered with red roses. Two enclosed white tents stood side-by-side several yards to the left of the gazebo, and red carpet flowed from the one labeled for the bride.

I knew better than to wander the park when my only impulse was to kick in the white tents.

I hope Abby's happy. Repeating the mantra did not improve my mood.

I'd spent the past two days snapping at Anuli

until she cried, which made me scramble to apologize, give her a raise, and tell her I might be coming down with something. My five o'clock shadow had become a prickly stubble only a straight razor would tame. I hadn't slept. Every waking hour I second guessed my decision to reject Abby again. Which, I didn't kid myself, I had done. Her sister had asked me to take a chance, completely abandon my comfort zone, think outside the box, or any other bullshit saying people use when they want you to make a bad decision. Yet, I had lost.

I was lost.

⊕

"What's that burning smell?" Anuli poked her head in the roasting room, where I struggled to clear a ruined sack of beans.

"Me in hell, Anuli. It's hell." I didn't bother to look at her, and from my peripheral vision, I saw her leave. My rudeness would cost me another raise and apology. All I seemed to do lately was apologize and feel like crap. Now I'd ruined an entire batch of coffee beans because Abby was getting married tomorrow to a man I supposed would make a *great* husband.

Bullshit. Underneath my fake good will, I wanted her with me. Fuck the other guy. I reached for my phone to call Karen before realizing nothing had changed. Abby and I still didn't know each other well enough for marriage, and I still didn't want to be part of a media circus. Fuck my life.

The shop would close soon, leaving me with fewer distractions from my tortured thoughts. Other than drinking or working out, I couldn't think of anything to keep me busy and distracted. One more day. Then the decision would be made for me. Abby would be married, and I'd get the hell out of town until I felt human again.

By the time I dragged myself upstairs, I'd cleaned the roasting machine and worked through a new batch of beans, creating an acceptable but not great product. It was nearly midnight, and my body felt exhausted, while my mind was wide awake. I ate leftover chicken salad standing in front of the fridge with the door open, tossing my fork in the sink after three bites. Across the room, my TV was as dark as my mood. I wouldn't find distraction there. After brushing my teeth and avoiding my reflection in the mirror, I crawled into bed with my phone. I told myself, only for tonight, I wouldn't read about Abby's project. But because her posts were as close as I could get to her, I unlocked my phone.

Teasing myself, I scrolled and read posts offered by the app, deliberately avoiding Abby's. The doomed game lasted almost a minute before I read the day's Random Husband posts. Abby reminded her fans about the wedding, inviting everyone to attend and send her good wishes for a successful marriage. Her fans responded with comments full of support and love. Later she posted a hint about the wedding, telling followers not to expect a traditional ceremony but one that put "Women First." Clever.

I remembered the deal I'd made with myself. If I wasn't willing to marry Abby, I'd send good wishes for her happiness with someone else. Tonight, I couldn't do it. The wedding loomed over me, and I'd be there tomorrow to wish them well, but tonight I wanted to wallow in self-pity and send white-hot hatred to a man I didn't know. He was probably a great guy.

Fuck him.

CHAPTER 23—ABBY

The night before my big day, I insisted on sleeping alone at my house. I wanted one last night to myself before I married Luis. Handsome, smart, comfortable Luis. At nine, I made a cup of tea and sipped it while reading a romance novel, skimming chapters to find the happy ending. At nine-fifteen, a time I'll never forget, Edith called.

I jumped up and started pacing before I answered. "Hey, are you calling to congratulate me?"

"Sure, why not? Congratulations." Edith paused for an exhale. "Look, Abby, Luis is out."

My mug fell to the floor and shattered, just like my dreams. "*What*? Why?"

"Schtupping his grad student and wants to see where it goes."

Son of a bitch. My lips felt frozen. With effort, I asked, "What now?"

"What do you mean, 'what now?' You're with Trent. He's already agreed. In fact, he's eager."

She acted like my life was no big deal. I needed time to think, to adapt. This time I ended the call without another word. Let her wonder if I'd stick with the plan. Well, it had been *my* plan, not Edith's. She'd agreed to Random Husband, but the project was my baby.

Shit.

I don't know how long I stared into space, slack-jawed and probably drooling, trying to locate the resilience I'd come to expect.

Okay, okay, I could do this. Trent was a perfectly nice man. I texted the news to Karen, told her I was happy about marrying Trent and was going to sleep, and turned off my phone. I spent the next several hours reviewing Trent's application, video, and any notes I'd taken after our meeting. He had several redeeming qualities, including hard-working and innovative in his business.

We'd be fine.

Just fine.

I don't know what time I fell asleep, but I woke up on the couch with a cramped neck and a pounding headache made worse by the bright sunshine. When I turned on my phone, I saw it was nearly ten o'clock, and Karen had called eight times. Before I could return the call, someone pounded on my front door.

"Open up, Abby! Come on, right now!" I turned the knob, and Karen burst in. "Get in the car. I have everything you need at the house, and I want you where I can see you."

I had no energy to argue. What was the point? After pulling on my flip flops, I let her herd me to the car, tuck me in, and slam the door. The drive went way too quickly. I felt the wedding racing toward me and wanted to sleep for another twelve hours until the entire ordeal had passed without me. The heart that should have been racing felt like a rock in my chest, heavy and lifeless.

At Karen's house, I vomited twice, trying to purge the bile clinging to the lining of my empty stomach. Karen held back my hair while I leaned over her toilet. She put a cold cloth on my forehead. "Abbigail, are you okay?"

Her question asked about more than my physical health, but I wasn't ready to concede. With as much strength as I could manage, I pushed back from the toilet and sat against the wall. "I'm fine. It's fine." I smiled weakly. "I'm getting married today."

Karen didn't respond. After tossing the cloth in the sink, she pulled me up and led me to her bedroom, where my gorgeous dress fanned across her bed. I heard Ricky calling the children to eat so he could get them dressed, and the normality of it struck me. My sister, Ricky, Eli, and Prissy would be nearby most of the day, offering their strength without knowing I leaned on them. Well, Karen would know, but as the matron of honor, it was her job.

My arms dangled by my sides as I stared at my beautiful dress. Karen fidgeted beside me. Without looking at her, my voice droned the all-important question. "Are we having red velvet cake?"

"Honey, I'll always do my best to get what you want." Her voice sounded strained, like her throat wanted to hold the words inside.

I needed to brush my teeth.

◎

Karen helped me get cleaned up and into the limo waiting in front of her house. We arrived at the park and were escorted to a white "bride" tent to get ready, and I was grateful for the portable air conditioner on what promised to be a hot day. The commitment ceremony, or "wedding," for viewers, was still a few hours away, but already the park bustled with people. Vendors served food, children ran through crowds, and couples stretched out on blankets in open spaces of grass. The air was festive.

Why did I feel like I walked toward slaughter?

Security sent a never-ending parade of guests into the tent, and photographers refused to give us a moment's peace. Edith showed up with magazine nobility, ad sponsors, and devoted fans, ushering people toward me as though she owned my time. Okay, she did own my time today, but give me a break. Karen moved people aside to bring in hair and make-up experts who insisted on making me "pretty." They remarked on how bad I looked before working their magic, transforming me into a bride, complete with false eyelashes and enough hairspray to send Karen into a coughing fit.

"Enough!" She yelled to the tent, in general.

234

"Everybody out!"

Edith opened her mouth to protest, but my bossy sister saw it coming and said, "*Everybody out, including you.*" She'd pay dearly later, but I loved her for it.

When we were alone, she whispered, "We have to get you dressed." I didn't know why she seemed so sad.

"Wait!" I needed a minute. Or longer. "Karen, I don't think I can do this." I swallowed the lump in my throat. "What am I doing? I don't want to get married. The idea seemed great, but now that it's time, I can't do it. Please."

"Oh, honey." Karen's eyes filled with tears. "Of course you don't have to do this." She pulled me up for a long hug. "Let's get out of here." And before I could say anything more, she put her arm around me and marched us from the tent toward the limo.

Edith called to us, "Where are you going?"

Karen didn't turn around, shouting over her shoulder, "Getting old, new, borrowed, and blue." She kept pushing us forward, moving through the parting crowd like she was in charge. I guess she was.

I saw the door of the limo. Sweet freedom.

A woman stepped in my path. "Abby." We had to either push her aside or stop. I froze and gazed at her, feeling like a ghost of my former self. She reached for my hand. "Abby, I want you to know what you've done for us." She gestured at a group of women nearby. "Because of you, I took control of my life, forced myself to open up and meet people, and now I'm engaged to a wonderful man." She held up her hand to show me a small diamond ring. "You're brave. You made *us* brave."

Another woman came to stand beside her. "I stopped waiting for the universe to bring Mr. Right, and I went looking for him." She giggled. "I proposed last week."

The group surrounding us applauded. From my left, a woman said, "I plan to propose after your wedding today. We bonded over your adventure."

More applause and women saying, "Thank you, Abby! We love you!"

Wide eyed, I looked around. The women smiled and nodded. I turned to Karen and tried to telegraph my resolve. She waited, frozen in her tracks like someone trying not to spook a frightened animal. I stared back at the women. Did I help? Was I brave? I didn't feel brave. Running away wasn't brave...breaking my promise.

I straightened my spine and found my smile, even if it felt painted on. "Thank you for your love and support. Thank you for trusting me." To Karen, I said, "Let's go make me a bride." She kept a blank expression when she turned and walked us back to the tent. Around me, people waved and shouted encouragement.

In the blink of an eye, music cued me to walk the red carpet toward my future. I played the part of a bride, with my professional make-up, hair swept into a French twist, and breath-taking wedding dress. If I didn't exactly feel like a bride, the problem would solve itself. In a few seconds, I'd stand beside my soon-to-be husband and commit myself to him, then we'd race to the courthouse to make our marriage a reality in the eyes of the law.

I'd be a wife.

Trent's wife.

I walked forward, alone except for more fans than I could count. No one gave me away because I belonged to no one but myself. As I stared at my shuffling feet, I saw red rose pedals strewn across the carpet. I looked up to see Karen waiting with Trent and the officiant standing in the gazebo.

I'm brave.

When I reached the steps, a man in a tuxedo held out his hand to make sure I didn't trip, and before I could back down again, I stood in front of Trent.

He belched.

The ensuing smell nearly knocked me over. I searched his face for some explanation, but his eyes refused to focus. In fact, they were half closed. Trent swayed on his feet as though we rocked on the bow of a ship in the middle of a storm.

He was drunk.

I don't mean I-had-a-glass-of-champagne tipsy, but so drunk I wasn't sure he'd make it through the ceremony.

I gawked at Karen in horror. Did she see what I saw? Her face told me she did. She tilted her head toward the parking lot as though to ask, "Want to run?"

For a full minute, I examined the crowd, reminding myself why they were here, why *I* was here. Most people wore huge smiles. I swiveled to scan more faces, stopping only when I saw Ricky at the base of the stairs. Like Karen, he had a question on his face. What did I want to do?

CHAPTER 24—MAX

Alone on this sunny day, I'd walked to Forsyth Park. I had taken the time to shave and put on khakis and a button-down blue shirt because, hey, I was attending a wedding. The thick crowd chatted in tight groups, and I weaved through them toward the gazebo. The ceremony had already begun. I'd deliberately avoided arriving early because I couldn't trust myself to leave Abby alone.

From where I watched, I saw Abby in profile. Her dress shimmered around her, clinging to every curve and pooling at her feet. I'd never seen anything more stunning, and I closed my eyes to brace against the loss. In my agony, I saw our future...late mornings in bed, her laughter over coffee, vacations at the beach, holding hands at the fountain, and our kids tumbling over us on Sunday mornings.

Abby was everything. And she was marrying somebody else.

This man she'd chosen would live what should've been my life. But she *had* chosen, and he would make her happy. I'd grow old and grumpy knowing the man was braver than me and earned the prize. He'd be a good husband because she deserved a good husband. He'd treat her well.

To torture myself, I walked near the base of the stairs and saw her face. Her beautiful face. Except she looked confused and panicked, not like a glowing bride on her wedding day. She turned to her sister and then scanned the crowd as though searching for an answer or deliverance. Soft music faded away, and people around me whispered, "What's happening?"

Abby turned toward the stairs, where I floundered in my misery. When her eyes met mine, I stepped forward, but she closed her eyes as if to say, "No."

She inhaled, her chest rising, and handed her bouquet to Karen before turning back to the groom. He seemed unsteady. With some urging from the minister, the groom repeated his vows, slurring and swaying through every word. Was the son of a bitch drunk? I told myself it was nerves or the heat, but I watched for any clue he was a loser. He kept swaying through Abby's vows. They didn't exchange rings, but moved on to the moment I dreaded.

The minister declared them husband and wife. That's it. Done.

I felt proud of myself for not fucking up her wedding because I'd *really* wanted to. Next, they would walk past me, and I'd let go of fantasy Abby. I stared at my shoes and waited.

Someone next to me yelled, "Gross!" and the

crowd erupted in shouts of disgust.

I looked up. The groom had vomited on the minister. I knew he'd vomited because he currently was holding a hand over his mouth and still vomiting. Great gushes of brown liquid spewed between his fingers until he gave up and leaned over the edge of the gazebo. Unfortunate fans wore the brunt of his purge. Abby backed up against her sister, who held her around the waist. While I watched, Karen urged Abby toward the stairs, calling for someone named Ricky to help her down. Abby seemed hesitant to go, but I saw Karen push her toward a man who met her halfway down the steps.

Ricky grabbed her around the waist and practically carried her to the bride's tent, with Karen yelling after him, "Keep her there!" Meanwhile, the groom held the railing and crumpled to the floor. I glanced at Karen to see why she'd stayed in the mess, and she caught my eye, shrieking, "Max! Come help me!"

I charged the steps two at a time and met her by the groom's side. At Karen's direction, I lifted his smelly body from the floor and half dragged him down the steps and to the groom's tent. I swear, if the crowd had carried rotten fruit, the guy would have been covered in more than vomit. Karen and I moved quickly, both knowing the crowd wouldn't stay back for long, and I pulled him into the tent right before he passed out completely. I let the piece of shit crumble to the floor.

A security guard poked his head in. "Can I help?"

"No, keep everyone out." Karen turned to me. "And you. Come with me." She led me to chairs on the other side of the tent, away from the reeking drunk. "Sit." I sat, but Karen paced.

Head down, she talked to herself. "What now, what now? Abby is okay. Maybe she'll put a hard stop to this right now."

From my obedient corner, I said, "How? An annulment?" *Please say yes.*

Her head jerked up like she'd forgotten I was there. "Annulment? What?" Frowning, she shook her head. "No, no, they're not married. You saw a commitment ceremony for fans, not a wedding."

I could not have been more confused. What the hell was a commitment ceremony? What was she talking about? I'd watched them get married. Answers were more important to me right now than leaving Karen to her musings. I stood but stayed frozen to the spot, breathing like I'd run a marathon. "Explain."

She dropped her hands to her sides and huffed at me. "The magazine kept changing the groom, so how could we get a marriage license? In less than an hour, we're supposed to be at the courthouse for the license, and Abby and Trent will get married for real."

Trent. Well Trent was dead on his ass. If

he hadn't been, I'd have laid him out. But they weren't married. Abby wasn't married. Damn, that felt good. Excitement rose up in me like a tsunami. My subconscious knew the words before my mouth did. "What about me?" As I asked, my gut clenched into a knot.

"What *about* you?" She nearly growled at me. "You mean the man who refused to marry my wonderful sister?" She waved my words away and returned to pacing. "How do I get her out of this? She's too stubborn to walk away. Too damn stubborn." She stopped and eyed me again. "Okay, help me try to wake him up and wipe him down. He needs to get to the courthouse." While she talked, she crouched beside Trent and shook his shoulder.

In the rank tent stinking of vomit, I marched toward the source where Karen busied herself wiping goo from his mouth. Was I doing this? I waited for the fear and uncertainty to come, but I found only hope. Hope Karen would leave Trent to rot and let me marry her sister. After months of plowing through my life, I was ready to admit I wanted Abby, and if marrying her today was the only way to keep her in my life, that's for damn sure what I was going to do...assuming she said "Yes."

I stopped a few feet from Karen, blood racing through my veins and pounding in my ears. "Let me marry Abby."

She shook her head. "It's too late." She stood

and nudged Trent with her toe. "Wake up, already."

"Stop!" I wanted to pound my chest and bellow like a caged animal. "Listen." Karen glared at me like I'd grown a second head. "It's not too late. Do you want your sister with this loser?"

Karen folded her arms across her chest. "You're saying you should marry my sister as the lesser of two evils? Not exactly an expression of undying devotion."

Okay, I could see her point. I ran my hand down my face, took a deep breath, and tried again, this time holding nothing back. "I'm sorry I said no before. I was a dumbass, but I won't pass up another chance. I don't know how many more chances I'll get." I channeled all my energy into showing her the desperation in my eyes and stepped closer to give her a better look. "Think of it as the universe bringing us together."

"Like soulmates?" I saw the grin she tried to hide. She was giving in; I was sure of it.

Relief nearly brought me to my knees, and I couldn't stop the smile from spreading across my face. "Like whatever you want to call it."

She shook her head, and for a few seconds I was pretty sure I'd vomit right beside Trent. Karen muttered, "I can't make it work." But I could see she wanted a way.

"I've seen you in action. You can do anything." I grabbed her hand and held it in mine. "Please." Begging didn't come easily to me, but I was willing to sacrifice my pride.

We stood in silence for a full minute, me holding Karen's hand, and her staring over my shoulder with unfocused eyes.

"Oh my god, this is crazy!" She smiled and glanced around the tent like she thought someone would stop us. "Oh my god. If we're doing this, you'll need a tux." Holding up her phone, she stepped back, snapped several pictures of me, and asked for my measurements.

I laughed, allowing joy to fill my body, and gave her sizes. Karen typed on her phone, glancing at me every few seconds and smiling from ear to ear.

Then all hell broke loose.

From outside the tent, a woman screeched, "Karen, you'd better be fixing this!"

Karen yelled back, "On it!" She rolled her eyes. "Perfect. The gargoyle is Edith, the editor. No way are we getting this by her. But if you'll help me drag puke-boy to the limo, we can make everything appear on track." She inspected Trent, prodding him with the pointy toe of her flats. "Wake up, Trent."

He groaned and sat up slowly. "Oof. Who shit in my mouth?"

I reached down to help him up. Hoo boy, he stunk. "Come on, buddy, stand up. We're taking a walk."

"To The Rail?" The bar was a popular hang-out for locals. Trent sagged against me.

I held my breath. "Nope. You've had enough for today."

Karen glanced toward the front of the tent. "Okay, I'll lead us to the limo and do the talking. Right now, I need your muscles."

I hauled Trent to his feet, but by the time we left the tent, he walked under his own power. His arm stayed around my shoulders for support, but we needed to let people see everything was okay. Photographers blocked our path, and a shriveled gnome shoved her face in front of Karen. "What the hell is going on?" The screech labeled her as Edith.

Loudly, Karen explained the "minor" glitch. "The groom ate some bad shrimp, but he's already feeling better."

Edith screamed to the crowd, waving her hands. "Not here! The shrimp here are great!"

Karen pushed through, leaving photographers to snap pictures from behind. No matter, fans held their phones up and captured the entire walk of shame on video. As we tottered forward, Karen chattered like she was on stage. "Every wedding has a problem, right?" She laughed as though a drunk groom was the most natural thing in the world. "We need to get this poor guy to the reception. Abby will be right behind us." En masse, the crowd turned their attention to the bride tent, leaving us to maneuver Trent to the limo. We shoved him in the back and told the driver to lock the door until

Abby arrived. Tinted windows afforded some privacy.

Karen leaned against the limo and pointed to a silver minivan. "There's our car." She clicked it unlocked. "Give me five minutes. Ricky will drive you to the courthouse."

My logical side tried to screw things up again, but I had to ask, "Karen, are you sure Abby will be okay with this?"

"Absolutely positive." She grinned and ran off into the crowd.

I was getting married today.

To Abby.

Today.

Anticipation washed away months of heartache. I leaned against the minivan, letting my mind wander through a much more interesting future. Mom would give me an earful, then my family would welcome Abby because it's what good people do. She would be loved. As for me, I wasn't sure what romantic love was, but for now I'd take the win and be thankful. Maybe Abby was right about everything—love grew from kindness, an open heart, and a shared commitment. Based on reading thousands of Abby's words, I trusted we'd get there.

Now that I was fully committed to the wedding, I wanted it to happen as quickly as possible. Every chance I got was a gift, and gifts can be taken away.

CHAPTER 25—ABBY

He vomited. My drunk future husband vomited. I'd needed a predictable ten minutes in the gazebo, but the universe had to give me one more horrible surprise. As I paced the tent. Ricky stood in the center with his arms folded across his chest, a frown letting me know his mind was somewhere else. My niece and nephew sat quietly behind him as though they felt the tension.

I stopped pacing. "Ricky!"

"Yep?" He faced me but didn't unfold his arms.

"What now? Where's Karen? Where's Trent?" I covered my eyes with a hot hand. "Oh god, I'm marrying Trent." I dropped my hand and froze, feeling more than a little lost in this maze I'd created.

"You don't have to." He shrugged like breaking a promise was no big deal. He loved me more than any decisions I made, and in his mind, my happiness was all that mattered.

Yes, I was miserable, but I kept telling myself Trent would be okay later. We'd start over, maybe at the courthouse, as long as he wasn't covered in vomit. "It's fine." My lingering wish, my *belief*, was pinned on Karen. Where was she? We'd been in this tent for at least fifteen minutes, and Edith had already demanded we move forward on schedule.

Karen barged into the tent. "Ricky! Can I see you a minute?" To me, she barked, "Get your stuff together so we can head to the courthouse."

I trudged to my chair in the corner of the tent and gathered my purse and a bag of clothes I'd worn to the park. Karen gestured wildly, fixing everything, I assumed. Ricky nodded. They both looked serious, but then, this was a seriously messed up day, one not half over yet. Dread washed through me when I thought about what we needed to accomplish before I could go home, and home meant being alone with Trent.

I dropped into the chair, not sure I'd ever get back up.

Maybe I'd bail on the whole project. What's the worst that could happen? Edith would be furious, but I didn't mind. My followers would be disappointed, and I'd feel shame for abandoning them. I could say goodbye to my career... But, somewhere along the line, I mattered too. I'd endured Rob and Luis bailing, and the mantel of "husband" falling to Trent, a man who, if I'm honest, I did not want to marry, especially after he'd puked on the ceremony.

A quiet, insistent voice in the back of my head whispered, *Max*.

I felt more for Max than I had for any of

the candidates, including Rob and Luis. The day we'd kissed, a passion pulled us together and wrapped us in our own world. The passion made me want him still. I yearned for Max, which, under the circumstances, was about the worst timing possible. During and after his rejection, pain ripped through me then settled into a dull ache that weakened over time but still made its presence known in the early morning hours.

Wanting Max was like wanting my mom back. It wasn't going to happen. People who dwell on the impossible end up broken, and I refused to break.

Which left me with Trent.

When I stopped feeling sorry for myself, I noticed Ricky and the kids were gone. Karen waved me toward the front of the tent. "Let's go!"

As I had most of my life, I followed her. She led me through crowds of well-wishers, most of them cheerful but others looking concerned. Photographers snapped pictures, and I tried to smile, knowing they expected bridal bliss. But come on, they'd seen Trent's performance. All was not well.

Karen practically shoved me into the limo, where Trent's odor nearly made me gag. I moved as far away from him as possible, but nothing hurts the feelings of a sleeping man. Karen climbed in beside me and smiled. What the hell was she smiling about? We needed to have a talk.

I inhaled through my mouth. "I'm not sure

I can do this." These were the same words I'd said to my sister when mom was dying and I didn't want to say goodbye. Today I got the same response.

"Yes, you can." She stared at Trent as she said it. Her demand hurt, maybe more than it should have, but she'd always been on my side. Throughout the Random Husband project, she'd let me know I could stop at any time. Tears formed in my eyes, and I turned away. I didn't think this day could get worse, but being abandoned by Karen left me more alone than ever.

She turned her attention to a call. I gathered she spoke with Hao, asking him for the favor of a tuxedo delivered to the reception venue. When she stopped talking, I heard the whisper of Hao's gentle voice, but I couldn't make out the words. Karen promised to text pictures of the groom and some measurements. At the very least, a fresh tux would make Trent smell better, and I was grateful for a small miracle. She ended the call and hummed. *Hummed.*

After a few minutes, Karen tried to chat. "Abby, we should talk about—"

"Nope. I need to sit quietly for a while." Hurt feelings spread through my ribcage in waves.

"But I really—"

I stared at the back of our driver's head. "Please. It's important. Please."

We didn't say another word during the ride.

My fate was sealed, and I was on my own. I desperately wanted to hide in a bathroom and cry the grief out of my body, releasing enough to march on. Hitting "rock bottom" would be an exaggeration and insensitive to people who live on the street and don't know where their next meal will come from, but this moment felt like rock bottom in my little corner of the world. I had to get through this cursed day and find a way to build myself back up. While married to Trent.

He snored, and I swear his breath amped up the putrid odor. I would have given Karen a wilting look, but I didn't want her to see the tears or my pain. If we both knew I had to do this, I wouldn't make her feel worse about playing her part.

We parked at the courthouse, where Karen jumped out. "Come on, come on, we're going to miss the appointment."

I tried not to feel annoyed with her happy energy. Could she not sense my misery? I crawled over Trent on my way out the door. "What about him?"

"Later. Ricky will be here soon. Right now, we need to get you inside."

Okay, so now she was illogical as well as insensitive. Not her best day. Screw it. At this point I was a pawn to be moved from place to place by someone else, totally out of control.

I followed Karen inside and through security in what now felt like an absurd wedding dress.

She led me down a wide green hallway to a door marked "Firearms and Marriage Licenses." With a point at the sign and a chuckle, Karen opened the door and ushered me inside. For the life of me, I couldn't understand why she acted like we were on a fun adventure.

I stood behind my sister and waited passively for her to chat with the clerk, announcing I was the bride here for my appointment. She asked for my driver's license, and I produced it, handing over my ticket to despair.

The clerk acted like a doting grandmother. "Congratulations, sweetie. Found your soulmate?" I didn't answer, but she kept talking anyway. "Where's Mr. Right?"

Karen jumped in. "He's outside, but can you go ahead and get my sister's signature?"

Grandma smiled. "Of course!" She pushed the marriage license across the counter, and I signed without feeling too much of anything. If pain gets too strong, we tend to shut down emotions as a survival mechanism. When an apathetic person has dead eyes, they've been deeply hurt and are trying to make it through another day. In my case, another hour.

I needed to close myself away from everyone, including Karen, for a few precious minutes. The only option I could think of was a bathroom stall. In a monotone, I announced, "I have to use the restroom."

The kind older woman looked up from

reviewing my signature. "You can use the one back here, sweetie. Pre-wedding jitters, I can see them a mile away." She opened a door to her inner sanctum and pointed toward the bathroom. Karen followed me in, but thankfully there were two stalls. I shuffled into one and closed the door, carefully sliding the lock like I was dismantling a bomb. I didn't trust myself with sudden movements. Fully clothed, I sat and bowed my head. Tears were banned by the dead space in my heart, but I sought peace and strength.

The minutes passed.

Karen asked, "Abby? Are you okay in there?" When I didn't answer, she peeked under the door. "Honey, let me in." I stared down at her. "If you don't let me in, I'm going to crawl under, and my belly is getting too big to fit."

Damn. I didn't want her to hurt herself. I leaned across and unlocked my cage. She opened the door, knelt in front of me, and held my knees. "Abby, I need to tell you some things."

"I can't. Please let me get through this quietly." I avoided her eyes. "Otherwise, I might break."

"No, no, no. It's good news." How could she think anything about this was good news? She squeezed my knees. "Abby, right now Max is signing the marriage license. Not Trent. He's a train wreck. It's *Max*."

I searched her face and tried to understand.

"How?"

"I might have gone to see him and ask if he was interested." She giggled. "Okay, I asked if he wanted to marry you."

My heart beat a little faster, reminding me I was still alive. "He said 'yes?'"

Karen studied her hands and shrugged one shoulder. "Kind of. He was interested but wouldn't commit to marriage." I buried my face in my hands and shook my head. What the hell? "But Abby, when he saw the ceremony and Trent, he changed his mind."

"He has a savior complex? 'Look at the screwed-up woman and her disaster. I can save the day.'" After this little exchange, I'd have to push down the pain again. "No thanks." If I was going to suffer, at least let me keep a shred of dignity.

She snorted, a noise she makes when she's exasperated. "It wasn't like that. He's waiting for you right now. Just say 'yes.'"

I wanted to believe her. I wanted to dive into a fantasy with Max, but I'd been devastated too many times today to open my heart again. If I let myself dream, pain would blossom like blood from a fresh wound. "The last time I saw Max, he was crystal clear about not wanting me around."

Karen stood. "Well, you can't hide in the bathroom forever. Let's get going."

She was right. One way or the other, I had to move. I felt the pressure of responsibility, knowing people waited at the reception for us, and I was due to get married in the venue's dressing room. I could drag Trent from the limo and urge him to sign the marriage license, or I could take pity from a man who rejected me in no uncertain terms.

Time ticked by.

I left my perch and walked out, leaving Karen to follow. I heard her pick up my driver's license and thank the clerk, but I kept walking, praying I'd make a decision before I reached the limo. I pushed open the door to leave "Firearms and Wedding Licenses."

Max and Ricky had their heads together a few feet outside the door, and the kids swung their legs on a bench against the wall. Everyone looked up. Max's blue eyes focused on mine, and I felt one glorious moment of clarity. In a heartbeat, I knew he regretted hurting me, rejecting me. His gaze asked my forgiveness. And something else, a gift too big for me to understand without words.

Max walked to me and paused a few inches away. I could touch him, but I didn't. I waited. Karen slipped out beside me and stood by her husband, the door closing softly behind her. Down the hall, security chatted with visitors. The background didn't matter, and soon it faded away.

I tried to read the message in those intense eyes. Max knelt on one knee and reached for my hand, pressing warmth into my frozen fingers.

I held my breath.

"Abby. I know it's been a crazy day, and you're probably confused right now. But I need you to know I'm not confused. I know exactly what I want. If you'll marry me, I want—I need—to be your husband. Since the day I met you, you've been in my head, and when I turned you away, I broke my own heart. I thought I was being noble, but I was being an ass. If I'm lucky, we'll have years to talk about the details that brought us here. But for now, today, I'm hoping you'll say 'yes' and marry me. I promise to be kind, faithful, dependable, passionate, loving, and sober. Every step of the way, I'll participate. I want to be your husband, and I'm asking you to be my wife. Please."

With every word, I let myself believe, a little at a time, this was real. My hands warmed, spreading heat through my body. Max knelt before me. He wanted to marry me. On this chaotic day, nothing else mattered. The beautiful, sexy man at my feet would be my husband. All I had to say was—

"Yes."

My sister spoke. "Yes, what?"

I turned to her. "Yes to what he asked."

"Yes, you want to what?" She nodded like when we had played charades as kids, encouraging a closer guess.

"Yes, I want to marry him." When she kept nodding, I added, "I want to be his wife. I want him to be my husband. I agree to his proposal."

"You both agree to be married to each other?" She barely suppressed a grin now, and I thought maybe the stress of the day had gotten the best of her too.

In unison, Max and I said, "Yes."

Karen laughed. "Then by the power vested in me by the World Church Organization, I now pronounce you man and wife."

Max rose and hugged me, picking me up and swinging me around while my heart came back on line. Ricky slapped him on the back, the kids screeched and ran in circles, and Karen stood back and smiled.

I spoke into Max's hear. "We're married." Awe reduced my words to a whisper.

He kissed my cheek, slowly lowering my feet to the floor. "Yes, wife, we're married."

Karen held out a pen and the marriage license. "Sign here, please." Max signed first, then me, and Ricky signed for good measure although Georgia didn't require a witness. Karen, being Karen, had already signed it. She'd never doubted the marriage would happen.

God, how I love her. Everybody should have an ally like my sister in their lives. A guardian angel.

She beamed. "Come on, come on, we've got a few hundred people waiting to see the bride and groom." With a final squeeze on my arm, Karen prodded her little family toward the exit.

Max and I walked toward the limo, hand-in-hand. I wanted to stare up at him, take in his gorgeous jawline, but I also wanted to walk without tripping in high heels. He squeezed my hand, letting me know we were in this together. The limo driver opened the door for us, and I bent to climb in, only to be hit by a wall of foul odor. Trent sat awake and smiling through his hangover.

He reached out for me. "Baby! Are you ready to get married for real?"

I flinched back, but not before his fingers touched my arm. Trent was cold water on my warm glow of happiness.

Max leaned around me. "She is married for real. To me." With my husband's face close to mine, I saw his jaw tighten and realized he could be the violent type. I didn't need to worry, though, because he reached in the door pocket and pulled out a bottle of water, handing it to Trent. "Here, you probably need this."

Trent looked too pale and tired to be confused by the turn of events. "Thanks, man." He fumbled to unscrew the cap. "I'd stop getting wasted if it wasn't so much damn fun."

Behind us, Karen said. "Take the minivan. Drive around to the service entrance. Security will be there, but they'll know to let you in. Max, fingers crossed there's a tux in the men's dressing room for you."

I didn't care if we made our grand entrance

with Max in casual clothes, but I liked Karen's style. Either way, eventually I'd have to deal with Edith, our guests, and readers. My plan, like always, was to tell the truth.

Ricky handed Max the keys. I asked, "How will you get there?"

Karen shrugged. "The limo."

We considered Trent, who was sucking down the last of the water. The kids nudged past us, eager to take their first limo ride. Eli saw Trent first. "Ew. He upchucked." Prissy stuck her head inside. "He *stinks!*"

My sister put a hand on each of their heads. "Don't be rude. We're going to give the poor man a ride home." With a giggle, she whispered loudly, "Hold your nose."

Max opened the van's passenger door and helped me tuck my dress inside before taking us on the next leg of our journey. Over the console, he opened his hand, palm up, in an unspoken invitation. I laced my fingers with his, enjoying the butterflies tickling my stomach. We rode in silence, probably because neither of us knew what to say, but I assumed we were both intensely aware of each other.

I swallowed and broke the silence. "The reception. My editor and other magazine people will be there, and an army of photographers will take pictures of our every move." With a glance at Max's face, I reassured myself he was okay so far. "And some fans who won a contest for invitations...and maybe the local news will ask some questions."

"Okay. I'll follow your lead." He turned to me and smiled, causing a thrill to run from my stomach to my neck. I couldn't convince myself the reception would be fun, but we'd get through it—as long as Max was beside me.

CHAPTER 26—MAX

When we'd left the courthouse, I had opened my hand on the console and waited to see what would happen. I didn't want to push. Abby, my wife, put her soft hand in mine. At that moment, I'd move heaven and earth to make her life easier. My first challenge came when we neared the venue. Cars filled every spot and lined surrounding streets, requiring me to squeeze through nearly impossible lanes toward the service entrance. Once there, I parked near the building and came around to help Abby from the car, offering my arm.

In what would probably be our last quiet moment for a while, she pressed my arm to her side and whispered, "Thank you."

Since "you're welcome" didn't quite cut it, I settled for looking down at her with a smile. I'd always known she was beautiful, but now she glowed in my eyes, and I wanted to stand there and appreciate her all day. While I tried to stretch the moment, a security guard opened the door and ushered us inside. He pointed me toward what I assumed was a dressing room before leading Abby away to prepare for our impending debut. I watched her go, the gentle swing of her hips against the silky dress hypnotizing me.

"You will come with me?" A small man held out his hand from a doorway. I followed him into the room, where several tuxedos were displayed. The man bowed. "I am Hao." He mimicked me removing my shirt and turned toward the wall of tuxedos. His voice drifted toward me. "Hopes and dreams?"

I froze in the middle of unzipping my pants. Hopes and dreams? Like world peace?

Before I could answer, he said, "Hopes and dreams of the heart."

At this moment, all I could see was Abby and the commitment I'd made to her, this crazy arrangement I'd freely entered and would have to explain to my family in the near future.

Hopes and dreams?

"Abby."

Hao nodded once and chose a tuxedo. He helped me dress, and although I could have done it myself, his touch was oddly calming. I stood still and waited for him to shift and fiddle with the jacket, add cufflinks, and tie a bowtie around my neck. When he turned me toward the mirror, I watched James Bond smile back. Hao walked behind me, and with a final brush of my shoulders, blessed me with a benediction. "Happy life for you."

"Thank you." I turned to tell him how much I appreciated his help, but he was already walking out the door. This day kept getting stranger and stranger, but not in a bad way. In fact, the day had been full of positive events, leaving me with faith the reception might go well even though—

"Nice work!" Edith bellowed from the doorway before advancing toward me. Instinctively, I stepped back. "You and Abby managed to derail the entire project in one fell swoop!" Sarcasm dripped from the words. She shook a stack of papers in my face. "I'm doing damage control, and you *will* cooperate." After pulling up a chair, she plopped the stack on the seat and handed me a pen. "Since you're the husband now, you have to sign these so we can take pictures, report on the next three months of your life, etcetera, etcetera, etcetera."

I stared at the pages, leaned against a wall, and settled in to read.

Abby's boss continued her rant. "You're *reading* them? So *now* you get slow and cautious? Little late, isn't it?" She threw her hands in the air. "Great. I'll be back in ten minutes to pick up the *signed* documents."

Alone in the room, I read contracts promising I'd allow my life to be an open book for the next three months, complete with photos, interviews, and daily—hourly—reporting of my life, including any intimacy with Abby. And there would be intimacy. Another contract promised a big payout if we divorced. I tossed it aside.

No divorce.

Marrying Abby was one thing, and I'd wanted to do it, but losing my confidential life was a problem. I couldn't think of any reason why I'd sign off on such a self-sabotaging plan.

I went to find Edith. In the hallway, I heard her ranting at someone from another room. "He signs or else."

Abby's softer voice drifted into the hall. "Max can make his own decisions. I won't interfere."

Edith sputtered, "*Won't interfere*? Tell you what, he signs, or you're fired!"

In the silence that followed, I strained to hear Abby's voice. The quiet stretched, and I realized there was, in fact, one reason I'd sign the damn papers. I scribbled my name on the documents in the few required places and entered the sitting room. Abby sat with her arms crossed like a determined child, and Edith paced the thick carpeting. When I walked in, Abby stood, clasping her hands in front of her like a defendant waiting for the verdict.

I handed Edith the papers. "All signed."

CHAPTER 27—ABBY

Max calmly handed Edith a stack of pages. I would have thrown them at her, but I suspected he had more self-control than me, a theory we'd test out through the years. The thought made me smile, and when Max offered his arm, my attention focused entirely on him. I tucked my hand in the crook of his elbow, and he covered it with his own, leading me from the room. Alone in the hallway, we paused to stare at each other before entering the reception. My stomach flipped with the realization I was already half in love with him.

When he leaned down to kiss me, my stomach flipped again, and I closed my eyes, ready for this man to wow me. I opened my lips a little, trying to be enticing. Only when he hesitated did I realize he'd intended a modest peck. Was I embarrassed? Yeah, sure, but I forgot to feel foolish when he slipped his tongue in my mouth and shoved the boisterous party to the distant background. I wanted everyone to leave. *Let's go home*, I whispered in my head. *Let's go home so I can have you to myself.*

Instinctively, I turned toward him for more contact, pulling him closer with my arms around his neck. He smelled so good—a clean smell like freshly washed linen dried in the sun. His strong shoulders under my arms, his chest against my exposed skin, the rigid need at our hips, and the honeyed taste of his tongue, all swirled together in a fog of pleasure. I felt protected...wanted. *Let's go home.*

When Max ended the kiss, I nearly fell over. I was pure sensation and no bones. While he held me up, he studied every feature of my face. My cheeks burned from the blood pumping through me double-time, and my mouth gaped open. I would have felt like a goof, but the heat from his eyes promised we'd continue our exploration later.

I closed my mouth and grinned, remembering my goal to entice him. In a move completely uncharacteristic of me, and therefore completely thrilling, I noted his bulging erection and said, "I'm looking forward to it."

After stepping away, he mumbled, "I, ah, might need a minute."

I laughed out loud, a joyful noise that might have lifted my feet off the ground if our host hadn't brought me back to reality.

A man in a burgundy tuxedo jacket tapped Max on the shoulder. "I have been instructed to avoid using your name until Ms. Abby can break the story to readers." With a sweeping gesture toward the party, the man said, "Your fans await."

We emerged from the hallway and were greeted by photographers and people yelling "congratulations!" The crowd shimmered and shone, dressed in their party finest. Men strutted in suits or tuxedos, and women modeled their cocktail dresses, everyone eager to celebrate. From the looks of things, an extended cocktail hour had amped up happiness and lowered inhibitions.

A woman shouted, "He's the wrong guy!"

Our host ignored the interruption and spoke into a microphone. "Allow me to be the first to present Ms. Abby Lynn and Mystery Man. Wife and husband."

Cheers followed us to the main room, where tables covered in white cloth and red rose pedals glittered with candlelight, and jazz music drifted through the air. My stomach growled when I smelled roast beef wafting from one end of the room, and I realized I hadn't eaten today. Funny how the body makes its needs known.

Most of my attention strayed to Max's arm and the occasional brush of our hips as we walked toward the band, my bustled skirt swishing behind me. Our host announced the first dance. In a moment of panic, I realized I didn't know if Max could dance. I examined his profile for clues, but I only saw the hard jaw I wanted to stroke and kiss. A five-o'clock shadow darkened his face, invoking fantasies of a dangerous pirate. When I squinted, I could almost imagine him with an eye patch and a curved sword, swashbuckling and whatnot on the bow of a ship. Then he'd take me below deck and rip open my dress before—

"May I have this dance?" Max stopped in the middle of the dance floor, and I moved into his open arms. The band played a slow, sexy rhythm, while a singer crooned her rendition of "Till There Was You." I won't say Max whisked me around the room in an elaborate waltz, but he danced well enough, taking command of my backward movements and ending with a dip.

The crowd applauded.

Cameras flashed.

Mentally, I checked one more reception event off the list and crossed my fingers that the meal, cake cutting, and farewells would move quickly.

Edith rushed to the dance floor and handed me the microphone. "Here you go, princess, explain *this*." She gestured vaguely in front of Max as though he was a stray dog who had wandered inside where he didn't belong. With a final comment under her breath, she left us.

Max and I exchanged a look. I shrugged. "Back to work." I turned toward the audience and did my job. "Thank you, everyone. Please get comfy at your table. I'd like to explain the latest Random Husband developments."

Photographers crowded closer while other guests found their seats. My husband, God bless him, put his hand on my waist, reminding me he would stay beside me, ready to provide anything I needed. Or at least I interpreted his gesture as allegiance. When he kissed the top of my head, I knew I was right.

The room quieted other than clinking glassware from the kitchen. I scanned the crowd, hoping for inspiration, a fairy godmother, or someone going into labor, but none appeared. Only one approach seemed viable. Be honest. Then I would deal with any fallout. I glanced at Max and couldn't help but feel grateful for my chance to break the rules. I inhaled deeply and started a speech from my heart rather than my pen. "Thank you, everyone, for joining us on this happy occasion. You've probably noticed my husband is not the same man I committed to in the park." The guests tittered at their tables, processing what they already saw. "I'm sure Trent is a good person, but it seems he was not in a condition to marry today. And I have to be honest, I didn't want to marry Trent. Because I wanted to make everyone happy, I'd have tried to find a way, but I'm grateful for the final-hour pardon."

A woman yelled, "It's not like Trent was a death sentence!" Panic seized me when I realized the woman might be Trent's mother, a woman certainly on the guest list.

"No, um, you're right. I'm sorry." I was messing this up. My face grew hot. I might have excused myself, but Max gently squeezed my waist.

Karen stepped into the room, drawing attention away from me. "How many of you are happily married?" Most people raised their hands, some who honestly believed their marriage was happy and others who dared not cross the spouses sitting beside them. "If you had been forced to marry someone else, wouldn't it have felt like the end of life as you knew it?" The room quieted as people nodded. My sister turned to me. "Carry on, Abby."

I smiled my thanks and held up the microphone again. I could do this. "For months, my heart has belonged to this man." I peeked up at him and reached under his arm to hold his waist. "Through all the applications, interviews, and planning—through all of Random Husband —I wanted only him." I paused to let my confession sink in. "But he did not apply. In fact, I doubt he heard about Random Husband until after the applications closed, which means he was never a candidate."

In the back, Karen held up two thumbs and smiled. Ricky came to stand next to her, with Eli and Prissy leaning against their parents.

"I rode the wave of Random Husband to the tenth yard line—"

Max chuckled at my football reference, and tension eased out of my body.

"—but I couldn't make a field goal."

He snickered again, sounding like someone

opening a shaken soda. But he squeezed my waist and mumbled, "Carry on, Abby."

"Then, when I almost reached home plate, I had to stop and ask myself what I wanted. When the articles and posts are written, I'll still be married, and I'd like to think it's forever. I want a happily ever after." I scanned the room. "So please meet the groom, my forever husband. My happily ever after."

When the cheers and clapping died down, a reporter shouted, "Is he your soulmate?"

I grinned and shook my head. "Oh no you don't. If you want to know what comes next, read my next article in *Women First*."

A photographer knelt in front of us for a photo and asked Max, "What do you have to say about all this?"

I glanced at Max and read his playful smile. "Abby is beautiful, ethical, kind, intelligent, and funny. Plus, her sports references guarantee we'll watch games together. I'm a lucky man." The crowd erupted in laughter, and although I wasn't sure what was so funny, I trusted Max to tell me later.

⊕

After a dinner of roast beef, asparagus, potatoes, and yeast rolls, courtesy of Edith's arrangements with the caterer, people crowded on the dance floor to work off their steady stream of cocktails. I sipped champagne at our private table, and Max came back from the bar with a bourbon. Every time I lifted my glass, I pretended to survey the room so I could surreptitiously glance at my husband. The trouble with my plan was Max always watched me, leaving me red-faced and short of breath.

We talked about the food, the decorations, and the dancers. Every boring word helped fill the space between us and fostered a comforting sense of familiarity. When Max mentioned cooler weather, he touched my back. I commented on the asparagus and touched his forearm. We played our subtle game until Karen approached the table.

"You both look adorable." She clapped her hands. "But I know you want out, so now's the time to walk around and make small talk with your guests." Obediently, we walked around the front of our table while Karen explained her plan. "In a few minutes, I'll get the host to announce cutting the cake, then we'll set up a farewell, complete with sparklers. The limo is already waiting out front to take you home."

Wait, where was home for us? The plan dictated my house, but... I tugged Max's sleeve. "Is my house okay?" Anxious to show off my home, I opened my eyes wide before adding, "Please?"

He shook his head but smiled. "Should I count on seeing those puppy-dog eyes every time you want something?" He pulled me closer and kissed me; this time I left it at a peck. "Your house is fine with me."

Karen rolled her eyes. "Get going, married couple."

⏻

"Time to cut the cake!" The host bellowed at the room. "Everyone gather around the cake and enjoy something *sweet*." A loud groan rolled across the crowd, followed by scattered laughter.

We strolled over, and Max handed me the knife, covering my hand with his. I noted the differences between our hands; mine was small and white, and his was large and tanned. Such a simple observation sent a thrill into the pit of my stomach, excitement growing when I realized we'd be home soon. We cut a piece of cake, revealing the deep red center, and I sent a silent "thank you" to my sister. Max tucked a bite inside my mouth, his eyes on mine. When it was my turn to feed him, I dropped his bite before aiming a second time. I tried to look anywhere other than his eyes, but they seemed to draw me back in.

While everyone clapped, Max leaned down and whispered in my ear, "Thank you, Abby."

His breath made me shiver, and I knew he meant more than gratitude for a piece of cake. Although, to be fair, it was red velvet with whipped cream-cheese frosting, a delicacy almost as perfect as bacon.

We stepped away from the cake to make room for eager guests. After a few smiling minutes observing, Max led us back to our isolated table, where Karen waited with two plates full of cake. She sat one in front of Max before positioning the other in front of me and handing me a fork. "I'll always do my best to get what you want."

Of course. I looked at my sister, then Max, and back again, trying to restrain the rising tears of gratitude. Like she'd said in the bakery, my breakdown was about more than cake, and yet she'd found a way to let me have my cake and Max too.

An hour later, my husband and I walked through a long line of sparklers, their tiny embers dropping harmlessly to the ground, and climbed into the limo. I waved from the window as Max poured two glasses of chilled champagne. Because there was too much to say, we didn't speak. I sipped from my glass and laid my head on Max's shoulder, feeling his kiss on my head. As we turned onto Cohen Street, he reached his arm around my shoulders and pulled me closer, quietly sipping champagne and watching the city go by.

CHAPTER 28—MAX

We arrived at Abby's enormous house just after nine o'clock. My wife must have taken on some serious debt for this place, and although I couldn't believe she earned enough to afford what amounted to a mansion, I made enough profit at the coffee shop to chip in.

The sun had set, leaving only the porch light to guide us.

When I helped Abby from the car, she winced. "High heels."

Without thought, I swept her off her feet and carried her up the wide front steps while she laughed. Her arms around my neck brought her close enough to kiss, but I didn't trust myself to stop at one. As a distraction, I said, "Nice house! A family home?"

I felt her facing me in the near darkness. "No, just mine."

After we'd gotten to know each other better, I'd ask more probing questions. Our backward courtship started with a wedding and would trickle down to thousands of conversations about our families, past, and plans for the future. It never entered my mind we wouldn't figure out a way to make us last. Abby was my wife.

Karen hadn't asked us to repeat vows of "for better or worse" or "till death do you part," but marriage, for me, included those vows. I'd always be one-hundred percent Abby's husband. If our commitment included helping pay off her debt, so be it.

At the front door, I stood her next to me and asked for the key, which she pulled from a white purse. When she handed me the key, she grinned, and I assumed she was thinking of our next hours together. I sure as hell was. Her key looked like an artifact from an ancient haunted house, but it fit into the lock smoothly. I turned it and tried the knob, only to find the door wouldn't budge. I tried again. Beside me, Abby covered her mouth, but a giggle escaped between her fingers.

I gave her my full attention. "Wrong house?"

"No, it requires a little work and magic. Kinda like us." She giggled again. "Try this. Insert all the way, as far as it will go—"

I leaned back and smiled at her. "Phrasing, dear. Phrasing."

"Right, right, I hear it too." The shared laughter wrapped us together in a secret club. "Then wiggle it around before you jerk up on the handle and turn."

While I followed her instructions, I offered, "Maybe you should lubricate the mechanism."

The door opened.

Abby snickered. "Lubrication isn't a problem.

It only needs a little coaxing."

I picked her up again. "You did that one on purpose."

Across the threshold, I set her on her feet, and she immediately kicked off her shoes and dropped them in a basket by the door. With the flick of a switch, two lamps came on near the couch, casting a yellow glow in their confined spaces.

Abby gestured toward the couch, cleared her throat, and dropped her purse on a table. "Would you care to have a seat?" She sounded like royalty receiving guests, and I half expected her to offer me a spot of tea.

I put my shoes in the basket and sat at one end of the couch. Abby walked past me toward a room in shadows, and while I watched her hips sway, she called out, "Do you want some tea?" She poked her head into the living room with raised eyebrows.

"No, thank you."

"A beer?"

"No."

"What can I get for you?"

I patted the couch beside me. After hesitating (damn, she was cute), she padded over to me and sat where my hand had been. We stared at each other, and her brown eyes widened with an innocent, unspoken question. Already her cheeks turned pink.

My cursed memory flashed back to her

articles and the intimacy rules. She'd marry a random husband, but sex wouldn't be a requirement. The last thing I wanted was to start my marriage with a subtle, or not so subtle, message that she had to perform. But I did want the door open in case she chose to walk through it.

I stood. "How about a tour?"

The relief in her eyes deflated my ego, but I handled it like a man. In other words, I scowled as I trailed after her upstairs.

At the landing, she flipped on several lights. Open doors revealed beds, an office, and a den with a spiral staircase. I followed her into a large blue bedroom, which she identified as her room, but before I could learn much about her from this private place, she returned to the landing.

The next room was painted light gray with a darker gray comforter. Abby wrung her hands beside me. "I was thinking this could be your room. It's the manliest bedroom, and you're a man, so..."

I took pity on her. "It's a nice room, Abby. Thank you."

She smiled, and it was like the sun emerged from behind a cloud. With regained confidence, the pride in her home broke through. "I call this next bedroom the green room." With a wave, she ushered me inside. "I had to convince the decorator to use celery green, but she picked out the fleur-de-lis green and chocolate bedspread."

Although I had no decorating sense, the room looked nice to me. "It sounds like you had fun decorating the rooms, and they look great."

"Wait till you see my office and the den." She grabbed my arm with both hands. "Oh! You can use the office and the den if you want a place to work. I don't mind."

I didn't have the heart to tell her I'd have to spend some time at my own home to stay connected with the business. My agreement to stay here tonight was temporary—another issue we'd have to work out together.

In the office, a huge cherry-wood desk extended under two windows, ensuring Abby would be able to daydream in the sunlight. The comfortable space held a lamp, an empty "in" box, and a computer docking station for her laptop. Recessed lighting in the ceiling cast a glow over creamy white walls and matching club chairs in a seating area surrounded by tall, full bookcases. I meandered across a thick pink rug looking like it had been salvaged from a castle and skimmed an impressive book collection. Her tastes ran from romance to horror but included classics by Hemingway and Dickens. I could see myself working here or reading a book while my wife worked.

The wife who sleeps in a separate bedroom, my grouchy ego reminded.

Abby had come to stand beside me. "What do

you think?"

I smiled down at her. "I think you have good taste in books." With a glance encompassing the room, I added, "And a comfortable office."

"Usually I work downstairs, but it's nice to know I have this room as an option." She grabbed my arm again and pulled me away. "Let me show you the den."

She'd set up the den as a TV room, with an overstuffed couch and chair in dark blue on a gray, white, and blue checkered rug. On one dark-gray wall hung a huge map of the world with pins in dozens of locations. One more thing I didn't know about my wife. "Have you traveled a lot?"

Abby joined me in front of the map. "Not yet," she sighed, "but I'd like to." She pointed to a pin. "These are my top choices." Markers decorated Paris, Rome, and Madrid, but destinations closer to home included San Antonio and San Francisco. I made a mental note to plan a trip. Although I'd haphazardly visited most tourist cities, I hadn't seen them with Abby, and I suspected she'd make a world of difference.

A black spiral staircase curled toward the ceiling in a corner of the den. "Where do the stairs go?" I asked.

"The smaller third level. I haven't gotten around to finishing the space up there. I have so many rooms already." She laughed at herself. "I know I don't need them, but this is my dream house. When I won the—" Her sentence stopped in the middle, and she stared at me like a deer in the headlights.

"Won the what?"

"Um, won the chance to bid on this house." Abby scuttled from the room, leaving me behind. From the hallway, she called, "Want to see the kitchen?"

I came to the doorway and watched her fidget her hands together. Mystery woman still held some secrets. I eased closer so I didn't spook her and caught her icy hands, warming them between mine. She felt soft, looked soft, in her white dress. Her big brown eyes and pink cheeks might have kept my attention if I hadn't been a man on his wedding night. As it was, my eyes wandered to the V of her dress and breasts slipping halfway from the fabric in a teasing display. While mentally kicking myself for staring, I pulled her closer to remove the temptation, only to create a more urgent need.

Under my nose, her hair smelled like fresh grapefruit. She wrapped her arms around my waist and laid her head against my chest, exhaling as though she'd found her perfect spot, and as far as I was concerned, she had. I admitted defeat. "I can't think straight with you in that dress."

Muffled against my chest, she laughed. "Could you think better with me *out* of the dress?"

Yep, all the blood in my body raced to fill a rock-hard erection. My mind had no trouble picturing Abby naked, but reality would put my imagination to shame. I wanted her naked and under me in one of the many beds or couches in this monolithic house. She couldn't miss my need pressing against her stomach. I held her shoulders and shifted her a foot away. "How about old sweatpants and a T-shirt?"

She grinned and went to her room, closing the door behind her. I paced the hall, focusing on nonsexual images, like roasting beans. Then I remembered kissing Abby in the roasting room and groaned. My rebel mind morphed the image to Abby on the blue couch in the room behind me, stretched out and inviting... I changed the image to Trent puking on the crowd, which did the trick. When Abby opened the door, I had control of myself...until I saw her cotton pajama bottoms and tank top, a scrap of cloth barely containing the braless wonder that was my wife.

Abby ran her hands down her hips. "Is this better?" A smirk said she knew it wasn't. She sauntered toward me, arms spread. "Are your thoughts straight now?"

Does every woman take lessons on driving a man insane? I know, I know, we're not allowed to touch without permission or look without hiding it, but good lord, I *required* my wife. Right now, I wanted her, no, I needed her, like I needed to breathe. With my private admission, Abby was in control, and I floundered.

"Hold on." I stepped back.

She advanced another step, leering with half of her mouth, definitely in control now. "It's our wedding night. We both know what we have to do." I ogled her body. Where to start? Her full breasts jutted against thin fabric; her hips curved toward a playground. My body had responded when she'd opened the bedroom door, and now I released the reins, grabbing her arms to bring our bodies together. My heart beat so hard against my ribs I almost didn't hear her next words. "Readers demand it."

A cold shower couldn't have killed my libido more thoroughly. The brain fog lifted, but my heart continued to hammer an urgent rhythm, this time in anger. I had no right to be mad at Abby, but I sure as hell was pissed off with myself. How could I forget our arrangement? I'd signed Edith's papers, and Abby had a job to do.

The job included me.

Abby must have felt my lack of participation. She leaned back and searched my face. "What's wrong?" The pain in her voice pierced my heart, but I wasn't ready to share our sex life with strangers.

"It's been a long day." I kissed her forehead. "Let's get some sleep and start fresh tomorrow." The expression on her face was more than I could bear, so, like a coward, I slunk to my "manly" room and closed the door.

I doubted I could hold out for three months, but I could avoid sex one day at a time. Something about the Random Husband publicity stunt made our marriage an experiment, a perception I didn't want for Abby or for me. She was my wife, my future, the foundation of my life, and I'd be damned if I was going to drag something so important through the mud. Holding self-control for three months was a small price to pay for a lasting marriage.

While I listened for any sounds from Abby, I undressed to my boxer briefs and brushed with a new toothbrush I found in the bathroom. Abby had prepared this room for another man. A stabbing jealousy almost send me charging to my wife's bedroom, but I held my resolve, at least for tonight.

⏀

I must've fallen asleep because a *tap tap* on the door woke me up. For a few seconds, I forgot where I was, then it flooded back to me. Abby was my wife, and I'd rejected her again.

"Max?" Her soft voice drifted through the door. "Can I come in?"

I sat up in the darkness and turned toward the door. "Yeah, come on in."

She slipped through the crack she allowed herself. "Can we snuggle? I'm lonely."

I thought I heard her voice catch. If she cried, I'd break like a dry twig. After shifting to one side, I lifted the covers. "Follow my voice. I'm right here."

Light footsteps padded across the floor, and a cold and soft Abby climbed in beside me. I covered her with the blanket, my heart already beating faster. I smelled her grapefruit-scented hair under my chin as she scooted her bottom against me to be little spoon. My heart wouldn't give me an out, instead sending messages from my brain to tuck my legs behind hers and pull her closer with an arm draped across her body.

She stretched like a kitten finding a warm spot in the sun before settling against me with a sigh. "Thank you, Max."

I stared into the dark, throbbing with a need I couldn't hide, until Abby's breath deepened into a slow rhythm. After what seemed like an hour, my body relaxed, and I pulled her sleeping form closer, resting my head against hers. Sleep lapped at my consciousness, carried on a citrus scent.

⊕

Sun streamed in the windows, but I could've slept through the glare. What I couldn't sleep through was Abby wiggling against me and kissing my bare chest. Her hands stroked my upper arms and shoulders before running down my back.

She spoke against my skin. "You're not hairy."

What could I say? *No, but I'm horny.* Since my erection pressed against her stomach, I figured she'd already gleaned that information, so I opted for a mundane response. "No, not much."

My arm lay across her body, and I struggled to stay still.

She kissed my cheek, traveling toward my mouth; my resolve would break when she got there. Already my body screamed at me to *participate*. I pulled back and mumbled a lie. "I'm not really a morning person."

I don't know what she heard, but she threw the covers back and jumped up, running from the room without a word. Would I ever understand this woman? I examined the ceiling while I planned this morning's conversation about privacy in a marriage. She had a job to do, and I'd support it as much as I could—as a platonic roommate until it was just the two of us. Our real wedding night, and the marriage, would start in three months minus one day. I had to smile when I thought about buying a calendar and marking off each day with a big red X.

Abby burst into my room and leapt on the bed, climbing under the covers in one fell swoop. "It was my breath, right?" She opened her mouth and made a *ha* sound so I could smell mint. "Fresh, right? I brushed my teeth."

I laughed out loud. God, she was adorable. Nothing could have stopped me from kissing her, but I kept it to a quick brush on the lips. She wrapped her leg over my thigh again and laughed. At this rate, our playful mood would turn serious in about thirty seconds, and I'd be lost. Surely I could hold out more than one night;

hell, it hadn't been twenty-four hours. *Get up, man. Now or never.*

I squeezed my eyes shut, sighed, and climbed out of bed, careful not to make eye contact. "How about some coffee? People tell me I make a great cup!" My attempt at cheerfulness sounded lame to my own ears, but I had to get out of there before I attacked my wife. And by attack, I mean have sex with her for the rest of the day. That thought almost sent me diving back under the covers, so I grabbed my tuxedo pants and rushed toward the door, leaving it open behind me.

Nearly an hour later, Abby came into the kitchen. I handed her a cup of coffee, and she put it in the microwave. At first, she refused to look at me. I sat at her kitchen island and waited, sipping my third cup. She stared at the microwave, obviously stalling, but when it dinged, she had no choice but to acknowledge my presence. After a cautious sip, she nodded toward me. "Thank you for the coffee. Are you headed to work today?"

Nice. In no uncertain terms, my wife dismissed me. I could sit there and have hurt feelings about it, or I could be a better husband and realize *her* feelings were hurt. No matter what she said, I didn't plan to leave her today, but I could see we needed to talk about the whale in the room.

I sat my cup on the counter. "Abby, we need to talk about Random Husband."

She lifted her chin a fraction. "I'm listening."

Clearly, she wouldn't make this easy, which, I suppose, was fair. "For the next three months, you'll write about us, right?"

Nodding, she sipped from her mug.

"Everything about us, including conversations, ups and downs, and what we almost did in my bed."

Abby shrugged one shoulder. "To a point, yes. I can gloss over some…" She waved a hand in the air before finishing, "details. If you disagreed, why did you sign the contracts?"

"So Edith wouldn't fire you."

After turning her back to me, she placed her mug on the counter and stood in silence. Finally, she murmured, "You heard her?"

She sounded unhappy, but I couldn't see her face, and every cell in my body screamed at me to *move*. I marched over and held her shoulders, pulling her around to face me so I could wrap her in a hug. Part of me feared she'd push away, but she didn't. Instead, Abby tucked herself against my chest, including her arms, and let me envelope her body. Her tears wet my skin.

I hugged tighter, desperate to ease her pain. "I'm sorry if I screwed things up. I want a private life with you, but I'm trying to be okay with sharing our days with fans. Give me some time, and I'll get there. The only part I can't share is our sex life. It's the one part making us a couple and not roommates."

Abby sniffed. Oh god, I sucked at this. What had made me think I could be a good husband? She sniffed again. Her arms crept around my waist. "You're a great husband, and it's only been one day."

I hadn't expected that. I stood there, shock and confusion mixed in with a rush of gratitude toward my wife. "I don't want to fuck this up."

Abby leaned back and gave me a watery smile. "Not possible. We're married." She stretched up and kissed my chin. "Let me get this straight. Rather than shaking the sheets and asking me to keep quiet, you plan to practice celibacy for three months and let me do my job without rules?"

"Shaking the sheets?" I laughed.

"Making the beast with two backs?"

I joined in. "Kickin' boots?"

"Horizontal refreshment?"

"A bit of 'how's yer father?'"

"Eww!" She lightly punched my chest, where I still held her captive.

We quieted, breathing in the scent of coffee and listening to a dog bark outside. I broke the spell. "Three months is a long time."

Abby sighed. "It is."

I lifted her chin. "I'm not going to make it if you keep climbing into my bed."

She looked down. "Judging by your reaction to, um, coffee, I don't think the bed is your only problem area."

As I backed away, I had to laugh because she was right. "Maybe we need to stay four feet away from each other. Any closer and you'll be in reach."

"We can try it." One shoulder came up in an unconvincing shrug. "But you have to wear a shirt." Her gaze roamed down my body and back up again. "I want you so much right now, I'm throbbing with it."

Groaning, I backed further away. "And you can't tease me. I'm in physical pain right now. Actual agony."

Abby held up both hands in surrender. "Okay, okay, I concede." With a glance around the kitchen, she asked, "Other than get you some clothes, what do you want to do today?"

"I'm glad you asked, wife, because I have a trip in mind."

CHAPTER 29—ABBY

When the door closed behind Max, I returned to the kitchen to think.

Last night, after Max had escaped to his bedroom, I'd stood in the hallway for a few minutes, waiting for him to return. When he didn't, I'd slunk to my own room and soaked in a hot bath for nearly an hour, trying to figure out what I'd done wrong. I was convinced he desired me, and I'd been clear about wanting him. Maybe my seduction game was clumsy, but he couldn't have missed my intention.

In the deep darkness, the house had felt empty, the quiet drumming against my ears louder than a sound could. After climbing into bed, I'd tossed and turned, burning with need, until I found relief while fantasizing about Max touching me. The climax rocked my body, releasing tension for thirty minutes of staring at the ceiling.

When I'd approached Max's door, I half believed he'd send me away, but I had to try. By the time I'd climbed into his bed and felt his need against my back, I'd convinced myself we'd have a proper wedding night. Somehow, I'd fallen asleep—probably the warmth of his body

—and made my big move this morning. Thank goodness I knew he wanted me or I'd have been crushed rather than *very* disappointed. What does a woman need to do to get laid around here?

Down in the kitchen, I'd avoided looking at him and nursed my bruised ego, remaining stoic to let him see my hurt feelings. Sure, it was childish, but this man, my husband, had rejected me too many times.

It all became clear when he'd admitted signing Edith's contracts to save my job. Jeez. I couldn't stay angry. Max's rejection only reflected his discomfort with Random Husband, not with me. He didn't want our sex life in the public eye, but I'd agreed to report *every* detail of our marriage. What a horrible position I'd put him in!

As icing on the cake, Max had agreed to keep his distance for three months and dive into our marriage (read, *me*) as soon as Random Husband expired. I can't say whether Max believed he could wait three months, but *I* couldn't. My marriage had started, and I wanted to be part of it, not playing checkers and making small talk with a roommate.

I knew what I had to do.

I threw on clothes and drove to beg Edith for amnesty. I'd appeal to her human side, if she had one. After parking near corporate headquarters, I trudged into the building and toward Edith's office, fingers crossed she'd be there and alone. I already felt the heat in my cheeks, and my heart raced ahead of me through the maze of hallways and offices.

She had to say "yes."

⑩

"No. Absolutely not." Edith slammed her hand on the desk. "After the schlock you pulled yesterday, I'm *stunned* you'd ask for a favor today."

"Edith, let me explain." I sat like a child in the principal's office.

"No! You have my answer." She balled up some poor writer's submission and continued to rant. "I met with the board this morning after your little stunt, and they said we're still on target with ad sales over the next three months. Readers ate up your last-minute switch for love, which is a lifesaver for you, princess."

I was far from done. *Ask for what you want.* "How can I get out from under Random Husband?"

"You can be under, over, or sideways with your husband, but the project continues." Now both hands slammed the desk before she sat back and smiled like a tiger about to leap. "If you can think of a magical way to bow out with zero repercussions, more power to you. That would mean ending the project without a dime of lost revenue and not one reader dropped."

"Come on," I practically begged. "Be reasonable." Like *that* was going to work. But I was out of ideas.

"That's rich. No matter that my job and the magazine is on the line. Let's focus on *you*."

This dramatic nugget wasn't new for Edith. Every time she wanted something from me, she said the magazine needed it to stay afloat, and I'd feel dutifully contrite. Not today. Today I'd focus on Max.

"If I can find a way out, I'd still have a job?"

"No repercussions to the magazine. We're limping along as it is." Edith picked up a pen and focused on paperwork, dismissing me. "Now get back to work, princess. I expect posts today and an article by Wednesday."

I strutted from her office, head held high; it felt good even though Edith wasn't watching. I was rich. I was creative. I was smart. Surely the combination offered a solution; I simply had to figure it out.

⬓

When Max picked me up from home, my suitcase was packed with casual clothes, per his instructions. We'd only be gone for two nights, so I assumed we wouldn't drive far. There he stood at my front door, smiling in jeans and a T-shirt. He looked good enough to eat. I remembered our deal and primly handed him my suitcase, keeping as much distance as possible. "Should I know where we're headed?"

"Macon, if that's okay." Before I could respond, he walked my suitcase to the car, with me following behind and admiring his...behind. He slipped the suitcase in the back. "My family wants to meet you, and I want you to meet my family." He paused and searched my face. "Are you up for it?"

Meet the family? Whoo, scary, but he'd gotten roped into a marriage without his family there, and I acknowledged the huge sacrifice. "I'd love to meet them! Let's go."

He picked me up and kissed me hard on the mouth. "Thank you, Abby." I froze, flushed and beaming, but he seemed to realize he'd broken his own rule. "Oh, sorry. I got carried away."

I smiled at my husband, feeling the sunshine down to my stomach, where a kaleidoscope of butterflies danced their approval.

◍

His mom opened the front door before we climbed out of the car. Her long hug communicated kindness, welcome, and acceptance. Her child had chosen, and his decision was good enough for her. Max's bear-sized dad waited inside and offered a briefer, stronger hug that reminded me of his son. Two men I assumed were Max's brothers, and a woman, also embraced me as a welcome to the family. In a small chair, a boy they called Natty waved shyly.

As newlyweds, we were given the guest room; the married brother, Frankie, and his wife insisted on a blow-up mattress in the "office," and the younger brother, Justin, would sleep on the couch. Natty would curl up against his grandmother in their king-sized bed. It seemed important everyone stay in the same house, probably to avoid drinking and driving, if our first night was any indication. We ate chicken and dumplings, drank beer and wine, and played poker with a quarter ante until after midnight.

The first awkward moment came when we closed the door to our bedroom and climbed into bed together. Max wore a shirt, which helped, but the double bed brought us way too close for comfort. We both shrugged our shoulders at the same time and giggled like teenagers sneaking away from our parents.

By unspoken agreement, we nestled into our pillows facing each other, grinning our delight at finding ourselves together alone.

Max spoke first. "Thank you for a fun day."

I dared to touch his cheek. "You have a wonderful family. I'm glad you brought me here."

Something soft in his eyes woke up the butterflies, but before I could figure out his secret, he turned over, showing me his broad back. "Mom will be up early. If you want any sleep tonight, it might work better if you're big spoon."

Laughing, I tucked myself behind him. I understood exactly what he meant, and although I might've enjoyed being poked in the back, lack of closure would've tortured us.

When I woke up the next morning, Max slept facing me, his beard stubble dark and intimate. I watched him sleep. With every breath, I wanted to run my hand across his cheek, but I held back, eventually abandoning my watch and padding from the room.

Max's mom scuttled around the kitchen, working on several different recipes at once. She noticed when I entered. "Good morning, Abby!"

"Morning, Barbara. You seem busy. Can I help?" I perched on a barstool.

"You're a Southern girl, so you know you're part of the family when you're invited to work in the kitchen. Let's get that little formality out of the way." She handed me a camouflage apron matching hers and laid a bowl, fork, and carton of eggs on the counter. "Beat the entire dozen while I pour you a cup of coffee."

For the next hour, we created a huge breakfast of bacon, egg-and-cheese casserole, homemade biscuits, and grits. Thank goodness my assigned jobs didn't include culinary challenges because I would've shocked and disappointed Barbara with my complete lack of skills. As it was, my helper role allowed me to shine.

While we worked, our conversation centered on food, the weather, and my recounting of the wedding. I wasn't sure how much of the sordid truth she'd already heard, so I glossed over Trent, the vomit, and Random Husband. Those parts were Max's story to tell, if he chose. I opted for painting a picture of Karen marrying us at the courthouse and the beautiful reception.

Barbara asked questions about Karen and my family, making me promise we'd get together soon. Since Max's mom and my sister proved to be kind-hearted people, they'd grow to love each other.

I was lost in thought imagining their meeting and turning the bacon over in the skillet when Barbara put a hand on my shoulder. "I know there's more to the wedding story, but we'll have plenty of time for gossip later." I couldn't meet her eyes. "Abby." I turned to face her, and she continued, "Thank you for marrying my son. I haven't seen him this happy since he opened the coffee shop."

The blush climbed my cheeks in record time. Max was happy? I had so little time for comparison. Barbara didn't wait for a response but bellowed for everyone to come get breakfast while it's hot.

And so went day two with Max and his family. Warmth, conversations about nothing and everything, and soft snoring as people dropped off to sleep while watching football. Max held my hand on the couch until the lull of penalty flags, instant replay, and men running in circles hypnotized me. I rested my head on Max's shoulder and joined the symphony of slumber.

Before dinner, I texted Karen and explained

I had a ton to tell her Monday. I apologized for not texting sooner, but I was on an adventure with my husband. She'd laugh when she read it, knowing my reference to "husband" meant I was happy with the outcome of Friday's craziness.

Cynthia and I helped Barbara with dinner, and our conversations brought Cynthia into the fabric of my life. She was quieter than Max's mom, but a keen sense of humor emerged when she made observations about the men and parenthood. So far, the only person I couldn't figure out was Justin. He rarely spoke but answered direct questions. Likely he'd remain enigmatic until Max and I grew close enough to ask about his brother.

Late in the night—actually, early Monday morning—Max and I crawled into bed, exhausted. He kissed my cheek and turned away, my signal to curl against his back. Soon his slow breathing let me know he'd found sleep, but I stared at the wall over his shoulder.

I was too excited to sleep.

I'd spent the past two days rolling ideas around in my head, considering ways out of Random Husband, until the solution coalesced into certainty. I had the answer. Simple but exciting. Every time I thought of my strategy to regain freedom from Edith and save my job, a delicious thrill arrowed through my stomach, reminding me of the time Karen brought home a kitten and said she was mine.

In every spare minute, I devised a scenario where I'd seduce Max. The seduction would probably involve slow music and a sexy negligee. Or naked. The familiar thrill shot through my stomach again, and I nearly squealed with excitement. I closed my eyes, willing myself to sleep. If I had my way, this would be the last restful night for a while.

The next morning, we went out to breakfast at the Waffle House before Max and I headed home, swapping more childhood stories along the way. A few miles outside of Savannah, Max asked, "Do you want kids?"

Whoa! That came out of nowhere, but his question deserved a serious answer. My husband had every right to know my wishes. "Yes. If I could choose, I'd say three kids, but maybe two." I held my breath in the silence, not daring to look over at Max. Impatient as always, I caved and saw him smiling.

With a glance at me, he said, "We're a good match, Abby."

But I already knew that.

⊕

During the afternoon, Max went to work for a few hours, with the plan I'd return to his apartment after packing some fresh clothes. I missed my house, but I'd miss Max more if we stayed apart. Besides, I had big plans for the evening.

I met with a lawyer and my accountant, and

we formalized details of my offer to purchase *Women First*. I made sure the offer was generous for a small, regional magazine. Like my Victorian home, this expense felt exactly right.

Next stop, Edith.

There was no reason to be nervous, but my heart pounded anyway as I rounded the corner to her office. She frowned when I entered. "Well, if it isn't princess. I haven't seen posts these past two days, and you have an article due soon. Can't wait to get to know your husband." Her smirk only made me smile.

"I have something for you." With flair, I brandished a one-page summary of my offer like I was holding a crucifix in front of a vampire.

She scanned the page and sprang up, ripped off her glasses, and sputtered, "Where the *devil* did you get this kind of money?"

I waggled a finger at her. "Ah, ah, ah, no you don't. I never agreed to divulge my sources." Sitting without an invitation, I said, "I'll give you a minute to process what this means, but you're a smart woman, so I don't expect to wait long." I handed her a letter of release from Random Husband. "Then you can keep your promise and sign this."

Edith narrowed her eyes and sat down, quickly reading the letter before eyeing me across her desk. "This letter says I agreed to the release, but legal will have to write a formal document."

"I understand. But it's enough for now that you sign on behalf of your employer." Besides, I wasn't willing to wait the weeks it might take for lawyers to draft paperwork.

Edith frowned and leaned forward. "You're willing to purchase the entire magazine rather than write about your marriage? *Why*?"

"I want a real marriage." I shook my head. "Not three months from now, not three days from now, but starting today. I don't want to share my husband with countless readers and followers while we maneuver through the tenuous early days of our relationship."

To her credit, Edith looked truly confused, flopping back in her chair as she surrendered. "But this was *your* idea. You were the one who wanted to write through the first three months until each of you decided if the marriage would continue." She threw up her hands in defeat. "What's changed?"

I'm not sure until that moment even *I* knew what had changed, but when she asked, I didn't hesitate in my answer. "I fell in love."

My brutal, no-nonsense editor laughed until she triggered a coughing fit. When it subsided, she said, "Would you write one more article about your happy ending? Obviously, you can write whatever you want and leave out as much as you want."

I smiled, feeling one more thing was right in the world. "I can do that."

With pursed lips, Edith signed the letter and came around the desk to hand it to me. "Abby, I figure this means I'll be out of a job soon, but right now, I'm still in charge. For your fans' sake, do you have a killer idea for another project?"

Grinning, I pulled notes from my purse. "As a matter of fact, I do."

CHAPTER 30—MAX

My first stop after dropping Abby at her house was the pharmacy, where I bought enough condoms to last a month at the rate of three a day. The entire afternoon, my mind swirled with thoughts of Abby and obsessed over when I'd see her again. I roasted beans, kidded around with Anuli until she asked if I was on drugs, and prepared to seduce Abby. After only a few days together, I knew beyond the shadow of a doubt I wouldn't last three months without touching my wife. I *needed* her. We'd spent days talking, laughing, and touching platonically, and although I'd loved every minute of it more than I could say, it wasn't enough. If I didn't bury myself in her, touch and taste every part of her, my head would explode.

She planned to stay at my apartment tonight, which gave me time to set a sexy mood, as if I had any idea how to accomplish the task. Women like candles, I guess, and R&B music might set the tone. Just thinking about such a transparent effort made my palms sweat. A ladies' man, I wasn't. But as a husband, I needed to try.

In the back of my mind, a little voice reminded me we had an unseen audience, but a louder voice rose to the challenge and ordered me to do a damn good job. Fans or not, confidentiality or not, I needed to make love to my wife.

After roasting a second batch of beans, I spent two hours at the gym trying to purge restless energy, then I cleaned and organized the entire stockroom.

Time crawled by.

Abby texted she'd arrive at seven thirty, which gave me a few hours to set up the apartment. Excited fizzes in my gut propelled me up the stairs, two at a time. I ripped the sheets from the bed and replaced them with clean ones, making the bed with the care of an Army recruit. Old, half-melted candles filled my junk drawer, but none were appealing enough to display, so I dumped the contents of the entire drawer in the garbage. I sat on the couch with my phone, knee bouncing with nervous energy, and shuffled through music options until I located a station for "smooth R&B." Smooth is good. In the kitchen, I opened a cabernet because she'd had a glass with my mom.

When I sat down again, sweaty and breathing heavily, only an hour had passed. I smelled my shirt and peeled it off on the way to the shower, where I deliberately kept my mind occupied with thoughts of dad working on the old Caddy. I had to calm myself down and stop thinking about sex, or I wouldn't last two minutes with Abby. And, good god, would she tell her fans? Knowing Abby, she'd gloss over any intimacy, but two minutes...hard to put a positive spin on it.

I texted Abby to let me know when she was out front so I could let her in the store, the only entrance to my apartment. Then I stood at the kitchen counter and tried to relax. When that didn't work, I downed warm bourbon and settled for *appearing* relaxed, not an easy feat while I paced the floor.

CHAPTER 31—ABBY

After leaving Edith's office with her blessing on my next project, I'd driven straight home to deep clean my house and work off nervous energy. Sure, buying a magazine was a huge deal, but I could only focus on Max.

Max touching me…me touching Max.

Late in the afternoon, I gave up on busy work in the middle of ironing a sundress and headed to Karen's house. After only three days apart, we had some catching up to do. Once again in her sunny kitchen, I leaned back in my chair and sipped fresh coffee.

At the sink, Karen rinsed a final dish before joining me. "Well, married lady, are you pregnant yet?" She giggled at her own lame joke.

"I think sex is required for that particular outcome."

"*What*? You and Max haven't sealed the deal?"

"Aw, sister, you make it sound so romantic." I held my nose in the air, channeling my image of British royalty. "But no, we haven't *consummated* the marriage."

"Why not?" She slammed her cup on the table, spilling half, with no regard for cleanliness. "What's wrong with him?"

I winced, not wanting her to think ill of Max. "Nothing. He's struggling with our very public arrangement. Random Husband for three months is a lot to handle."

"Oh! God, I forgot about the hype!" Laughing, she said, "Poor Max, worried about how much you'd need to share...and performance anxiety!" Karen laughed harder, thoroughly enjoying herself at my husband's expense. "And wondering if you'd take notes when he rummaged around for your G-spot. Oh, god, too funny." She wiped her eyes while I tried to send my steely gaze across the table rather than crack a smile. I failed.

"Yeah, you get the picture."

With a sniff, she became serious. "But three months..."

"Not exactly." I grinned at my sister, knowing she'd love the next part. "I made an offer to buy *Women First* today."

"What the—? You'll be your boss! You can run the project however you want." She threw her head back and laughed. "Oh my god, typical Abby." After wiping tears from her eyes again, she said, "I want to hear every detail of that gem later. For now, the important question: Where does it leave you and Max?"

I loved that she knew where my mind and my heart were.

"I plan to seduce him tonight." I jumped to my feet and tried to wiggle my hips like a belly dancer, with my hands clasped over my head. "How could he resist me?"

"Just do that." Karen smirked.

I plopped back in my chair, giggling and without a care in the world. My marriage would begin for real tonight. *Tonight!* "Okay, I'm open to suggestions. I was thinking candles and a negligee, but I've never seduced anyone." I grabbed a pen and her grocery list from the table, ready for direction. "Go!"

With a "stop" gesture, she shook her head. "Abbigail. Do you seriously believe you need to jump through hoops to get your husband's attention?" After waving a hand toward me as though dusting the air, she added, "Look at you." Karen shrugged like I had nothing to worry about. "Besides, when you tell him you aren't reporting, nothing will stop him."

"Thank you. But I want our first time to be special, memorable. We'll be at his apartment, so I can't do much to prepare."

"If it makes you feel better, wear the negligee." She got up and called to the kitchen speaker, "Hey Giggles, play Egyptian music," and the sound of drums and castanets filled the room. Karen belly danced to the music with her baby bump leading the way. "And if a sexy outfit doesn't work—" Her tongue protruded past her lips in a mask of concentration. "Try this little number on him."

"Ha ha, big sister." I tried to scoot around her

on my way out, but she blocked my path with her dancing.

"You think I could seduce Ricky with these moves?" Her face remained solemn as she undulated awkwardly.

I put both hands on her belly and darted past her, calling back, "I love you!" from the front door.

⚭

The saleswoman draped three more nighties across the dressing room door. "Here you go, sweetie! These will look *great* on you!"

On my own, I'd picked out a pair of pink silk pajamas with shorts and a short-sleeved top. The overly helpful saleswoman had ambushed me to ask the occasion. Since I assumed we'd never meet again, I answered honestly. "I'm a new bride." She'd squealed and clapped her hands, nearly drowning out the rest of my answer. "Um, and I want something he'll like."

The first two outfits she'd picked out resembled black cobwebs, sheer and impossible to wear without becoming trapped in a tangle of straps and lace. Now I waited nearly naked in the dressing room while Phoenix flitted around the store for "jaw-dropping" nightwear, draping her latest three discoveries within my reach.

I pinched the strap of one and pulled it toward me. This bright-red little number boasted open, ruffled circles for my nipples and a matching red G-string to *not* cover my rear end.

Whenever I feel shy about my body, I imagine what my forty-year-old self would say to me, and usually she talks me through any insecurities. But even if I managed to wear this outfit in front of Max, I wouldn't be able to stop laughing, a response not super conducive to sex.

I dropped the pieces on a chair.

Outfit number two glared a neon green, but at least the designer had added material in key places. I dragged it over my head and peeked in the mirror. Spaghetti straps led to a corset-style bodice ending in a skirt barely reaching to my thighs. I'll admit, the style wasn't terrible, but the color would work better as a Saint Patrick's Day costume than a seduction.

The final option held more promise. I tugged it on before I could change my mind. The silky powder-blue shift also had spaghetti straps and fell to the top of my thighs, with tiny blue bikini panties hidden under the hemline. Unfortunately, transparent netting material removed any mystery concerning the shape and color of my breasts. Maybe I could fold my arms over my chest during the *ta-da* moment. I couldn't picture myself brazenly strutting toward Max in this getup.

Forty-year-old Abby frowned in the mirror. *If I had the chance to be twenty-something again, I'd wear every one of these negligees and strut around in high heels!*

Okay, okay, stand down, older Abby. I bought

the blue ensemble, but I added the pink PJs with shorts too, not sure if older Abby would make an appearance tonight.

At home, I packed an overnight bag and included my recent purchases and a copy of the release letter from Edith. Since I still had some time before the coffee shop closed, I soaked in a bubble bath and pictured my seduction in the racy blue number. Anxiety blossomed in the pit of my stomach and spread to an unpleasant throbbing in my throat, complete with sweat not caused by the hot water. I allowed my mind to abandon the image, concentrating on what would happen *after* we touched.

CHAPTER 32—MAX

Abby texted she was on the way, and I scanned the apartment one more time, trying to see the place through her eyes. Damn! I should've bought curtains to cover the wooden blinds. My heartbeat kicked up a notch. *Relax, already.* Abby was my wife, not a temporary visitor. If she wanted curtains, we'd get curtains.

I ran a hand through my damp hair. Maybe I should've dried it, but I didn't own a hairdryer. My favorite old jeans and a Bob Dylan T-shirt suddenly seemed too casual for tonight. I should change.

My phone dinged again, another text from Abby. She'd sent a picture of the shop's front door and a waving emoji. Out of time, I raced downstairs in my socks and slowed my pace at the bottom, where she might see me. Play it cool. Her story might start with, "He approached me with animal grace, confidence oozing from every pore." I grinned and vowed to leave the writing to my wife.

I unbolted the front door and pushed it open. Abby wore faded jeans and a Stevie Nicks T-shirt, yet another hint we made a good match. I smiled, gesturing her inside, and said, "Welcome home."

When she walked past me, I winced. *Welcome home?* It had sounded way less cheesy in my head. "The stairs are over here." I pointed, but she probably remembered the store layout.

She glanced over her shoulder and smiled. "I remember." I watched her sashay up the steps with a backpack slung over one shoulder. Three steps behind her, I rewrote the article opening. "She walked with animal grace, confidence leaking—" Nah, Abby would never leak. But the juvenile thought lowered my stress a few notches.

At the top of the steps, I touched her shoulder to remind myself Abby was real, and she was my wife. "The door's unlocked." I followed her into the room and waited for her approval, staring over her head at the naked window blinds.

"Oh! Max, it's great! I love the colors, and everything looks so comfortable." She dropped her backpack by the door and hugged me, wrapping her arms around my neck. "I'm so glad I'm here." Her damp hair brushed my face, and god, she smelled good. I'd never been a fan of eating grapefruit, but her scent might change my mind.

My arms wrapped around her as though my body knew exactly what to do, and I needed to let nature happen. But my rebel mind filled with the words she might write. "Eager, premature, boyish," paralyzed me. Abby dropped her arms and stepped back, tilting her head in question. I walked past her toward the kitchen. "How about some wine?"

"Sure!" The squeaky response hinted she might not be the confident animal I gave her credit for. I heard her shoes drop to the floor, and she came to stand behind me, so close I could smell her hair. While I poured the wine, she stroked my back. "Can we ditch the four-foot rule for tonight?"

Wine slopped on the counter. What did she mean? How could she know what I had planned? I tossed a towel over the spill and, empty-handed, turned slowly to face her. Those big brown eyes pleaded with me for something... to agree? I sure-as-hell, one-hundred-percent, don't-look-back agreed.

I rested my hands on her shoulders, not wanting to rush her, and lowered my lips to hers. Her eyes closed, reminding me of the roasting room, where I'd fallen head over heels for this woman. My heart pounded in my ears, and I almost forgot ours was a public marriage. Or, more likely, I stopped caring. As my tongue tasted her mouth, she sighed like a woman finally getting her wish—although it was clear to me *my* wish came true. I slid my hands down her body and pressed her hips against me to show my intentions, hoping she still wanted what I offered. Thank god she wrapped one leg around my thigh for better contact.

Already I worried I wouldn't last long, but

I couldn't make my body slow down, not with Abby grinding against me like this. I'd never wanted a woman so painfully.

She whispered in my ear, "More," before reaching down to unzip my pants.

A switch flipped. I needed my wife *now*. The kitchen wouldn't give me enough access to her body, so I picked her up while she wrapped both legs around my waist and kissed my neck all the way to the bedroom. I bent to lay her on the bed and followed her with my body, doing everything in my power to maintain the contact threatening to drive me crazy.

When Abby pulled away, I felt the loss to my toes. She breathed heavily, which brought my attention to her breasts, as she said, "Max, I have some paperwork to show you."

She must be kidding. *Paperwork*? *Now*? I figured she was stalling or had changed her mind. I leaned back against the pillows, desperate for her to want me but knowing she had a right to stop. The next words choked down my disappointment. "Do you not want to...We can wait...I thought you wanted us to—"

"Oh! Nonono," she said, "I want you —desperately, desperately need you—touching me." She closed her eyes and swallowed, a cute blush on her cheeks. "Tonight, I don't want to sleep a minute because we'll be too busy— Never mind, I'll show you."

Abby, my beautiful wife, sat up and peeled

off her shirt and bra, then scooted around to drag jeans and panties down her legs. Just when I thought she couldn't surprise me more, she wiggled up against me and pulled my hand down between her legs so I could feel she was ready.

I didn't need more encouragement. I slipped a finger inside and stroked the folds, watching her face. She dropped her head back. I wanted to remove my clothes for more body contact, but I wouldn't stop her pleasure for one second. As long as she wanted me to keep stroking, I was at her mercy. I inserted a second finger and shifted to find her G-spot, knowing her body would tell me when I arrived.

"Oh! Max, I—" She jerked her legs closed, holding my hand in place, while her back arched. "I've thought about this all day."

I could tell. And thank god. I kissed her open lips, trailing down her neck while she whispered sounds of encouragement. Her hips bucked.

Every woman's body is a little different, but I intended to learn exactly what made Abby come. Judging by the increased pressure on my hand, she was close.

I murmured, "Is this good?"

"Yes, don't stop."

Not a chance.

She grabbed the blanket with her free hand and arched her back again. On an exhale that barely held words, she said, "I'm coming." Even without her confession, I'd have known she came, an orgasm that left her gasping for air.

Slowly, I removed my fingers, still watching her face. Her wild abandon fed my male ego, and though my body throbbed for release, for the moment I was content to focus only on Abby. I pulled her against me and said, "You're amazing."

Still out of breath, she turned her face into my chest. "Me? Your fingers are magic." Her soft hand ran down my chest and reached into my open fly. "Your turn." But I didn't want her to focus on me yet. I wanted to savor every second. Tonight, I'd fulfill at least a few fantasies I'd been having about Abby for the past few months, and she needed to be able to walk tomorrow.

I stopped her hand and undressed, repositioning myself next to her and following the curve of her hip. If she had shifted a leg over my thigh like she had on our wedding night, my jutting arousal would have entered her by accident.

I prayed she'd shift her leg.

When she twisted on the bed, I thought my prayers were answered, but she jumped up and darted from the room, yelling, "Hold on!" She hadn't gone to brush her teeth this time because she ran to the living room.

With her backpack, she scooted past the bed and into the bathroom. Intrigued, I leaned up on my elbows to see what my wife was up to, pulling a sheet over my hard-on to make it slightly less apparent. I shook my head and smiled at the wonder I'd married. Damn, what a great decision.

Several long minutes later, Abby walked out wearing an erotic blue thing. My jaw dropped. She fidgeted by the bathroom door and smiled, shifting eye contact away from me shyly. The top half of the nightgown lifted her breasts and displayed them, including hardened nipples and all. My mouth watered. I shifted from my elbows to my hands, wanting to get a better look.

Suddenly, she scooted back into the bathroom, calling out, "Nope, nope, can't do it. Hold on."

I had no idea what to do. Was she saying she'd changed her mind about tonight?

A few minutes later, Abby came out in pink pajamas, little shorts showing off her gorgeous legs. I already missed seeing her breasts, but we'd solve that problem soon. She pranced up to the bed and leapt in, playful until she saw my raging hard-on. "Hey!" With a giggle, she leaned back like it was going to bite her, and I joined in with a growl and pounced, holding my body up to avoid crushing her.

She laughed out loud when I nuzzled her neck. The scent of her hair filled me, and we both stopped moving. I whispered into her ear. "You're beautiful and sexy, Abby. Wear—or don't wear—whatever makes you happy, and I'll be grateful." I kissed her then, wanting her to know how I felt. I didn't have the words yet, but I trusted she'd understand.

With a gentle push, she moved me to my back and undressed again before climbing on my lap. Leaning down, she returned my kiss, sharing the same gentle intensity and meaning. I felt cherished. At first, her hips rubbed against the length of my shaft while she watched my reaction, then she opened a condom and rolled it on while nipping at my chest. I had to guess she'd brought condoms in her backpack, but I soon forgot to think at all. She sat up slightly and angled herself to take the tip, moaning her appreciation as she rocked forward and backward, taking me inside, inch by inch. Her eyes drifted closed. I watched her lose herself, squeezing her walls around me in a warm, slippery embrace.

I lost control. Shaking with adrenaline and need, I held her hips and thrust into her, burying myself to the hilt. She gasped but returned to her rocking motion, leading us both toward an explosion that would be the first of thousands. I'd crave this woman for a lifetime.

After our heartrates slowed and we held each other for a while, I offered food and pulled on my boxer briefs. Abby put on her pink PJs and followed me to the kitchen, where I made eggs over hard and bacon, both of which brought tears to her eyes along with a smile, so I guess she approved. I gave her barely enough time to eat before inviting her back to bed and indulging my fantasy of tasting every part of her body.

At her insistence, we showered near midnight.

At my insistence, we dirtied ourselves again.

In the early morning hours, I watched her sleep on her stomach, enjoying the smooth curve of her bottom in the light from curtainless blinds. My heart had calmed, bringing with it peace and awe. I'd let Abby sleep and recover until dawn before kissing her left ankle, an area I'd neglected earlier. For the next eighty-six days, when she wrote about our marriage and any intimate moments, I hoped she'd say she was satisfied. Because nothing mattered more to me than her happiness.

⬯

"What do you want to do today?" Abby asked from the bathroom doorway. She had showered again and wore the clothes she'd arrived in last night.

I gifted her with a lecherous grin from the bed, clad only in boxer briefs I'd pulled on while she showered. She knew full well what I wanted to do today. I had to laugh when she held up one hand to "stop," and the other hand tucked between her legs in a protective gesture.

She bit the inside of her cheek. "I might need a minute." Abby slid against the wall toward the bedroom door and relative safety from her amorous husband, pretending to be afraid of my intentions. "Um, maybe we could get something to eat."

I growled and slowly shifted my feet to the floor, stalking her like a wild animal smelling prey. On cue, she squealed and ran from the room, giggling until I caught her from behind and pulled her to the couch. I nuzzled her neck and kissed behind her ear, losing myself in the scent I had come to love. God, she smelled good.

Releasing her, I kissed her once on the lips and paused to stare at her face. A curtain of brown hair fell across one eye, and she wore a lopsided grin. Her face without make-up looked fresh and young. I wanted to eat her up. After allowing myself one small nip on her ear, I headed to the shower. "Give me five minutes," I called over my shoulder. At the bedroom door, I turned to catch her watching me with a lustful grin. "Later." I smiled, joy welling inside when I thought about having the morning with her, the day with her, my life with her.

Four minutes later, I hurried from the bedroom, already missing my beautiful wife. Abby sat primly on the edge of the couch, her face lighting up when I entered the room. She was great for my ego. I held out a hand to her. "Ready to go? The shop's been open for a few hours if you want breakfast there."

She beamed. "You mean do I want the best coffee in Savannah? Um, yeah."

Downstairs, I avoided Anuli because I wasn't ready to let anyone else into my bubble with

Abby quite yet; I wanted to have her to myself, just the two of us. The table I'd come to think of as "Abby's table" near the roasting room was empty, thank goodness, otherwise I might have had to boot some customers. I led Abby to her table and left her to get coffee and croissants, enough calories to replenish some of the energy we lost last night...and this morning.

I sat across from Abby and couldn't make myself stop staring. She was stunning. And she was my *wife*. When she added Splenda to her latte, I waited patiently for her to look up again so I could see those big brown eyes, but she seemed lost in thought as she stirred her coffee. Shit, she didn't seem like a happy bride. What had I done wrong? I thought we were a perfect fit in most ways—definitely in bed—but then again, every man wants to think he's delivering the goods. Maybe she planned to remind me that last night would be part of Random Husband. Sure, I'd come to terms with the publicity, but it would sting.

I shifted in my chair, uncomfortable with silent Abby; this wasn't the woman I'd come to know in, yes, a very short time. The news must be pretty bad. "Abby, is anything wrong?"

She jerked her head up, almost as though she'd forgotten I was there. So much for my ego. "Oh, no, no. Not wrong. I'm trying to think of exactly the right way to tell you some big news."

The tension in my shoulders released a

notch. Maybe she'd won an award for her writing. I sipped my coffee and leaned back, ordering my body to relax and be patient. My life was too close to perfect for worry.

"Maxie!" A familiar voice shouted behind me.

What the actual hell? I whipped around, sweeping my full coffee to the floor.

"Zoe?"

It wasn't a question because of course I knew her inside and out, but the word popped out of me like a reflex—or like the *Alien* movie where the monster rips out of someone's belly.

A little *kip* sound from Abby would have caught my attention if Zoe wasn't descending on us. What the *fuck* was she doing here? I stood to face her head-on and deal with this distraction. "What do you want?"

She reached me, and for a reason I don't understand, I blocked her view of Abby with my body. I guess I was still trying to keep our marriage, our time together, pristine. If anyone could sully the morning, it was Zoe. The blast from my past tapped me on the chest with one of her long, red fingernails. "Maxie! Is that any way to welcome me after our recent couch-time?" She put her hands on her hips and cocked her head to one side, trying to look cute but failing. "I told you I'd be back! You're the winner of Random Husband!"

CHAPTER 33—ABBY

Nearly hidden behind Max's bulk, I frowned. Although her hair was lighter, she looked like the woman Max had been with on Porsche night. What the hell did "recent couch time" mean? We'd come back to her comment later, but for now, how could this woman know the winner, and what did it have to do with her?

Max seemed to have the same questions. "Yeah, but— I mean, how do you— Why are you here, Zoe?"

His assumed ex-girlfriend huffed and rolled her eyes like Max was the dumbest man she'd ever known. "I told you I'd 'interview' ten men and marry the winner." She poked his chest with a talon. "It's you, silly."

My mind wandered in a dense fog, searching for the only reasonable conclusion: The woman was batty. I couldn't decide if I was dreaming or angry or shocked. Never one to sit on the sidelines, I stood and walked the three steps to Max's side before slipping my hand in his and pressing against his arm. I announced, "Max is with me."

Zoe laughed. Standing right there in front of me, she laughed in my face. "Oh, sugar pie, he and I have history."

Max squeezed my hand and tried to intervene. "Zoe—" But I had more to say.

"You can have the past. I get the future." Max turned to me, and we became the only two people who mattered. I spoke more for Max's benefit than for Zoe's. "He's my husband."

It was Zoe's turn to sputter. "Wh— But he — Your *husband*?" A light dawned in her eyes, and her perfectly painted red mouth gaped open. "You're Abby! From Random Husband." The woman seemed to forget about Max as she rummaged in her purse and pulled out a phone. "Abby! I can't believe it! Can I get a selfie with you?" Before I could answer, Zoe ran to my side, held her phone high in the air, and clicked a series of pictures, her cloyingly scented hair pressed against mine. She pulled away, stepping back slightly. "Max is the winner? How exciting! I can't wait to post about it! I'll break the story and be famous!"

"Wait!" I held out a hand toward her as though I had the power to stop her plan. "I haven't posted yet, so if you could please give me —"

Zoe practically danced away in her five-inch heels. "I gave you Max!" She giggled as she said it, delighted with herself for discovering the finale of Random Husband.

We watched her leave, locked in a spell until the closing door released us.

Max spoke first. "Fuck."

My heart raced at the likely fallout from being scooped on my own story. "Um, yeah. I'm so sorry, Max, but I have to go." I shifted from foot to foot. "This is bad." As I grabbed my purse from beside the chair, I gave him my pleading eyes and was rewarded with a grin.

He kissed me once on the lips, releasing me. "Go, go!"

By the time he reached the second "go," I was halfway toward the door, but I ran back and skidded to a stop in front of him. "Do I have your permission to write your name and the coffee shop?"

His eyes clouded, but he smiled down at me. "You have my permission to write whatever you need to write. We're a team." I stood there, mesmerized by how deeply I loved my husband. For every word he spoke, every kiss, every smile, I loved him. He kissed me again and laughed, "Go!"

⌼

Outside the shop, I ran to my car. Before I left the parking spot, I posted three messages to social media, desperately trying to regain control. I announced Max as my husband, including a picture I found online. I gave more free advertisement to the coffee shop. Finally, I promised readers a *Women First* story by the end of the day.

Once I was securely cocooned in my home once more, I sat at my desk and opened my computer to write. My mind was filled with Max, which wasn't a bad thing, but it got in the way of writing, so I texted him to say I might be gone a while. He immediately texted back, telling me to take the time I needed.

We're a team.

It took me three hours to bang out the first draft, then I soaked in a bubble bath to roll the words around in my head. By four o'clock, I sent Edith my article and explained the rush, although, to Edith, every story is an emergency. The more I thought about how hard the little nemesis worked, the more I realized I'd never fire her.

I doubt the article was what she expected, but she approved and posted the story fifteen minutes later.

We started this journey together, you and I. You supported my clumsy efforts to find a husband in a sea of wonderful men. You stood by me when I faltered, regrouped, and tried again. This article is a note to you —a "thank you"—for the goodness in your heart.

My note also must contain apologies. I lied to you about the ceremony in Forsyth Park, letting you believe it was a wedding, when in fact, it was a commitment ceremony with no legal obligations. As you know, I had chosen three men for my groom, and (this part is hard to admit) they kept bailing out, like I was a sinking ship. In retrospect, maybe I was. With constant changes, we couldn't get a marriage license before the ceremony because we didn't know the groom's name!

My second apology is for choosing Max, a man who never applied to Random Husband. Actually, I feel ingenuine apologizing for my choice because he's my husband, but more on Max later. I broke the rules, and you didn't deserve that. If I could do it over again, I'd have been more honest with you about meeting Max, about falling for him. But first I'd have needed to be honest with myself, a goal I didn't reach until my wedding day when Max stepped forward and asked me to be his wife.

My third apology is to the brave and beautiful men who applied to Random Husband. You're searching for love, a basic human need meant to lift our hearts and fulfill our lives. Ultimately, out of one-hundred and two eligible candidates, I chose none, a betrayal of your trust. For the next six months, Women First and I will contact every applicant and work with you, our readers and followers, to match you with a partner. Our project is called Savannah Soulmates, a name I chose because it makes me smile.

Before I end this message, I want to share with you the past few days of my life. I'm happily married to a handsome, kind, talented, funny man who makes the best coffee in Savannah (his wife's opinion). With his permission, I can share with you I met Max at Historic Coffee Roasters, where we conducted interviews for Random Husband. I know I promised to share the first three months of my marriage, but I learned that what happens between a wife and husband is private—not only the sex, but the talks, the trip home to meet the family, the long walks through Savannah, and even the disagreements. Every precious interaction becomes part of the fabric we weave together, just the two of us.

I haven't forgotten my premise. You must be wondering if Max is my soulmate. Maybe. Ask me again later. After we travel, face challenges at work and at home, stand by each other through wins and losses, and raise our second or third child, you can guess what my answer will be. Soulmates don't appear by magic. They emerge from hard work, commitment, and kindness. But first, you have to participate.

I sat on my couch and reread my article once more. I'd planned to tell Max I wouldn't betray his trust, I would keep our marriage private, but

Zoe interrupted my plans. Before she arrived, I'd been frantically tying together words to say exactly how I felt about Max and the marriage, all the while distracted by the sexy forearms he rested on the table. In the back of my mind, Karen's voice teased me into writing what I wanted to say, forcing me to curb my impulsivity and weigh each word.

I still had to figure out how to share my thoughts with Max, but maybe I could hand him my phone and let him read the article. Okay, too cheesy. Maybe I could read it to him… nope, worse. One thing was certain: I couldn't do anything from here. The thought of seeing him again set the butterflies free, which fluttered my heart into beating faster, which tickled a laugh in my throat. I let it fly, followed by a *eek* of delight as I raced upstairs to pack more clothes.

Twenty minutes later, I hauled a suitcase downstairs, still giddy with anticipation. Karen knocked on the door. I knew it was Karen because she always knocks too hard, pounding for me to let her in right away. Come to think of it, that's probably why I'm impatient; I learned it from her. I had so much to tell her!

I opened the door with a flourish, shouting, "I'm in *love!*"

Max stood on my doorstep. I don't think he could have looked more stunned if I'd slapped him in the face.

Still clutching the edge of the door, I stepped

back. "Oh! I thought you were Karen." I shuffled back another step. "Um, sorry about..." My heart plummeted, but those damn butterflies multiplied.

He stepped forward, chin down, lips pressed together, and eyes leveled at me. If I'd ever been spanked, I imagine the warning would have looked like this. With every step he advanced, I stepped back, dropping my suitcase along the way. Without breaking eye contact, he swung the door closed behind him. "Upstairs," he growled.

I'll admit, I felt jittery, not knowing what he was up to, but I wasn't afraid. Intuitively, I was certain Max would never hurt me. I clomped up the staircase, hearing his heavy footsteps right behind me. At the landing, he caught up with me and pressed a hand to my waist, herding me into my bedroom.

We stopped beside the bed. Slowly, so tenderly I almost cried, he cupped my cheek and slid his hand to the back of my neck while he leaned down to kiss me. Gentle at first, he deepened the kiss when I wrapped my arms around his shoulders and pulled him closer. Somehow, we managed to undress each other, helping along the way, while never losing the touch of skin to skin.

As he pressed me backward onto the bed, he mumbled, "Is this okay?" In response, I opened the bedside drawer and pulled out a condom, laying it on the table.

The full length of his body on mine told me he was more than ready for the condom, and I was more than ready for him. I'd probably been ready from the second he said, "Upstairs," in his growly voice. He tore open the foil packet and rolled on the condom, closing his eyes in the process. I spread my legs to let him know I was ready, but he slid down my body to taste my heat, inserting his warm tongue and instantly finding my G-spot. Unfortunately, at the exact moment, my mind wandered to my admission of love at the front door, and I froze as heat from embarrassment replaced the throbbing need for his touch.

Max stopped tasting me and lifted his head. "Am I hurting you?"

"No, no, it feels wonderful. Don't stop." *Get your head in the game, Abby.* I needed to concentrate on his mouth, not my impulsive stupidity.

He pushed my legs open further with both hands and grabbed my ass to press me tighter against his tongue—licking, touching, erasing everything from my mind and leaving only raw sensation. After teasing with motions that sent electric vibrations through my body, Max lengthened his licks, long and smooth against me, while his fingers pressed against my G-spot over and over. I felt the heat build, and every time a new pulse rocked me, I thought I had come.

But Max didn't stop, and I didn't want the waves to end, until a tidal wave crested, emanating from his tongue and his fingers. "Ohh!" Oh, god, I braced my thighs against the wave, locking my muscles to take every last drop of pleasure.

Without moving his fingers, Max slid up my body until he could replace his hand with an enormous erection. I gasped. Surely it wasn't this big last night or this morning. But after the first deep thrust, my body accepted his gift, closing around him with my swollen heat. The strength of my climax still clutched at the length of him in pulses, and he groaned as he slowly, slowly withdrew, only to slide in again.

He grabbed one of my legs and tucked it over his shoulder, opening me up wider, letting him press deeper. The self-control of moving slowly and holding his weight on bent elbows brought sweat to his chest and face, but he didn't rush. Incredibly, he hardened more, swelled more, until I wasn't sure he'd fit. He lifted my other leg onto his shoulder, still keeping a slow rhythm. Another wave built deep inside of me, where he kept forcing the tip to touch, pressing, pressing, sliding all the way in and all the way out to let my body learn the pace and respond.

My mind crowded with images of him inside, filling me and pulling me toward climax—my body reaching for release. This man controlled my body; I belonged to him, and he belonged to me. With a shaky inhale, I gave in, leaving my mind behind, and whispered, "Max, I want to come. Please." I didn't know what I was asking for. But Max did.

He reached down and stroked between my legs while his in-and-out hip motions increased their tempo. Faster, but still long strokes, he plunged, slick with sweat and control...until he couldn't hold out. I rode the wave of his fingers, tightening my legs against his shoulders as I lost myself in the purest pleasure. Vaguely, somewhere in the distance, I heard Max moan, "Abby, oh god, Abby. You're perfect." He came. Not for a few brief seconds but through pulse after pulse, jerking his hips against me.

When he released my legs and rolled to the side, his hand stayed on my stomach as though staking his claim to my body. I could have told him I was happy to be his and only his, especially after mind-scrambling orgasms. Well, and the whole marriage thing. I giggled at the thought.

Max smiled, still breathing heavily, and turned his head to me. "What's funny?"

I turned to stare back at him, my cheek nestled in the pillow. "I'm happy."

His smile softened. "I'm glad, and me too." Then he popped up onto one elbow. "Abby."

"Max." I grinned.

"We got married quickly." Oh my god, where was this going? My smile slipped away while I waited for the other shoe to drop. Max explained, "We should get to know each other."

"Oh! Yeah!" Relief washed over me—not as breathtaking as an orgasm, but great in its own way. "Can I go first?" When Max nodded, I asked a burning question. "Have you ever been in love?"

Max looked thoughtful, and I knew I'd get an honest answer. "I thought I was."

"Follow-up question: with Zoe?" I held my breath.

"You snuck in two questions, but yes, I thought so." He stroked my stomach. "But what I felt for her doesn't come close to what I feel for you." I watched his face, eyes full of meaning, and exhaled. Was he saying—

"My turn," Max jumped in. "Have you ever been in love?"

I might as well be honest. "Before now? No." We grinned at each other like we'd discovered our best friends. "Too easy. I'll give you another one."

Max studied his hand on my stomach. "I read your article."

"What? Which one?"

"All of them." He looked up, making eye contact again. "But I meant the one from this afternoon."

"Oh!" I don't know why his admission made me so happy. "What did you think?"

"First, you're brilliant and talented. Second, I'm grateful you sacrificed the marriage details for me, for us. But I also have a question."

"Hit me."

"Weren't you required to write about our marriage for three months?"

"I sort of bought my way out." I stopped after providing minimal information, then remembered I was talking to my husband. Hiding my wealth had become a knee-jerk reaction. Fine, I could do this. I sucked in a huge breath and rushed my words out on the exhale. "I put in an offer to buy the magazine."

Max jerked his body to a sitting position. "Wh — *Buy it*? Abby, how did you— Where did you— And the house—" His eyes scanned my room.

I laughed, savoring my secret for another minute. "Yep, all mine."

He looked down and rubbed a hand over his face. "Okay, let me think. I have some money in savings, and I can always take out a second mortgage on the store's building. I don't know if I have much equity built up yet, but—"

The new emotion I labeled "love" welled up in me again. The feeling was soft and warm and rounded at the edges. "Thank you, Max." I pulled him down and kissed him once, but I could feel the tension in his shoulders. I released him, and while his worried face hovered above me, I whispered. "I'm rich."

He sat up again. "What?"

I giggled. This was fun. He looked utterly confused, but I was finally able to share my huge secret.

"Earlier this year, I won the lottery." I

watched his face process the information. "At last count, I have five million, give or take." With a shrug, I tried to play it cool while thoroughly enjoying my revelation. "The miracle of compounding interest."

Max stared across the room in the general direction of a window. He said only, "Huh," like "go figure; I didn't see that one coming."

I nudged his chest with my hand. "Max, you're not talking. Any more questions?"

His mouth quirked up on one side as he returned his attention to me. "What's your favorite color?"

It was my turn to sit up in confusion. "*What*?"

He smiled at my reaction. Then chuckled. Then my husband fell back onto his pillow and laughed, dedicating himself to the job of happiness. I'd never heard him laugh like this, such a full-bodied, rich sound of delight.

I grinned and stammered, "F-favorite color? Favorite *color*?" Splaying my body across his like a wrestler bringing someone to the mat, I joined in his happiness until the room vibrated with our shared joy.

At some point, he rolled on top of me and kissed me, a challenge since I was still smiling. When he lifted his head, we stared into each other's eyes, both of us sharing secrets of love, trust, and kindness. "Abby," he glanced at my mouth then returned to my eyes. "I love you."

I craned my neck to peck him on the lips once, smiling at this man who was my future... my husband...one day my soulmate. In that moment, I vowed to myself I'd always be honest with Max. I'd be an open book filled with romance, adventure, and love. Wrapping my legs around his waist, I pulled his body closer and whispered in his ear.

"Purple."

Author's Note

Psst, hey there...

I want to thank you for reading my first book. If you enjoyed *Random Husband*, would you please leave a review on Amazon?

I appreciate you!

My website at www.janiegordon.org has other stories, coming novels and random thoughts about writing, romance, and life in general. I've been a psychologist most of my adult years, and although that doesn't necessarily make me wiser, it has given me a lot of time to study the human experience. The wonderful, resilient human experience.

Contact me at JanieGordon345@gmail.com any time (I'm not much of a sleeper) to share your stories, offer feedback, or just say "Hi!"

My next book, *Olivia!*, is steamier, so brace yourself. A shameless plug for my second book is on the next page, and right after that, I hope you enjoy the first chapter.

OLIVIA!
A novel by Janie Gordon

Coming Soon

Olivia! is a steamy contemporary romance about a young actress breaking away from her influential and controlling parents to find her path in the world. Along the way, Olivia trusts the wrong people, as they exploit her for sex, influence, and money.

Through it all, one man remains her champion. One man sees her true worth. Martin picks Olivia up from failure, sets her free, and loves her through it all. But Olivia's destiny is her own, and she won't accept help from a world she has learned to despise. Her inner—and outer—diva promises to leave her rich, in charge, and alone.

Olivia! is a tale of self-discovery, friendship, and steamy affairs of the body, if not the heart.

CHAPTER 1

Much of Olivia's childhood remained a blur, punctuated by flashes like scenes from movies she'd made. Nearly five years ago, on her sixteenth birthday, she'd stopped blaming her parents for treating her like a commodity. After all, they spent their lives in film and TV, creating for their child the only reality they understood.

In two weeks, she'd turn twenty-one. That special day would bring independence, including access to money held in trust for her beginning with her first acting job at the age of five. New York—no, the world—would open to her, glittering with unrealized opportunities, like choosing her own scripts, her own clothes, and her own apartment.

Two more weeks.

Fizzes of excitement tingled in her stomach, reminding her of the time she'd dropped mint candy into a liter of soda. An eruption seemed imminent.

Not yet.

Freedom must be taken by surprise; sneak up from behind and wrestle it to the ground. Otherwise, the elusive prize might slip away.

Fourteen more days of behaving herself, the

ever-dutiful daughter judged by the world as worthy, accepted by her parents as pliant. No one would see her jailbreak coming, as long as she left her eyes vacant and her manner docile. An obedient puppy, eager to please, exactly the way everyone wanted her.

Get back into character, Olivia. The voice inside her head was her mother's, but the voice would soon be evicted.

Olivia stood in front of three full-length mirrors and examined the gown her mother had chosen. The scoop neck, tight bodice, and floor-length flared skirt shimmered in teal, a playful color meant to highlight her youth. Always, her youth. Her straightened blonde hair swung to her waist. Behind her, pink walls, bedspread, and pillows offered a Pepto-Bismol backdrop.

She leaned forward, nearly pressing her nose to the glass. Someone had stopped by earlier in the day and applied heavy makeup designed to look barely there. She had to admit, her blue eyes sparkled under long lashes. Even for their little family, a makeup artist at home was unusual, but so was tonight. The McAllister Awards recognized the best actors under twenty-one, which meant this year was her last chance to win the prestigious honor.

She didn't bother to consider whether she *wanted* to win. It was expected of her. Maybe if she won, her parents would admit she was a great actress in her own right. They'd have to see her as a competent woman rather than their little shadow.

Olivia's mother appeared in the doorway and posed. As always, she wore her signature color, this time in a form-fitting black mermaid dress with a plunging neckline. Her dark hair was pulled into an elegant French twist that probably took hours to complete and would be nearly impossible to take down.

Her mother gushed, "Oh! You look fantastic!" After holding her pose another few seconds, she crossed the room but stopped short of a hug. The glamorous Natalia Knight would never risk mussing her hair or creasing an outfit. "Are you excited about winning?"

"Do you know something I don't?"

"Well, I *do* have connections, but no, I don't have that particular information." Her mother waved the question away. "I've been in the business long enough to know you outshine the other nominees. Your performance in *True to Life* was magnificent." She turned Olivia around to examine every angle. "Thank goodness you took advice from your parents on how to approach the role." With a frown minimized by Botox, she brushed an imaginary imperfection from Olivia's skirt. "We take some credit for your success."

Take credit? If she won tonight, her parents would claim the victory, and their opinion of her would remain intact. *I'm a commodity, an object of value, like their crystal chandelier and Tiffany lamps, and almost as fragile.* Why would tonight be different?

After biting the tip of her tongue, she met her mother's gaze in the mirror. "Can I have a glass of wine at the after-party?"

"Oh, my goodness, no, not where people can see you. You'd be on the front of every tabloid!" Her mother walked toward the door, and Olivia fell in behind her, trailing in the wake of heavy floral perfume. "Speaking of public perception, don't forget to thank your parents when you win. No one likes an unappreciative child."

No one likes a controlling mother, either.

"And if I lose?"

"Thank us anyway. You'll be ambushed by reporters, and we've taught you to be a graceful loser. At least on camera."

Olivia remained three steps behind her mother as they descended the grand stairway. From the foyer, her father called out, "Wow! What a pair you make!" He spread his arms wide, not for a hug, never a hug, but to display his own well-made tuxedo. "No wonder I only have eyes for two women in my life."

She choked down a giggle before it escaped. Surely her father had been caught with other women enough times for his comment to be ridiculous. Then again, both her father and mother were accomplished actors, adept at projecting whatever persona the moment required.

Olivia's mother beamed. "Thank you, Andrew."

⚭

The limousine stopped in front of Manhattan Center, a short drive from their home in Central Park South. Complete with welcoming red carpet and requisite paparazzi, the award venue popped with energy and bright lights. The driver opened the door for her father, who immediately turned to help Olivia slide out of the car, always the perfect gentleman, at least in public. She stood behind him, shifting from foot to foot, while her mother slowly extended first one perfect leg and then the other, unfolding herself with impressive ceremony.

Rather than roll her eyes toward heaven, Olivia forced a wider smile. The effort—or embarrassment for her mother's dramatic display—brought a hot blush to her cheeks that threatened to overtake her ears if she didn't distract herself.

The crowd cheered.

A reporter pushed into their personal space. "Ms. Knight. Natalia. Do you think your daughter will win tonight?"

Her mother rested a hand on the reporter's arm. "Well, my fingers are crossed, but all of the nominees are fine actors." She drew Olivia to her side. "We worked tirelessly on the role, and we hope the fans and judges enjoyed it." Turning to her daughter, she asked, "Right, Olivia?"

"Oh yes! And we had so much fun working with the team." Olivia widened her eyes and grinned, as she'd been taught. Here she played the eager young actress who never uttered a bad word about anyone. A regular Shirley Temple. She had to admit, it played well.

The reporter held his ground against the surging mob and smiled back. "We're pulling for you!"

Olivia's mother guided her forward as she called over her shoulder, "Thank you!"

After a round of pictures and a few more questions, they made their way to the Hammerstein Ballroom, which pulsed with red and blue roaming spotlights. An usher led them to a table near the stage, either because her parents were considered film royalty or the committee didn't want Olivia to walk far when she won. In the industry, each decision held meaning; each nuance required deep consideration.

Olivia mentally shrugged her shoulders. She'd leave speculation to the gossip mongers lining the edges of the ballroom along with waiters and dark-clad security guards who frowned and folded thick arms across their chests.

At their table sat Martin Lange, an up-and-coming director who brought a fresh new perspective to camera angles. The media called him "edgy," but Olivia called him "boring" since he rarely had much to say. At least he was pretty, with short black hair, green eyes, and a designer tux. He shifted his shoulders and craned his neck as though the bow tie might suffocate him. Poor guy, an introvert forced to play dress-up and make nice with extroverted—often narcissistic —actors.

Her father shook Martin's hand for too long, probably intent on making an impression. Then he waved over a server to order a Manhattan (what else?) and a dirty martini for his wife. For Olivia, he ordered a Shirley Temple. She hated cherries, but tonight was about image.

Several preemptive congratulations later, the ceremony began.

Maybe it was the excitement, bright lights, or snug bodice, but Olivia felt her head tighten. A migraine was imminent. Unfortunately, she hadn't brought a purse, which meant the tension in her head would grow to a pounding, nauseating headache before she located sumatriptan at home. Closing her eyes, she tried to relax her shoulders and imagine herself on a uiet stretch of beach. With each award given, she opened her eyes to smile and clap soundlessly.

Two more weeks. Six hundred and seventy more hours. God, it sounded like a long time.

Her mother squeezed Olivia's leg under the table; it was time for Best Actor in a Children's Film. She leaned forward, once again widening her eyes and smiling for the cameras, if not for the people behind them. The weight of admiring scrutiny threatened to implode her body.

The host's voice thundered through the room. "And tonight, we have a wonderful surprise. Each of our nominees began their journey in acting with their first director. The person who guided them and molded them into the professionals they became. For tonight's winner, the premier director has agreed to hand out the award as a treat for an exceptional young actor."

Olivia's smile froze.

Chuck Dawson couldn't be here. Not here. Not tonight. The pounding above her right eye nearly blinded her as she desperately scanned the stage. Chuck had started her journey, alright, but the journey had included lies and endless workdays not meant for any actor, let alone a five-year-old child.

He'd called her "Thing One" on the set, a label most people assumed was meant to be funny and affectionate, but Olivia never knew a second of warmth from the man. Each morning, one of her parents dropped her with a nanny and left for a day of whatever kept them busy, well-dressed, and perfectly coiffed. Olivia remembered falling asleep on set, only to be nudged awake by Chuck's shiny white tennis shoe. "Up and at 'em, Thing One. Lazy is for losers." Late into the evening, the nanny tucked her in a car and roused her from sleep after the short drive home.

One afternoon, a friendly background actor brought her a box of crayons and a coloring book; the box displayed a rainbow of beautiful colors, and the book held unicorns and fairies with butterfly wings. During lunch, she sat alone at a table, hunched over a fairy masterpiece of purple, pink, and green. She'd give it to the director as a present so he'd be nice to her. Before she could color the wings, Chuck ordered his assistant to "get rid of the distraction," and a soft-faced man slid the book and crayons away, whispering, "I'm sorry, Livvie."

She hadn't cried.

Before she left the studio, she rummaged through the trash near the snack area and found three of her crayons: white, black, and red. Still clutching them in one hand, she followed the nanny from the studio, intent on owning a piece of the fleeting happiness. The magic crayons would be good luck when she begged her mom to take her away from Chuck, the set, and acting. She pinched herself to stay awake on the way home, and when she walked in the front door, she approached her mother lounging in the sitting room, a full martini in her hand.

"Mama." She needed to talk, but the ideas in her head were far too big for a child. "I don't want to— Can I please...stay home tomorrow? Can I stay with you? I don't like—"

"Good heavens, Olivia, speak up. You're

supposed to be an actress." She sipped her drink. "Staying home tomorrow is out of the question. When you make a commitment, you don't abandon people who are counting on you. Besides, you have a contract." Olivia's mom turned back to her drink.

Discussion closed.

"But I—" Then the tears did come. She dropped her crayons on the antique jade rug. They weren't magic, after all.

"Get yourself together, child." Her mother looked everywhere but at Olivia. "You need to learn a work ethic."

After what seemed like years but could only have been weeks, Olivia stumbled onto the set for a scene requiring her to cry. In the script, her character was lost in a mall, and Chuck ordered her to curl up beside a fountain and sob for her mom.

The soft-faced man positioned her beside the fountain.

"Picture's up!" Chuck yelled. "Action!"

Olivia said her lines and tried to produce tears. She used a trick where she thought of something sad, like losing her coloring book under mounds of sticky food, but her heart felt nothing. After several takes, Chuck whispered to someone behind a camera and approached Olivia, hunching down beside her.

"I have some bad news, Thing One." His breath smelled like hot onions. "Your mom was in a bad car accident, and she died."

What was he saying? She'd seen her mother this morning. She couldn't be dead.

"Do you know what it means to die?" A hard glint in his eyes took her breath away.

Around the edges of her vision, the room turned gray, and a sharp pain wracked her tiny chest, ripping through her like the kitchen knife she wasn't allowed to touch. Her body curled itself into a ball, trying to get smaller and smaller until she disappeared. While she shrunk like *Alice in Wonderland*, sobs escaped, making way for more pain.

Her mama was gone.

She'd never again see her, hug her, or kiss her cheek.

Who would take care of her? Her dad? A nanny? Who would love her? Through a haze of confusion, cameras rolled forward. Were they moving? Or did they look bigger because she was shrinking?

It didn't matter.

Her mama was dead.

"Cut!" Chuck bellowed. "We got it." He approached Olivia again. "I was teasing, Thing One. Your mom isn't dead. A pretty good joke, right?" Whistling, he sauntered away, leaving Olivia to wipe her tears and try to fill the hole in her heart.

Through an eternity of filming, she learned to sit quietly and wait to be called to the set. She stopped imagining a way out, a happier place, or coloring books. Each night, she climbed into her princess bed and squeezed her stuffed bunny to her chest, trying to make sense of feelings her mother called "silly." By the time the film wrapped, her body felt as empty and shriveled as a raisin. Olivia had learned a valuable life lesson: She couldn't count on adults.

On her sixth birthday, the day of the film's premier, her first migraine ripped through her head, and she was sure she'd die. Her father had dragged her to the premier, dissuaded only when she vomited on a microphone shoved in her face. She'd seen her mother's shame before the famous Natalia Knight smile hid her true feelings. The rest of the night blurred behind boiling clouds of pain and dry heaves that left her stomach sore.

To this day, she'd never watched the film.

Over the years, through numerous roles, she'd worked hard to put the past behind her, locking it up in a little black box and storing it on a shelf in the far reaches of her consciousness.

Until now.

Maybe she wouldn't win the award. She could go home and huddle in her bed until the migraine released her.

The announcer continued, "And the award for Best Actor in a Children's Film goes to...Olivia Knight!"

The audience clapped and called out their

support for the judges' decision. Olivia's mother stood and waved to those around her, then hauled Olivia from her seat. The woman was stronger than she looked. "Go on, honey, get up there. We did it!"

In a daze, Olivia looked up at the stage to see Chuck Dawson holding her award and grinning at the audience, his dark-blue tuxedo offset by those damned white tennis shoes. Although his brown hair was shorter now, from this distance, he looked the same as he had fifteen years ago. Standing at the podium, he smiled and waved at her as though delighted by their impending reunion.

Sweat trickled down Olivia's back. She could march up there and punch him in the smile. Or kick his shin. Or nudge him with aggressive intentions. Yes, she might get away with nudging.

Applause continued.

Time ticked by.

Her mother tugged her toward the aisle. Without thinking, instead of turning toward the stage, Olivia turned toward the exit and took a step before her mother caught her arm. The audience laughed like it was a delightful joke.

Through clenched teeth, her mother hissed, "Get it together. You're a professional."

Right, she was a professional, and this was required of her. She pasted a smile on her face and marched up to the stage. Someone held her hand as she ascended the stairs, and soon she found herself facing the one person she'd hoped never to see again.

Chuck held her award and kissed her on the cheek, acting like a doting uncle. He reeked of sweat and whiskey. She stared at his profile as he turned and waved to the cheering audience. With his free hand, he clutched Olivia's arm and pulled her toward the podium, where he clearly planned to stay in the spotlight.

He leaned toward the microphone, yelling over the din, "This is one talented young lady!"

Olivia wrapped her fingers around the award. *Let go.* She tugged the award from his hand.

The crowd cheered louder and rose to their feet.

Thank goodness Olivia had a minute to pull herself together while the crowd settled and the room quieted. They expected a speech. She clamped her teeth together and reminded herself she had an image to portray. The world was watching.

"I'd like to take this opportunity to thank my parents, who have always guided me through a profession they themselves know well. I've had every advantage, and I'm thankful." Her headache surged again, and she swallowed hard, pressing her lips together against the vomit inching up the back of her throat. *Not now.* "I'd also like to recognize Chuck Dawson for opening my eyes to the torment of child labor. He taught me how to cry on set and on demand, how to push through twelve-hour days, and how to abandon the magic of childhood." She held her award aloft and smiled. "But as Chuck would say, 'Lazy is for losers.'"

The audience laughed again, treating her comments like a teasing roast of her mentor and choosing to believe all was well in their glamorous world. Chuck reached his arm across her shoulders for a hug, saying into the microphone, "Thanks, kid."

While he squeezed her shoulders, Chuck's fingers dug into her upper arm, and Olivia tried not to wince in pain. She scanned the beaming, dazzling crowd.

This was her world.

These were her people.

She glanced at her mother and saw the silent reprimand even as she smiled, playing the part of proud mama for the cameras. Her mother knew the brief speech wasn't playful. Olivia would get an earful later, but for now, her mother stood trapped by social expectations. Her daughter had won a prestigious award. The spotlight allowed only compliments.

Olivia backed up a step, breaking Chuck's hold on her, and waved to the audience. "Thank you, and God bless!" Before Chuck could reach for her again, she ran off the stage and back to her parents, where they, and those nearby, offered congratulations.

Martin held a chair for her, and as she settled in and turned to thank him, she followed his gaze to her upper arm. Chuck's fingers had bitten into her flesh hard enough to leave angry red marks. Martin frowned, and his lips pressed together, jaw flexing tightly. Apparently, Martin hadn't gotten the memo ordering everybody to play nice.

She whispered, "It's okay."

"No, it's not." His simple assertion let her know he saw her pain, judged Chuck, and was angry on her behalf. Maybe it was the headache or the stress of the night, but Martin's protective comment felt like the first normal response of her nearly twenty-one years. She choked down tears and tried to concentrate on smiling. Martin returned to his seat, bursting the protective bubble holding the two of them for a few precious seconds. What would it be like to have a man like him in her corner, anchoring her to a safe world?

She missed him already.

Her mother leaned toward her. "Are you feeling okay? You look pale."

"No, I have a headache."

"Another one? The doctor said they're psychosomatic. Take deep breaths. This is your moment!" Her mother looked up and smiled at the cameras.

Olivia mumbled, "I think I might get sick on the carpet."

"Oh, for goodness' sake! Go backstage and get some water and a snack. I'm sure they have a place to rest for a minute. And it would get you out of view until you feel better."

Thank god.

Olivia scooted toward the aisle and made her way through a side door leading backstage. The white walls showed the wear and tear of rolled equipment scraping deep, black, unforgiving furrows. This was a working area, where blemishes and damage would never be repaired; time would chip away more of the surface until a patchwork of black lines created art no one wanted to see. Years would turn to decades, and the once pristine walls would bear the scars of careless people.

Would she suffer the same fate?

Olivia found an empty dressing room reeking of stale cigarettes and stretched out on a brown pleather couch. When the light seared her eyes, she flopped onto her stomach and buried her face in the cushions, hoping for ten minutes of quiet.

When she awoke, memory lagged by a few panicky seconds. The room was unfamiliar, and a figure loomed over her, casting a shadow across the couch. Fear, quick and cold, jerked her head up. Instinctively, she braced herself, certain that danger was near.

Chuck Dawson smiled—an evil smile he'd reserved for her years ago. "Hey, Thing One."

She jumped to her feet and stepped away from him in the small space, suddenly feeling five years old. How dare he use the awful nickname fifteen years later. "My name is Olivia." She tried to channel fearlessness, show him an adult's self-possession and poise, but the long-ago helplessness was back.

He moved closer, standing over her so she had to look up. "Nice little speech you made out there."

Her tongue stuck to the roof of her mouth, dry and thick. Swallowing produced a defeated clicking sound Chuck must have heard. He looked ready to hit her...or worse. She could simper and scuttle around him like a cockroach, begging for mercy from her tormenter, or she could secretly admit defeat but go down fighting.

"It, um, was the truth. Working with you was a nightmare." Olivia tried to summon an indignant frown, but her face betrayed her with tears.

"Oh, so *now* you can cry!" He shouted, shaking the room with his intensity. "You were the laziest actor I ever worked with, and the only reason you've made it in this business is because I demanded good performances! You're probably still *lazy* and *entitled* and *spoiled*—"

The door banged against the wall.

Martin—handsome, strong, quiet Martin—stood in the doorway, shrinking the room with his bulk. His frown and tight jaw told her he hadn't forgotten the red handprint even now beginning to fade. Without taking his eyes from Chuck, he growled, "Olivia, I think your mom is looking for you."

She scooted toward the door. "Thank you." He moved to let her pass, and her full skirt brushed against his legs on the way out. She touched his shoulder briefly, hoping he'd understand the meaning she tried to convey. *Thank you for caring. Thank you for seeing me. Thank you for being here right now.*

Martin graced her with the force of his sharp green eyes, and although he didn't smile, his anger wasn't for her. In his eyes, she saw the compassion of a champion, a man who would take on a bully and win. She almost felt sorry for Chuck.

Almost.

As she backed away, Martin slowly closed the door.

Before Olivia walked far down the corridor, she heard deep male voices from the room, followed by a loud crash. Curious, she tucked herself around a corner and watched the door. Within a minute, Martin emerged and walked in the other direction, shaking his right hand as though he'd hurt his fingers.